TRACES OF Mercy

MICHAEL LANDON JR.
& CINDY KELLEY

David C Cook®

transforming lives together

TRACES OF MERCY
Published by David C Cook
4050 Lee Vance View
Colorado Springs, CO 80918 U.S.A.

David C Cook Distribution Canada
55 Woodslee Avenue, Paris, Ontario, Canada N3L 3E5

David C Cook U.K., Kingsway Communications
Eastbourne, East Sussex BN23 6NT, England

The graphic circle C logo is a registered trademark of David C Cook.

This story is a work of fiction. All characters and events are the product of the author's
imagination. Any resemblance to any person, living or dead, is coincidental.

LCCN 2013946265
ISBN 978-0-7814-0869-1
eISBN 978-1-4347-0715-4

The Team: Alex Field, Jamie Chavez, Amy Konyndyk,
Nick Lee, Caitlyn Carlson, Karen Athen
Cover Design: Dog-Eared Design, Kirk DouPonce
Cover Photo: iStockPhoto

Printed in the United States of America
First Edition 2013

1 2 3 4 5 6 7 8 9 10

080113

For Our Moms

CHAPTER ONE

April 1865

The assault came in the dusky-pink dawn on a Sunday. The lone soldier, who slept forty yards from the rest of the bedraggled Confederate company, bolted from his bedroll and was on his chestnut-colored horse in a matter of seconds—urging the bay toward a hill to the east.

Looking over his shoulder, he could see his boys in gray awaken and stagger into a defensive position against the surprise attack from the Yankees. His brothers in arms referred to him as the sharpshooter, the crack shot, the skirmisher. But the soldier, bending low over the neck of his horse, thought of himself by one name only: sniper. He'd heard the term from a British colonel who had told tales of one man's supreme marksmanship. He'd tried the name on for size then—wore it in his mind and came to love it. It defined him. It was what he did.

The first blare of a Confederate bugle filled the air, and the sniper had the fleeting thought that the bugler should be picking up a rifle instead of his horn when he saw the enemy—the dreaded tide of blue—spilling out of a haze that hung over this piece of Tennessee land nestled between two hills and a meandering river.

The sniper knew from the enormous sound of the war that his boys were vastly outnumbered and the battle would be over almost before it began. He heard the otherworldly rebel yell split the dawn. The cry had always reminded him of an angry, wounded animal baying its intent to fight to the death. If the sound of his own men could send chills up his spine, he could only imagine what it did to the nerves of the Yankees.

He kept riding up the rise and away from the crash of musketry and the storm of leaden hail. His trained ear picked out the distinctive sound of the howitzer pummeling the troops as he reached the summit of the hill. He jumped from the saddle with his rifle and dropped to his knees behind a heavy patch of wild, knotted vines, practically becoming part of the landscape in his dark-brown shirt and green trousers.

From his vantage point, the scene below him was shrouded in clouds of gray smoke that rose from the ground. He nestled the long barrel of his rifle on top of the thick vines and looked into the high-powered scope made especially for the nine-pound Whitworth. At the sound of another thundering boom from the howitzer, he swiveled the rifle around until he located the artillery soldier who was manning the cannon six hundred yards in the distance. The sniper caught the buttons of the blue Union jacket in the crosshairs of his scope and fired. The force of the shot blew the Yankee off his feet and knocked him into the soldier behind him. *One hundred twelve.* As the sniper dropped a new bullet into the muzzle of his rifle, another Federal stepped into the space to fire the howitzer. The sniper squeezed the trigger and watched through the scope as the Yankee dropped. *One hundred thirteen.*

The sniper turned once again to the panorama of activity below him, where sulfur smoke moved around the soldiers like a living force to be reckoned with. After reloading his weapon, he used the scope to pan across the swarm of blue and gray colliding amid thrusting bayonets. A Union officer with a crust of gold braid on his shoulders charged through the thick of the battle, a rebel cap arrogantly dangling from the tip of his raised bayonet. The sniper adjusted the position of his rifle, momentarily taking the sight off the officer by raising the barrel a hair's breadth. He cocked back the hammer, braced for the recoil, and squeezed the trigger just as the officer moved back into his view. The bullet hit the man dead center in his forehead. He didn't even have time to blink before he died. *One hundred fourteen.*

The sniper figured he had one shot left before he'd foul the barrel of his rifle. With alacrity that was second nature, he reloaded. Through his sight, the sniper saw a Union cavalry officer, a captain, he thought, galloping wildly through the fray. The officer reined in his horse and jumped from the saddle. Seemingly oblivious to the barrage of lead flying around him, the man bent toward a wounded infantryman on the ground just as a rebel soldier wielding a bayonet came at him. The soldier managed to ram the tip of the bayonet into the captain's shoulder, but the Yank swiftly proved himself the better combatant by turning and running his sword into the rebel's chest. As the captain shoved his sword back into its scabbard, the sniper fixed his sight on the ribbons that decorated the man's chest. *One hundred fifteen …*

He felt the pressure of the trigger under his finger and squeezed off the shot just as an artillery shell exploded. Blue-tinged smoke filled the air and obliterated his view of the captain. As the smoke and debris from the shelling cleared, he searched the ground for his target, cursing when he realized that the captain wasn't dead— he was riding off with the wounded infantryman lying across his saddle. Heedless of the peril, the sniper stood and looked out over the field of battle to watch the Union officer galloping along the river.

The sniper jumped on his horse. Seconds later, as his own company bugler sounded retreat, he was flying down the hill with but one objective: to kill his intended target.

As he neared the bottom of the hill, the sniper dismounted and tied his horse to a low tree branch before creeping the last few yards toward the river. He heard the Union officer's deep, commanding voice before he saw him. "You're going to be fine. That's an order."

The sniper moved even closer and heard a weak reply. "Your rank doesn't have authority over me right now, Captain."

The sniper used the barrel of his rifle to part the tall reeds in front of him, revealing the two men. The infantryman was lying prone near the water's edge, and the captain was kneeling beside him. From his vantage point, the sniper could see that the officer was powerfully built, with chiseled features and a square jaw. As the sniper watched, the captain pulled at the buttons on the soldier's blue coat, then turned his face away from the sight that met him. The sniper used the opportunity to continue forward.

"You can't do this to me, Jed," the captain said. The sniper could hear the quaking emotion in the Yank's voice as he spoke. "I promised her I'd bring you back, and I won't let you render my word worthless."

The sniper took another step, thinking that for the first time, he would see the terror in a Yank's eyes before he fired the shot that would end his life. He was so intent on the position of his rifle, he failed to notice the dry branch under his foot. When it snapped, the captain glanced up, and their eyes locked for just a moment before the sniper braced and squeezed the trigger. But there was no recoil. No report of a bullet whizzing through the air. His rifle had jammed, and the captain hadn't flinched. The officer seemed to summarily dismiss the sniper as he pulled a kerchief from his pocket and dipped it into the river.

The sniper would not be denied. He put his rifle down and, with a trembling hand, pulled his bowie knife from a back pocket. With feet that felt as if they were encased in lead, he took a step forward while the captain washed the grime from the infantryman's face. The wounded man struggled to lift his hand, and the captain caught it between both of his own. The sniper could hear the effort it took for the young man to utter his next words.

"They were right, Eli. This dying. It doesn't hurt."

As close as he was now, the sniper could actually see the captain tighten his grip on the young man's hand. "Good."

"Pray me home, Eli." The voice was nothing more than a whisper.

The captain seemed to hesitate before he dropped his head. "Yea, though I walk through the valley of the shadow of death, I will fear no evil, for Thou art with me."

The sniper watched the officer shudder with the effort of his task as he continued. "Thy rod and Thy staff, they comfort me."

The sniper drew up the image of the captain killing the rebel soldier on the field. He inched toward the men and raised his knife.

"Thou preparest a table before me in the presence of mine enemies."

The sniper felt his heart thudding in his chest, echoing in his ears with a roar of anticipation as he mentally calculated where best to plunge his blade.

"Thou anointest my head with oil. My cup runneth over."

One hundred fifteen … one hundred fifteen … one hundred fifteen. The sniper kept his eyes on the Yank as he brought his knife high over the man's back … *thrust down and turn … down and turn …* and then reversed the arc. His arm propelled the knife toward his enemy. He braced for the resistance he knew he'd feel when his blade hit flesh.

The captain's head remained bowed, his voice strong. "Surely, goodness and mercy …"

No mercy! No mercy! The sniper veered from the knife's trajectory and swung the blade wide of the captain.

"… shall follow me all the days of my life, and I will dwell in the house of the Lord forever."

The sniper saw the young man's arm slacken, and the captain slowly released his hold. Somewhere in the distance, a lonely bugle played as the captain leaned over to place a kiss on the dead soldier's forehead.

The sniper, stunned and ashamed at his own failure, didn't move a muscle when the Union officer stood to face him with anguish in his eyes.

"He was Jedidiah Francis Hale. He was eighteen. He was a poet and had an affinity for dogs. He was my mother's second son."

The captain seemed to forget the sniper for a moment. A dark stain of blood spread outward from the bayonet wound to his shoulder, but he seemed oblivious as he stared past the sniper and rubbed a knuckle across the stubble on his cheek. When he looked back at the sniper, the pain in his eyes had been replaced by sad resignation.

"I am grateful I was able to tell my brother good-bye."

The captain reached behind his neck and pulled a medallion on a long silver chain over his head. He let the medal dangle from his fingertips as he stared at it.

"My mother gave me this before I left home," he said, his voice husky with emotion. "She said it would keep me safe."

The Union captain slipped the chain over the end of the Confederate soldier's knife. Then he turned back to his brother, hefted the lifeless body, laying it across the saddle on his horse, and led the animal away.

The sniper sat alone near a clump of bushes, cleaning his gun. The familiar mechanics of pushing the ramrod in and out of the barrel helped calm his mind and still his pounding heart. He hadn't yet gone to look for the remnants of his company after his encounter with the Union captain. *Mercy. He should have been one-fifteen. I let him walk away. Mercy. I let him live when so many of my own people have died.* It was the first time he had failed to perform his job—his duty. To kill the enemy who had stolen so much from him—from his family. The captain's face flooded his memory. The palpable pain in the man's voice; the look of sadness in his expressive eyes. The bravery he displayed as he completely discounted both a rifle and a knife so he could be with his brother in the final, terrible moments of the young man's life.

The sniper pulled the ramrod from his gun barrel and was about to get up when he spotted the medallion on the ground next to him. Picking it up, his thoughts returned to the captain and the deep, emotional timbre of his voice. *My mother gave me this before I left home. She said it would keep me safe.*

The sniper's horse whinnied softly behind him, and he knew it was time to find what was left of his company and trail them the way he always did—at a distance. He slipped the chain over his head and tucked the medal under his shirt. He heard his horse whinny again just before something solid smashed into the back of his skull. Pain shot through his head. *Stupid medal,* was his last thought before he sank into darkness.

His mind slowly came awake with tumbling, confusing thoughts as the familiar drawl of voices around him rose and fell against the monotonous creak of wheels in motion. The sniper opened his eyes and knew immediately that he was in trouble. He was lying on his back in a prairie schooner crammed with other miserable-looking Confederate soldiers. Turning slightly to the left, the sniper could see the blue coats of the Union soldiers on the buckboard as they drove the horses. The thought of his own horse's fate made him jerk around to look out the back of the wagon. Bars dashed any hope of escape, but he felt a measure of relief when he saw his bay traipsing in a line with other horses behind the wagon. He struggled to sit up, stopping for a moment to wait for the world to quit spinning.

He tried to focus on the soldier across from him. When he spoke, the sniper's voice came out scratchy and hoarse. "Where are we going?"

"Gratiot." The soldier shrugged. "Rumor says we'll be dead inside a month. The green-apple quickstep runs rampant through that place. And if that don't getcha, then the shakes do. Thought I'd die from a bullet—not from diarrhea in a Yankee prison."

The sniper vomited, and the men around him barely noticed.

As one day folded into the next, the sniper couldn't decide which was worse: the misery of the wagon ride under the unseasonably hot sun, or the dread of what was to come once they reached Gratiot Street Prison. The throbbing in his head had gone from pounding to almost tolerable, though he had yet to stomach his daily ration of food without getting sick. He looked around at the grimy faces of the soldiers in the wagon and wondered how many of them would survive the Yankee prison. Not for the first time, he wished that blow to his head had killed him. The thought of being locked up with thousands of men who were doing nothing but marking time was almost more than he could stand.

"Hey, buddy?"

The sniper cut his gaze to a scraggly soldier sitting opposite him.

"You gonna eat that or not?"

The sniper looked down at the piece of salt pork in his hand, briefly pondered how long it would take to starve to death, then tossed the pork to the soldier. The man grunted his thanks before stuffing it into his mouth. A guard walking alongside the wagon issued a sound of disgust. "Typical reb," he said. "Taking something that rightly belongs to another man."

A few eyes went to the guard who, for days, had been purposefully picking at the soldier chewing the salt pork. The sniper had heard rumors that the two were related through marriage, but that ideology and geography had put them on opposite sides of the war. Hate came off them in waves.

The rebel soldier turned and glared at the guard. "I expect that ol' skeleton y'all call president would know a thing or two 'bout that, seein' as he's taking our homes and our land."

The guard drew his pistol from a side holster and brandished it toward the wagon. "You speak more respectful of Mr. Lincoln, or you'll be eating dirt instead of pork."

"Says the yellow-bellied Yank holdin' a gun on a man who ain't armed," the rebel said.

"Once we stop, it could be a mighty long walk between the back of this wagon and the front door of Gratiot."

"If you're thinkin' that a bullet in my back would be a surprise, then think again. It's what I'd expect from you."

Though the threats and insults had become commonplace between the two men, the vitriol had escalated. Tired of the whole thing, the sniper closed his eyes and willed his thoughts to another place and time. He let memories parade through his mind and, for the time being, found solace in the fact that he'd once been very happy.

A burst of loud bugling filled the air the next day. The incongruent sound burrowed into the sniper's subconscious and roused him from sleep. He looked toward the noise and saw an American flag streaming proudly from the staff on the lead horse of a group of Union soldiers riding up fast upon the wagons. The soldiers reined in their panting animals.

"The war's over!" shouted a Union captain. "Lee surrendered to Grant at Appomattox yesterday! It's over, gentlemen. As God is my witness, it's over!"

While the Union soldiers cheered their victory, the sniper felt palpable shock at the words. The South had fallen. Everything he had fought to preserve would be gone forever. He felt tears sting his eyes as loss overwhelmed him. Looking around, he saw the same emotion on the faces of his Southern brothers.

"What about the prisoners?" a Union guard asked.

"Turn 'em loose."

In mere moments, everything changed. The same faces that had been etched in defeat, now conveyed relief. Confederate prisoners of war would be released to go back to their lives as farmers, teachers, storekeepers.

The sniper felt his numb feet hit the dirt, and he had a moment of panic that his legs wouldn't work at all. He looked around and could see that others were having the same problem as men started to disperse in all directions but the one they had been heading. The sniper had one thing to do before he'd join them. He made his way through the confusion of soldiers—blue uniforms, gray uniforms, men who wept and men who cheered.

The horse danced in place at his master's appearance. The sniper ran his hand down the length of the bay's nose.

"Time to go home, boy," he whispered.

"Leave the horse."

The sniper turned to the guard behind him—the same pistol-brandishing guard who seemed to hate rebs more than all the other guards combined.

"He's mine." The sniper's voice was low. He had to work to keep it steady. "I'm taking him."

The guard cocked his revolver. "I don't think so, Secesh."

Before the sniper had time to react, his wagonmate came from nowhere and bowled over his Union rival. The men scrabbled on the ground, fists finding purchase, hate finding relief. All around him, similar skirmishes were breaking out.

A gunshot split the air. Then another. Men started yelling. Some of the former prisoners hadn't turned to leave at all—some would rather die here than go home defeated. The short-lived calm of surrender had become thick with the tension of war once again. In the sniper's line of sight, he watched two boys in gray fall and a blue coat stagger back from an attacking rebel. The sniper wished for a gun but wouldn't take the time to try to find one. Instead, he worked frantically to free his horse from the tethered line. But he didn't have time before an onslaught of Union men rushed toward him.

The sniper was left with no choice. Willing his half-starved, wounded body into action, he turned to run away from the chaos and smoking guns. He felt a sharp sting in the back of his calf and nearly fell face-first, but somehow recovered his balance. Somewhere in his brain he registered the warm blood gushing down his leg, but in mere seconds he had a new worry: a rumbling tremble underground seemed to be nipping at his heels. He glanced back to see two horses still tethered to a wagon careening straight for him. He kept running with the hot breath of the horses on his neck, then felt the power of the animals as they charged past, tangling him in the harness rigging. In moments, he was ripped from the ground as the horses became airborne. He heard wood splintering, the terrified noises of the horses as they fell; the world tumbled past in bits and pieces of grass, rock, and dirt. The face of the Union captain who'd given him the chain around his neck flashed before him just before his head slammed into a boulder. *I think he knew this thing would kill me!*

It was well past midnight when Dr. Abe Johnson yanked open his clinic door and scowled at the two middle-aged men standing outside. In the dark it was hard to make out anything about them, other than the fact that one of them had a slight man wearing a brown shirt and green pants thrown over his shoulder.

"We found this fella 'bout five miles outside a' town."

"Bring him in." The doctor stepped back from the door, and the two men entered the clinic. Doc pointed at a table. "Put him right down there."

They did as the doctor asked and stepped back a couple of feet. Dr. Johnson lit a lamp and moved it closer to the table to peer down at the man.

"Tell me what happened," Doc said. He lifted each of the man's eyelids and then turned his face from side to side to examine it.

"It's a miracle we saw him at all," one of the men said. "We pulled our wagon over because Tom there had to relieve himself."

The man called Tom picked up the story. "I got myself off the road a ways and remember thinking I needed to be quick about it, on account of Dan gets testy when we stop."

"Seems like we gotta stop every hour fer that peanut of a bladder you got."

"*Anyways*, I was just finishing my, uh, business, when I heard something in the dark. Something below me. Turns out I was standing on the edge of a ridge."

"Dang lucky you didn't step off into nothing and kill yourself, Tom."

"I called over to Dan so we could both listen, and that's when we figured out we was hearing horses that had somehow wound up at the bottom of the hill," Tom said. "We could tell they was hurting pretty bad."

"We made it down to them in pretty good time and saw right away that there was no saving 'em. Never seen animals beg to be shot before—but those two surely were." Dan shook his head. "I sure hate to hear an animal suffer."

"We was just about to start climbing back up when we saw … him," Tom said, directing his gaze at the injured man. "He was stuck under the rigging—must have gotten tangled up in the wagon as it went over."

"He wasn't moving, but he was breathing," Dan said. "We hauled him back up the hill."

"He been awake at all since you found him?" Doc asked.

Both men shook their heads.

"No," Tom said.

The doctor continued to run his hands along the man's arms, then his shoulders.

"You think he'll live?" Tom asked.

Dr. Johnson began unbuttoning the man's shirt. "I don't know how badly he's hurt yet. There could be internal bleeding, broken ribs."

"I think he's about starved to death too. He's light as a feather," Dan offered.

The doctor peeled back the material, and the three stared at a thick binding wrapped around the man's chest.

"Let's get him up so I can undo the binding," Doc said.

They pulled the man into a sitting position. The doctor slowly began to unwind the binding. As the last of the cloth came off, Dr. Johnson cleared his throat. "Well, that explains the 'light as a feather,'" he said. The three men stared in stunned silence.

"Gentlemen," Dr. Johnson said quietly, "it seems we have been mistaken about the gender of the patient."

"Mistaken about the sex, too," Tom said. "That there is a full-fledged woman."

CHAPTER TWO

She opened her eyes and found herself in an unfamiliar room, looking at the back of an unfamiliar man, who was whistling. She must have shifted, moved, made some kind of noise herself, because he turned and looked at her, his lips still pursed in mid-whistle. The sound died on his lips as he started across the small room toward her. He was older, with an average height and build. His shirt and trousers looked rumpled—as if he'd been sleeping in his clothes.

"Good. You're finally awake," he said.

She realized she was reclining on a cot, and when she tried to lift herself on her elbows, a heavy, throbbing pain in her head made her moan and sink back into a pillow.

"Where?" she managed to croak out of her parched throat.

"At my clinic in St. Louis," he answered. He pulled a chair next to the cot and sat down. He reached for her wrist, but his touch made her jerk away. Her instinctual reaction caused her to grimace in pain. "Who?"

"You're asking the right questions. That's good," he said. "I'm Doctor Abe Johnson. I've been taking care of you for the past three days."

Three days?

She was confused. "Why?"

He frowned and studied her. "There was an accident. Don't you remember?"

She stared at him without answering.

"I'm going to check your pulse now," he said.

She felt him lift her arm with a confident touch.

"Excellent," the doctor said with satisfaction. "Steady and strong." He lowered her arm to the cot. "How is your pain?"

It was as if the question jarred her further into reality, and she quickly became aware of a myriad of things that didn't feel right. Her head throbbed, her ribs ached, and when she stretched out her leg, she felt something akin to a lick of fire run up her calf. She felt bruised and battered and tender.

"Pain ... everywhere." She lifted a hand to her head and gingerly ran her fingers over the thick wrap that ran across her forehead and, as far as she could tell, all the way around. She swallowed. All she could think of was water. "I'm ... thirsty."

"Of course you are."

He pushed to his feet and went to a pitcher on a table across the room. He poured her a cup of water, but he handed it to her with an admonishment. "You're going to be tempted to gulp this down, but I'll advise against that unless you don't mind vomiting."

She nodded her understanding, and he helped her sit up. She tipped the cup to her lips. The water felt like liquid heaven running down her throat.

"Easy does it," he said. She forced herself to stop drinking and gave him back the cup.

"How did I get here?" she asked.

"Two men brought you in."

"Where are they?"

"Long gone. They were just passing through this area when they found you tangled up in some wagon rigging at the bottom of a pretty steep hill about five miles outside of town."

"I was alone?" she asked after a moment.

"Yes, as far as I know," he said. "Had you been traveling with someone else?"

She searched her memory for the answer. "I don't remember."

"Where were you going?"

"I … can't say." She looked past him, her big brown eyes filled with worry as her mind raced.

Intrigued, Dr. Johnson leaned forward in the chair and rested his forearms on his knees. "Your secret is safe with me."

Her eyes flew back to his. "Secret?"

"I am obligated as your doctor to hold anything you say to me in confidence," he said. "So whatever you were doing—whoever you might have been running from—you can tell me. Maybe I can help you."

She felt as if she'd come into the room in the middle of a conversation. *Your secret is safe with me.*

"How long did you say I've been here?" she asked.

"Three days. But I have no way of knowing how long you were lying there unconscious before those men found you."

Lying there unconscious. Your secret is safe with me.

She shifted again on the cot and sucked in a sharp breath when a ripple of pain shot through her body.

"You have several contusions on your skull," he said. "The most significant is just above your left temple. I also found one located near the crown of your head—but I'd say that injury is older than the others. You have some bruising consistent with a bad fall, but as far as I can tell, nothing is broken." He hesitated for a moment, as if carefully giving weight to his next few words. "It very well may be that the binding you had around your chest kept your ribs from breaking."

Why is he talking in riddles?

"Binding?"

He raised his brows. "Yes. As I said, your secret is safe with me."

Frowning, she shook her head, then immediately regretted the action. "I don't know what you're talking about. I don't understand."

He studied her for a moment, then said, "You have another significant injury that we haven't discussed. A gunshot wound to the back of your calf. How did that happen?"

"I don't know," she said, more to herself than to him. "I don't remember."

"All right. I understand. I'm a stranger and we just met and, understandably, you don't know if you can trust me or not."

"No. You *don't* understand. I don't remember anything that you're talking about. I don't remember an accident, or falling, or being shot!"

He tented his hands together, tapping his fingertips while he studied her. "Your mind is most likely protecting you from what was certainly a traumatic experience."

When she didn't respond, he pressed on. "Let's start with simpler things, shall we?"

She licked her dry lips and dipped her chin in agreement.

"I can hear a trace of the South in your speech," he said. "Where are you from?"

She searched her mind, but it was filled with dark corners that seemed to be hiding the answers. *I don't know. I don't know … how can I not know?*

She uttered the words aloud. "I don't know."

He stroked his chin thoughtfully but sounded skeptical when he asked, "No recollection of that either?"

She tried again and reached inside herself for the information, but it wasn't there. The moment stretched, and silence boomed in the small room. Panic started to swell in her throat.

"We'll leave the geography questions for later, shall we?"

She swallowed and nodded.

Dr. Johnson offered a confident smile. "Let's start with the very basics. What's your name?"

She automatically opened her mouth to reply with the answer. Surely she knew her own name. But trying to retrieve the memory in the deep black chasm of her mind was like trying to catch the wind. There was nothing. Not a shred of anything to grasp and unfurl like a sheet where all the minutes, hours, days, and years leading up to this moment might be hiding. With frightened, heart-pumping adrenaline, she whispered her answer.

"I don't remember."

The admission hung in the air between them. Her large, frightened eyes studied the man sitting by her side as he studied her. It dawned on her that he was the only person she ever remembered having a conversation with. The thought stabbed through her, and she fought the urge to scream. Despite the splitting pain in her head, she swung her legs over the side of the cot and pushed herself to stand on her injured leg.

"Be careful now," he said, slipping a steadying hand under her elbow. Even with the terror rising up inside her, she was cognizant enough to hear the intrigue in his voice.

"What's happening to me?"

"As I said earlier, your mind might be trying to protect you from something you don't want to remember."

She turned to face him. "But my own *name*?"

He didn't answer—just kept looking at her in a way that was becoming increasingly irritating.

"Let me reiterate—you *can* trust me," he said. "I know we just met and you are likely skeptical about confiding in a complete stranger ..."

Her voice was shaky when she replied. "You're not hearing me. I don't know what you're talking about. I don't know where I was headed, why I was traveling—where I'm from or even my own name!"

She looked down at the white gown she was wearing. Down at her bare feet on the floor. She wiggled her toes and shook her head at the same time.

"Those might as well be a stranger's feet because I don't recognize them!" She raised a shaking hand to examine it. "This could be a stranger's hand." A new thought took shape, and the tears she had held at bay spilled down her cheek. "I don't even know what I look like."

"What is the last thing you remember?" he asked, clearly more intrigued by the second.

She took a deep, steadying breath and looked up at him. "I heard whistling, opened my eyes, and saw you."

He went to a small closet in the corner of the room and pulled some clothing from a shelf. Carrying the clothes back to her, he put them in her hands.

"You were wearing these when the men brought you in," he said. "They are clothes that would be worn by a man, not a young woman."

She inspected the wool shirt and pants. "If that's true, then why would I have been wearing them?"

"Your chest was bound, and your hair is cut in a masculine style. My hypothesis is you did all of it on purpose in order to be perceived as a man."

Tears slipped down her cheeks as she ran her hands over the rough wool of the brown shirt. "But why?"

"That's a good question," he said. "One I was hoping you would have an answer to when you woke." He crossed his arms over his chest and slowly shook his head. "Your cognizant skills seem fine. You can carry on a conversation and have knowledge of everyday things, have reasonable expectations—have a healthy fear level of what's happening to you. It is as if only one part of your brain has been traumatized by your head injury." His expression went from perplexed to revelatory. "I've read about cases like this, but in all my years I've never seen it firsthand. A once-in-a-lifetime thing, really."

"Cases like what?" she asked. A feeling of deep foreboding settled over her like a drape.

"Amnesia," he said. "It's the loss of one's memory—usually due to a brain injury or sometimes even a terrible shock."

She frowned. "That sounds—very bad."

He pressed his lips together, and she saw pity in his expression. She dug the heels of her hands into her eyes as if she could press her memories back inside her head. *Try harder! Remember something. Remember!*

Moments later, she felt him gently pull her hands away from her face. He leaned closer to her as if the very action would help convey the sincerity of what he was going to say.

"It might very well be temporary."

A ray of hope leapt up inside her. "Temporary?"

"Yes. I'll need to do more research, of course, but I know the condition can last anywhere from minutes to hours to ..."

"To what? Days? Weeks?"

"I don't see the point in speculating about that right now," he said. "Let's just concentrate on the present." He pulled something from his pocket and held up a silver medallion dangling from a silver chain. "You were also wearing this."

She reached for it. Feeling his scrutiny, she fingered the medal and willed something to come back to her. The black drape across her mind remained firmly intact.

"It's beautiful ... but I don't remember it."

He reached out for it, but she tightened her fingers around it. "You said it's mine."

He withdrew his hand. "Yes."

Careful of the bandage around her head, she slipped it on.

"There is something else we haven't tried," he said. "Something that might jar your memory."

"What?"

"I have a mirror in the next room. Let's go have a look, shall we?"

She didn't answer. It wasn't vanity that made her hesitate. It didn't matter to her if she was homely—if her nose was too big for her face or her chin too weak. What mattered was her quicksilver hold on sanity and how fast that might disappear when the face of a stranger stared back at her from the glass. What if the shock of seeing herself did nothing to help her remember?

"I promise you won't be disappointed in your reflection," he said, leading her to the next room.

Her first impression of the woman who stared back at her from the mirror was that she looked lost. Lost and terrified and sad. Her hand went to the short, dark hair cut above her chin. The bandage wound around her forehead served only to make her eyes look huge. Her nose was fine. Her chin was chiseled like a porcelain doll. Her memory stayed locked up tight. She shuddered with disappointment.

"Nothing, eh?" the doctor asked.

She barely managed to shake her head.

"Steady does it," he said, peering over her shoulder. "We'll sort it all out." She saw him frown into the glass. "You are a handsome young woman. I would surmise you've barely had twenty birthdays—if that. Somewhere, someone is probably frantic about you."

She continued to stare at the woman in the mirror. At a face that might have been anyone on the street for all she knew. She spoke to her own reflection as if she expected a reply. "What are you going to do?"

Dr. Johnson became pragmatic. "First things first. You'll need more time to recover from your injuries. Perhaps as your head heals, your memory will return."

"And if it doesn't?" Her voice was laced with fear.

"Let's not borrow trouble," he said.

She shifted her gaze from her own reflection to his. "I hardly have to borrow it. I'm consumed with it. I have no idea where to go or what to do next."

"Let's just take things one day at a time," he said. "The mind is a fascinating thing. A mysterious part of the body I could spend a lifetime studying and have only a scintilla of answers for the questions I have."

"That's what worries me most," she admitted. "That I'll spend the rest of *my* lifetime looking for the one answer I need." She found her own eyes in the glass again. "Who am I?"

CHAPTER THREE

I have woken up thirteen different times without a name. The doctor taking care of me has a name—it's Abner—but he says to call him Abe, or Doc.

Abe is very nice, and he is trying to help me. Every day he leaves the clinic to go from place to place and ask people if they are missing someone. I don't go with him. I stay behind at the clinic, where it is safe. And quiet. And I don't have to be in the busyness of the streets outside the window. So far, no one is missing me.

Doc gave me this book called a journal, with a quill and ink. He asked me if I remembered how to write—and it turns out I do. He said that means I have some kind of education, which seemed to make him happy. He told me this book would be a good place to write down all my thoughts—the things I am feeling and seeing. He said it can be like a paper memory. I think it's a good idea. There are a few things I didn't remember, but now I know:

When you put your finger into a cup of hot tea—it burns.

Women are not supposed to wear trousers—but I do.

Old men like Abe snore loudly when their mouth falls open, and they aren't very happy when you wake them to let them know.

I do not like red beets.

A gunshot wound hurts a lot more than the size of the hole it makes.

Outside, people were yelling in the street that the president was dead, and Doc cried for a man he told me he'd never even met. He said his name was Lincoln.

Questions can be tiresome if you are not the person asking.

There are times when Abe says, "Let's have a few moments of silence, shall we?" and he isn't teasing.

A lot of people come to Doc for help. There was a man with shoulder pain and a little girl who had a sore throat and an old woman who complained of a bellyache. He helps them and sends them on their way, and they look happier when they go than they did when they arrived.

Tomorrow, we are going to ride in a horse-drawn wagon. I asked Doc where we're going, but he said it's a surprise.

I don't remember if I like surprises. I hope I do.

St. Louis hummed with activity as Doc steered the wagon through heavy horse-and-buggy traffic on Main Avenue. The day was warm, and it didn't take long for the girl to feel the sun heat up the wool of her shirt, making her wonder why she had chosen such heavy material for her clothes. The relative quiet of the clinic seemed like a haven to her in contrast to the hustle and bustle of the people, wagons, horses, and buggies along the city street. Everywhere she looked she saw busyness. Merchants unloading wagons, women in brightly colored dresses making their way along the road, soldiers in different uniforms standing together in clusters. Loud clanging bells sounded behind them, and she jumped. Doc slapped the reins against the horse's back as a wagon filled with a half-dozen men careened past them.

"Fire somewhere," Doc observed as he fell back in line with traffic. They continued up Main past several businesses, and she frowned. "The windows are all covered in black."

"As a sign of respect," he said. "The country is in mourning over President Lincoln's death."

But she'd already turned her attention to two black men weaving their way in and out of the buggies on the street. He watched the way she studied them.

"I'm guessing you don't remember seeing Negroes before?"

"Negroes?"

"Colored people. Black-skinned."

The girl kept her eyes on them as they passed close by their buggy. "No, I don't."

"They're a good part of the reason we just came through that bloody war," he said.

"The fighting was over black men?"

"In part—yes," Doc said. "The Southern states who wanted to secede from the Union believed that a white man has the right to own a black man as his slave. Slave labor has been a part of the Southern way of life for as long as I can remember."

"You mean the black man would be—property?"

"Yes."

"Who won the fighting?" she asked.

"The Union, my dear. The Union prevailed, and slavery was abolished by Mr. Lincoln, and now, supposedly, all men are equal."

"You don't sound as if you believe that's true," she said. The same black men she'd been watching disappeared into a building displaying a sign that read The Freedmen's Bureau.

"I believe it's how it should be," he said. "But I also believe it will take more than my lifetime for everyone to come around to that way of thinking."

A man staggered past them and heaved right on the ground. The girl recoiled from the sight and grimaced.

"Doc—he's sick," she said, pointing to the man as he wiped a beard of vomit from his chin.

"He's sick all right," Doc retorted without sympathy. "Sick on whiskey."

"Aren't you going to stop and help him?"

"I'm afraid it's pointless," Doc said. "I imagine a man like that is drinking to forget something."

"That hardly seems fair," she said.

"What do you mean?"

"He's drinking to forget, and I forgot without drinking."

Thirty minutes later, Doc slowed the horse and turned down a long dirt road lined with trees. They stopped in front of a nondescript whitewashed building.

"We're here," he announced.

The girl examined the building. "So—*this* is the surprise?" she asked, her voice tinged with disappointment.

"Part of it."

"Why are we here?"

"That is the other part of the surprise," he said. "There is someone here I want you to meet."

She turned troubled eyes on the doctor. There was something he
wasn't saying—something that he didn't want to say. She could sense
it. And it made her stomach flip with worry.

"I don't want to meet someone."

"Yes, of course you do. It's always good to meet new people," he
said. She could hear the sound of pounding from somewhere behind
the house.

He jumped down from the buckboard and offered her his hand.
"Come on now. Here we go."

She ignored him, choosing instead to look straight ahead.

"Please, Missy. Get down."

"Why?"

"Because I think it would be a good idea for you to stretch that
injured leg of yours," he said. He wiggled his outstretched fingers in
the air, and she reluctantly grasped his strong, weathered hand so he
could help her from the wagon.

The pounding grew louder as they approached the back of the
building. And then she heard voices—women's voices raised over the
noise.

"Where are we?" the girl asked as he hurried her along. "What
is this place?"

But he didn't answer. Instead, he ushered her around the side
of the structure until she was looking at several women all dressed
exactly alike. They wore black tunics that brushed the ground and

white headpieces that fit closely around their faces. Some of them had pushed up the sleeves of their tunics so they bunched at the elbows, and more than a few of them held hammers.

"My, my, my. The addition is nearly finished," Doc Abe muttered, obviously impressed by what he saw.

"Addition?" the girl asked.

"They've added this part onto the house, you see," he said, gesturing to an L-shaped room shooting off from the back of the house. However, it wasn't the building that interested her. Instead, she focused on the activity in the yard. Several women were gathered around a horse, a beautiful bay, and some had formed a semicircle around a rough piece of wood on the ground. The beautiful chestnut-colored horse was being tethered to a heavy rope around his harness, while the women around him spoke in a steady stream of encouragement.

"Top a' the mornin' to you, Doctor!" a voice called out from above. The girl and the doctor looked up to see two women straddling a crossbeam centered on the edge of the roof. Their black tunics rode up on their legs, allowing everyone below them a glimpse of black stockings and sturdy black shoes.

"Good morning, Sister Martha! Sister Ruth!" Doc Abe said.

"They are your sisters?" the girl asked.

"They are *nuns*," he answered.

She searched her impaired memory for the word, testing it out. "Nuns."

"Yes. The sisters here," he said with a touch of impatience. He called out to the women on the roof. "Where might I find Mother Helena?"

"Right there," one of the sisters said, pointing to a small woman kneeling beside the wood on the ground. She pulled a long nail from between her lips and positioned it for striking.

"Mother Helena?"

Mother Helena gave the nail a few sharp raps and then turned toward Doc. It was plain to see she was older than the other sisters; her face was etched with lines and life, and nothing about her seemed soft or feminine.

Doc gave an absent pat to the arm of his companion. "You stay right here, Missy. I'm going to have a word with Mother Helena."

The girl watched Doc walk until he was standing close enough to the older nun to presumably have a private conversation. A conversation, she assumed, that would be about her.

Mother Helena was both thankful and irritated that she had to take a break from the time on her knees. The sun was climbing higher and the day growing hotter, and though she loathed admitting it—even to herself—her joints were throbbing with a steady heartbeat of pain. Several pairs of hands reached down to help her when it became evident she was going to stand. Wasn't it only a few months ago that she could be on her knees for hours in prayer and never feel a twinge of discomfort? She allowed the sisters to help her to her feet and turned to face her friend Abe Johnson, taking care to dust off her black habit and straighten the rosary beads that hung from a cincture around her waist.

"Abe! This must be divine timing!" Mother Helena said in a voice rich with an Irish brogue. She looked past Doc to his companion, who stood several yards away. "You've come to help and brought an able-bodied young man with you!"

"Not a young man, Mother," he said. "A young *woman* in need of your help." He lowered his voice. "She's got nowhere else to go. No means to support herself."

Mother Helena couldn't hide her surprise. She narrowed her blue-gray eyes and looked again with more scrutiny, even as the young woman started to make her way closer to the activity in the yard.

"I'm sure there is a story here," she said, "but the fact of the matter is that I don't have time to hear it right now."

"She needs a place to stay," Abe said.

The nun shook her head. "I'm sorry, Abe, but I can't take her in. We honestly don't have room." She looked from Abe to the two nuns on the roof. "Sister Martha! You need to move back a bit. You're dangerously close to that edge."

"Yes, Mother," Sister Martha said, carefully inching herself backward on the beam.

Satisfied, Mother Helena looked back at Doc. "I don't mean to be rude, Abe, but the day is growing warmer, and we've still work to do before the heat forces us inside. Surely there is someone else who can take her in? Doesn't she have family? Friends? Even a distant cousin somewhere?"

"I honestly don't know—and neither does she. She was brought to my clinic two weeks ago, unconscious. When she woke up, it quickly became apparent that she's suffering from amnesia—probably due to a head injury. She remembers odd things—can read and write. She's obviously been educated—seems quite intelligent—but has no specific memories about herself. I've been calling her Missy because she can't even remember her own name."

Mother Helena lifted a brow that disappeared beneath the bandeau of her headpiece. She turned her attention back to the young woman. "And the clothes?"

"She was found in them, and she's refused my offer to buy her something more appropriate."

"Pride, I suppose," Mother Helena said. "The clothes she's wearing may have been all she could find in some unfortunate circumstance."

"I don't believe that's true, Mother."

Mother Helena glanced over at the young woman. "Oh? What makes you say that?"

"Pardon my candor, but her chest was tightly bound under that shirt," he said. "I suspect her identity is perplexing to her in more than one way. I'm sure she intended to pass herself off as a man."

The horse whinnied impatiently and snorted loudly. Mother Helena's attention went to a young postulant kneeling by the horse's harness. "I believe that horse is the Devil incarnate," she said.

"How did you end up with him?"

Mother Helena rolled her eyes heavenward and shook her head. "We had limited funds to procure a horse. The liveryman gave us a choice from some animals rounded up from captured Confederates. He looked the strongest, and we were assured he had an even temperament. He said his name is Lucky, but if you ask me, it's the liveryman who got lucky when he sold us that unpredictable animal!"

The horse snorted again and pawed at the ground. Mother Helena called out, "You know what happened last time, Oona! Make sure that knot is secure!"

"Yes, Mother, I will."

Mother Helena saw the young woman in the trousers move even closer to the activity.

Abe's voice took on a pleading tone. "Please, Helena. As one friend to another, take her off my hands. I can't keep her on at the clinic any longer. It's not proper."

"I'm sorry, Abe, I truly am, but all of our energies are focused on getting the orphanage ready. The horror of the war is over, but the new horror is how many children have been left without parents. The orphans are coming. The Lord has told me to hurry, and that's precisely what I'm doing."

"For all intents and purposes, *she is* an orphan, Mother."

"She's a grown woman."

"Yes, but more importantly, I know you would concede she is a child of God, and who better to see to her spiritual and physical needs than God's humble servants such as yourselves?" he asked with an innocent look. "Turning your back on one of God's own must break a dozen or more commandments."

"There are ten commandments, Abner," Mother Helena said. She arched a brow at the doctor. "If you're going to use the Good Book to argue your point, at least get the number of commandments right."

"Then you'll help her?"

Mother Helena issued a heavy sigh. "She obviously needs more time and help than I can give her. Besides, I can't imagine how she would fit in here."

The level of excitement in the yard grew exponentially with the readiness of the horse. Mother Helena turned her attention to the bay as he danced in his harness.

"'Tis time to say a silent prayer to the Father that all goes well with this attempt, Sisters," Mother Helena announced. For the moment she forgot about Abe and the mysterious young woman and took her own advice to direct a prayer to God that the horse would have a complete change of personality and—for once—cooperate.

Reaching up to open the collar button of her wool shirt for some relief from the wet heat, the girl nearly tripped over the huge piece of wood on the ground. Chastising herself for almost falling in front of all the strange women, she quickly realized that they weren't even looking at her. They were all focused on the beautiful horse. She watched as a woman gave a final tug on the rope knotted around his harness. This woman was young and dressed differently from the others. She wore a black lace cap, black skirt, and white blouse covered in dust and dirt. The young woman got to her feet and looked up at the sisters on the roof.

"Are you ready, then?" she called out in a voice that practically lilted like a song.

The sisters hollered back down. "Ready!"

Though the girl was grateful her presence seemed to go unnoticed, she would have liked to ask one of the women what they were doing. She could see that the rope tied around the horse's harness was also looped up and around the beam on the roof. That rope went down and was attached to one end of the wood.

She heard one of the sisters say, "Let's hope that this horse has found his Catholic roots!"

The horse started to move forward, straining from the weight of the wood. She watched as the nuns moved on either side of the horse, encouraging him—cajoling him—willing him to keep moving away from the building. The rope grew taut, and the end of the wood came off the ground. Gaining momentum, the horse dug in and continued to move. The rope around the beam groaned and creaked, and as she watched, the wood inched higher and revealed itself to be *two* pieces of wood that were crossed in the center. The wood wasn't smooth—it was like living bark that seemed regal and tall and imposing as it came completely off the ground and ascended.

She couldn't take her eyes from the beauty of the bare wood lifting into the cloudless blue sky. Her breath caught in her throat, and for a moment, she heard nothing but the sound of a breeze sighing over the crossed boughs now poised in the air above the roof. The only sight in the world was the sunlight burning around the edges of the cross suspended from the wide expanse of the heavens. Inexplicable longing made her choke back tears, and she wondered at the power of that simple piece of wood.

Then her reverie was shattered when the wood began to dance erratically in the air, swinging to and fro from the rope. The nuns behind her started to yell—panicked cries of "*Whoa! Whoa!*" On the roof, Sister Martha seemed to have but one objective—to grab the cross. She scrambled to her feet on the beam. The horse whinnied and snorted and stomped hard enough to cause the sisters around him to scatter back in fear. As the cross swung wildly toward her, Martha got her arms around the wood. Ruth, on the opposite side of the beam, sat frozen and unmoving.

"Let it go, Martha!" someone shouted, but the nun hung on with fierce determination. And then the horse skittered backward. The nun screamed as the cross plunged off the roof. The sisters tried frantically to gain control of the horse, but he seemed oblivious to everything as he reared in the air—causing the heavy wood to swing back and forth over the ground, the nun hanging on for dear life.

In the chaos of the moment, the girl's eyes connected with the horse as his front legs crashed back down against the ground. *He's looking straight at me*, she thought. *That horse* sees *me*. She could hear the nun on the cross praying out loud; she could see the nuns around the horse back away in fear from an animal who had lost all control. Yet she went toward him, lessening the space between them in a purposeful stride, and raised a hand in the air while he continued to stare at her.

"Easy now," she said to him, and he instantly calmed. His flaring nostrils were the only indication of his excitement as she grabbed hold of his harness. He responded readily to her commands and then strained under the weight of the wood again as he found purchase on the ground and dug in to raise the cross back above the roof.

"Pull it over, Ruth! Pull it over!" Mother Helena called out.

Seemingly jarred out of her shocked reverie, Sister Ruth reached out a hand for the sister clinging to the cross as it inched past the apex of the roof. Between them, they guided the heavy wood behind the parapet of the wall made for the sole purpose of housing the cross. Making quick work of the heavy rope, the sisters loosened it from the wood and threw it to the ground.

The horse's sides heaved with exhaustion, but he stood stock-still while the girl stroked his nose and whispered in his ear. It took a moment for her to remember that they weren't alone, and she looked up to see all the women in black staring at her in reverent silence.

"Glory be to God the Father," Mother Helena said.

"And to a young woman who seems to have a way with horses," Doc said with a definite smile in his voice. He turned to the older nun. "Can you imagine how she might fit in *now*, Mother?"

CHAPTER FOUR

Doc Abe is gone, and I am here in a place with thirteen women. It is embarrassing to cry in front of strangers, but I couldn't help myself as I watched him leave. I was mad and scared and wanted to run right after the wagon and go back to the clinic with him.

The sisters left me alone on the porch with my tears for a good while, and then when my head felt as if it would split wide open from misery, Mother Helena, the sister in charge, came to sit by me. She told me that sometimes God takes away all of the options but the one staring us in the face. I think that sounds like a dirty trick, but she knows God a lot better than I do. I followed her inside, hoping that her God knows what He's doing with me.

Mother Helena is small but quick, and I had to hurry to keep up with her as she led me through the house. She said the other sisters were having their afternoon prayers and then would have supper. I didn't want to do either, so she brought me to the room I am going to share with two sisters that she said are close to my age. Someone had already brought some nightclothes into the room and put them on one of the two beds. Mother Helena told me that tomorrow is a new day and we would "sort things out." I don't know what that means, but I am grateful to be alone now, doing what Doc Abe said to do—writing things down so I won't forget.

I feel lonely in the pit of my stomach and homesick for a place I can't describe.

A day can start out one way and end up in a way you can't even imagine.

I found a horse who can speak to me without words—and who seems to understand me better than people.

I like the end of the day the best—and the dark that covers me up so I can sink into sleep and not have to think about the puzzle my life has become.

The girl was already awake, dressed and sitting on the edge of the narrow cot, when Mother Helena knocked briskly on the door and then entered.

"Good morning," Mother Helena said. "Did you sleep well?"

"I slept fine," the girl lied.

Mother Helena studied her. "Good. Then let's have a wee look around the place before we'll be having breakfast."

She followed Mother Helena down the hallway from the bedrooms into an austere common room.

"We're an order of nuns from Ireland," Mother Helena said. "Women devoted to serving God. Our community is called the Little Sisters of Hope."

"What do you hope for?"

Mother Helena smiled, and her face transformed. "Right now, I hope you will come to feel like this is your home and we are people you can trust."

Once out of the common room, they moved through a kitchen and then into a narrow room where various pairs of galoshes were lined up against a wall and overcoats hung from pegs. Mother Helena pointed through the window on the far side of the room.

"We have a large garden we all tend to," she said. "And presently, we are in the process of adding on to the existing structure. Well, you saw that firsthand now yesterday, didn't you?"

The girl nodded. "There is a lot of pounding."

"Yes, lass, and I might as well be warning you now, you'll be hearing it morning, noon, and night until we get the place completed."

"Because you need a bigger house?"

"Because we're going to open an orphanage soon and need more room to accommodate the children who will be coming here. We will be a place for children who have lost their parents and have no one else to take care of them," Mother Helena explained. "Even though your circumstances are a bit different, they are like you."

"I'm not a child," the girl protested.

"As a wise man reminded me, you *are* a child of God, lass. If you don't remember anything else—remember that."

Moving through the house on the heels of Mother Helena, the girl met the sisters she would be living among. Engaged in various activities, each one stopped, glanced at the young woman in the dirty trousers and shirt, and nodded her greeting.

By the fourth sister she met, she detected a pattern. "All their names start with Mary," she said.

Mother Helena smiled. "Yes, at least *almost* all of them start with Mary. We have Sister Mary Agnes, Mary Gertrude, Mary Margaret, Mary Martha, Mary Ruth, Mary Constance, Mary Sarah, Mary Rachel, Mary Rebecca, and Mary Marie."

"But you are not Mary? You are Mother?"

"I am Sister Mary Helena," she explained, "but because of my position in the convent, the others refer to me as Mother. Deirdre and Oona are the other inhabitants of the house. They are called postulants—beginning nuns, if you will. They spend about a year with the community, studying and learning, and at the end of that time, they reconsider if they really have been called to this holy way of life."

They arrived back at the small bedroom she'd slept in, and Mother Helena led her inside. "We let you have the room to yourself last night, but I'm afraid that isn't a luxury we can continue. Tonight, Oona and Deirdre will be back in the room with you."

Another sister appeared in the doorway, carrying a bundle of clothes. Sister Agnes had lively blue eyes, and her fair skin had a generous dusting of freckles across her nose and cheeks. Her face looked far less serious than her habit.

"Here they are, Mother," she said, handing off the clothes and offering a quick smile at their guest.

"Thank you, Sister Agnes."

Sister Agnes disappeared as quickly as she had appeared, leaving the two of them alone again.

"Can we discuss your clothes?" Mother Helena asked.

The girl offered a small shrug.

Mother Helena pushed on. "Abe tells me that you were found wearing that shirt—those trousers."

"He tells me the same thing."

"And you don't know why?"

"I know you're not supposed to go around naked," she said. "I suppose that's why."

"Well, that's true," Mother Helena answered with a smile. "I meant do you have any idea why you would be wearing clothing meant for a man?"

"No. Doc kept asking me that too, but I don't see why it matters so much."

"Clothing is a uniquely human characteristic. It's a way to communicate to people who we are and what we value."

"I don't understand."

Mother Helena unfurled a simple blue dress from the pile of clothes in her arms. "What we wear usually defines our gender, our place in life—what we consider to be important. Even what we consider to be beautiful," she said. "Women usually wear dresses like this one."

"You're a woman."

"Yes."

"But you don't dress as a woman?"

"Not as *you* will dress, no. My clothing—my habit—tells the world that I am a woman who has decided to commit my life fully to God. Sisters dress alike because we value the conformity in it and the fact that it sends a message that we are living in our community for a sacred purpose."

"What do *my* clothes tell the world?" she asked.

Mother Helena hesitated for a moment. "I think that you were trying to tell the world that you didn't want to be known as a woman, lass."

The girl didn't respond to the statement, simply because she didn't know how to. She had no idea if the sister was correct. For a moment, she wondered if she'd ever know the answer.

"Am I to be lass, now, instead of Missy?" she asked, changing the subject.

"No. You need a proper name until you remember the name given to you at birth," Mother Helena said, taking the hint that the clothing discussion was over. "Just as I told you, when a postulant takes her sacred vows, she relinquishes her worldly name and takes the name of a saint to signify her new life in the church. Is there a name that has some kind of significance to you that you might remember?"

The girl shook her head. It made no difference to her what they called her. "No. You pick one," she told the nun.

Mother Helena nodded. "I will promise to give it some thought. Now, I'll have someone bring in a basin with some water for you to bathe, and then you can change into something clean for breakfast."

"The dress."

"Yes," Mother Helena said. "Sister Gertrude is a wonder with a needle and thread, and we'll have her make a few things that will be appropriate for you."

The girl hesitated. "I'll change into the dress, but I want to keep these clothes. Besides my journal that Doc gave me, and this chain"—she withdrew her silver medallion from under her shirt—"they're the only things that are truly mine."

"Of course," Mother Helena said. "We will have Sister Ruth wash the clothes and put them away for you." The sister crossed the few steps between them and gestured to the medallion. "May I have a closer look?"

"Yes."

Mother Helena lifted the long chain and palmed the medallion. "I don't suppose you remember what this is?"

"No," she said. "Doc Abe just told me I was wearing it when I was brought into the clinic."

"'Tis an Our Lady of Mercy medallion," Mother Helena explained, "meant to remind the wearer to pray for safety." She let the medallion drop against the shirt and smiled. "I take this to mean you're a believer."

"A believer?"

"In God."

"If I was," the girl said, "I don't remember."

Mother Helena nodded. "'Tis a hard thing you've been saddled with for sure, lass. But I have faith that the Lord brought you here for a purpose we have yet to know—and I believe He's just provided us with your new name."

"He has?"

The old nun nodded. "From now on, we'll call you Mercy."

CHAPTER FIVE

My new name is Mercy. I think I like it just fine. Maybe even better than my old name—whatever that was. I am sleeping in a room with Deirdre and Oona. They are much younger than the other sisters here. They wear black skirts and white blouses and black caps. When Oona takes her cap off, she has very long hair that hangs in a braid down her back. They left their families in Ireland to come to America and work with the Little Sisters of Hope. Did I leave my family? Do I even have a family? Oona told me the sisters are her family now.

Everyone here stays very busy. Mother Helena says God likes hard workers.

I don't care much for darning. If I ever did it before, I don't care now that I don't remember it.

It's possible to miss the sound of something that you didn't think you liked—even snoring. Quiet can be very loud.

Some of the sisters do the inside work and some do the building work, and all of them do the work of praying. Talking to God. They do it all the time.

God, if You're listening to me, I would like to have my memory back, please.

The dark room enveloped the three women, and for a moment, the only sound was a breeze pushing through an open window. An earthy scent filled the room, probably from the large garden beside the house. Mercy thought about how different it was from the chemical smells of Doc Abe's clinic. She gave herself a second or two to remember the sound of Doc's snoring and how it made her feel as if she wasn't alone in the world. But, she reminded herself, she wasn't alone. She was now living in a house filled with women. As Mercy's eyes adjusted, she could make out the forms of the young postulants. Deirdre lay opposite her on the only other cot in the room, and Oona was prone on a pallet on the floor between the cots. Mercy propped herself up on her elbow and whispered toward the dark form below her.

"I'm sorry you have to sleep on the floor, Oona. I should be the one down there."

"Stop your apologizing, Mercy. 'Tisn't your place to be on the floor. Mother made it quite clear that Deirdre and I will take turns with the cot."

"But this is your room," Mercy objected.

"'Tis your room too, now," Oona told her.

Mercy loved the sound of Oona's voice. Of all the women, Oona had the most lyrical Irish brogue. It almost sounded as if she were singing instead of speaking.

"Maybe Mother Helena doesn't have to know if I take my turn on the floor," Mercy offered. "I won't tell her."

"We can't be lying to Mother," Deirdre spoke up. "She'd know for sure."

"We can't be lying, period," Oona said reproachfully.

"I *know* that," Deirdre responded. "I've taken the same simple vows as you, Oona."

"How come you aren't Marys?" Mercy asked.

"We'll both take on Mary when we begin the novitiate and choose our new names," Oona said.

"Novitiate? Is that another name for nuns?"

"No, it's our formal training to prepare us to take our sacred vows," Oona said. "We will be known as novices then. I have already chosen my new name. I want to be Sister Mary Magdalene."

"I may not be Mary," Deirdre said quietly. "I may choose something else."

"You can't do that, Deirdre," Oona said in a scandalized tone.

"I can—and I might."

The room went quiet for a moment, and Mercy heard the soft, resigned sigh from Oona. "Your decision is between you and the Holy Father, of course. 'Tisn't for me to judge."

"Wouldn't it be something, if when I remember my real name—it turned out to be Mary?" Mercy asked. Both of the postulants were quiet for a moment before Deirdre giggled.

"That *would* be something."

"I have a younger sister named Mary," Oona offered. "Truly. Her name is Mary."

Deirdre giggled again. "You never told me that."

"Does that mean if she wanted to be a sister, she would be Sister Mary Mary?" Mercy surmised, causing both Deirdre and Oona to laugh.

"My parents were never worried that one of their daughters would join an order of Catholic nuns," Oona said, "considering they are Protestants."

"What does that mean?" Mercy asked.

"It means that Oona grew up rich in a country that hates and persecutes Catholics," Deirdre said.

"I don't understand. Why would people hate you?"

"I don't understand it either," Oona said. "One group of people hating another because of the way they choose to live their lives and worship God. Catholics were left without rights. No property—no voice in their country. No education for their women. No hope for their future. I'm thinking it has to cause tears in heaven for sure."

"Does that mean that your Protestant family hates you now, Oona?" Mercy asked.

Mercy barely heard Oona's covered whimper in the dark. Then came Deirdre's apologetic voice over Mercy's unguarded question.

"She didn't mean anything, Oona," she said. "She doesn't know any …"

"No, I don't believe they hate me," Oona said quietly. "I was quite young when I told them God had called me to serve. Children want to be all sorts of things when they grow up, and I don't think they took my quest to become a nun any more seriously than my brother telling them he would be a great knight and slay dragons."

"Ah. Dragons. Giant fire-breathing beasts that can tear you limb from limb," Mercy said.

Mercy could hear the smile in Oona's voice when she answered. "My brother did not grow up to become a knight and slay dragons."

"But you grew up to become a nun," Mercy observed.

"They tried to convince me otherwise. Year after year of arguments, but it didn't matter. I knew God wanted me, and that was more important—*even* more important than my parents. Finally, my da and I made an agreement. I would spend one year after school contemplating my future, and then at the end of that time, if I still felt the call in my heart, I would join the church."

"Was it hard—to say good-bye?"

"So hard," Oona whispered. "My ma and da, two brothers and sister, Mary, took me round to all my relations for a final farewell. We knew by then that I would be joining the Little Sisters of Hope here in America."

"Ireland is a long ways off?"

"Another world," Deirdre said wistfully. "Across water wider than you can even imagine."

"My family brought me all the way to the little seaside town where I was to board a ship for the journey," Oona recounted. "We arrived the night before, and there was a dance. A lovely band played waltz after waltz, and I danced with my da round and round in a barn that had been made to look like a fairyland. My green silk skirt twirled about my ankles and my da looked so handsome and my ma wiped tears away when she thought I didn't see. We danced until they put the fiddle away and the candles went out, and my da put a kiss on my cheek and told me he couldn't be there the next day when I traded my silk for the black skirt of the postulant."

"And then she met me at the ship," Deirdre said, "with enough family there to tell both of us farewell."

Oona laughed softly. "True enough."

"Your family was happy to have you leave, Deirdre?" Mercy asked.

"I am the oldest of thirteen brothers and sisters. From the time I was a wee girl, I knew I was supposed to become a nun. 'Twas my ma's dream for me. In Ireland, the best a little girl can hope for is to marry a farmer who has a big enough plot for potatoes to keep his family alive."

"So being a nun is better than being a wife of a potato farmer?"

Deirdre hesitated. "I almost married a potato farmer."

Mercy heard Oona's surprised intake of breath. "You never told me that before," Oona whispered.

"Patrick O'Leary." Deirdre breathed his name into the dark. "Handsomest man in the county, but as poor as he was charming. My ma said 'twas like looking in a mirror of the past and seein' my da standing there. Handsome and charming got her a house filled with hungry children and a husband who worked from sunup to sundown and a life that never changed for the better."

"Patrick O'Leary never had a chance, did he?" Oona asked.

Mercy heard the soft rustle of the pillowcase under Deirdre's head as she shook it in the dark. "He may as well of been the Devil himself, according to my ma. She wanted me to have an education— see the world. Have more out of life than worrying about how to feed hungry babies and wondering when the next potato famine will happen."

"But I thought God had to call you to be a nun," Mercy said.

"He did," Deirdre said quickly. "He did. I just didn't hear it as clearly as Oona."

"Maybe that's because He told your ma first, and then He told you," Mercy offered.

Deirdre didn't answer right away. Mercy heard the soft clearing of her throat and then the sound of her shifting on the cot. "Maybe."

Chapter Six

Four weeks, two days, and five needlepoint lessons is how long I have been with the Little Sisters of Hope. I have learned many things since my arrival. I confess I'm worried I may go to sleep, then wake up with my new memories as gone as my old ones, and I don't think I could stand that. So I will continue to write things down in this book just as Doc Abe told me to—so I can always remember.

Someone is stealing jams and sweets from the larder behind the kitchen. Sometimes I catch the sisters watching me. I heard Sister Constance tell Sister Ruth that things started to disappear just after a certain someone arrived. I think they may believe that I am the certain someone.

The orphans' house is almost ready, but there are still no beds. Mother Helena says, "God meets the needs of those who trust Him completely."

She's not worried. She says the beds will arrive when God wants them to arrive.

I despise sewing. All of it—even the needlepoint they keep trying to teach me.

Horses have their own language. Lucky talks to me, and the sisters let me take care of him. He is the one thing I love.

Mother Helena gave me beads like all the sisters wear. It is called a rosary. There are prayers that go with each bead, and honestly, I can't remember them all. Oona and Deirdre said someday I'll be able to say all the prayers like they do, but I'm not so sure. Sometimes when I touch each bead, I'm thinking of other things instead of talking to God. I'm thinking how good the rooms smell when Sister Sarah bakes bread. How Mother Helena looks like she's stern and angry sometimes but then her face cracks in a smile and she is beautiful. How weeding the garden with my hands in the hot dirt makes me lonely for something.

I have three dresses Sister Gertrude made for me. The sisters all looked so relieved when I started wearing them—but I feel like an impostor. I am ashamed to admit I felt more at home in my old clothes than I do in my new dresses. I miss the scratchy wool of the shirt and the comfort of those trousers. Is there something wrong with me?

Several nuns swarmed over the orphans' large room with a level of activity that Mercy found exhausting. It was midmorning, and they had been at the work of painting the walls since just after sunrise.

Mercy, in a pale-blue dress, stood out in the room filled with sisters in their black and white. She dipped her brush into the last of the paint in her bucket.

"How do you know that orphans will be coming?" Mercy asked.

"God has told me," Mother Helena answered.

"In actual words?"

The other sisters stopped painting and looked at Mother Helena as she answered. "Yes."

"Out loud and talking like we are right now?" Mercy persisted.

"No, Mercy. Not like this. It's a different way of talking. It's communicating in prayer."

"So in a prayer—you heard God's voice."

"That's right," Mother Helena said, dipping her brush into a bucket of paint.

"But He didn't say when? He didn't say today or tomorrow or next Friday?"

"He said there will be a need and we are to meet it," Mother Helena answered. "I take it on faith that if we don't dillydally, neither will the orphans."

She looked at the sisters, who had stopped painting to listen to the exchange, and raised an eyebrow. "Is everyone's paint bucket empty?"

"No, Mother," chorused the nuns, who went back to painting. Mercy stood with her brush dripping over the floor.

"But what if they come and we aren't ready?" Mercy asked. "What if God sends them early and there are no beds and the room still smells like paint and there isn't enough food for everyone? What if …"

"God's timing is always perfect," Mother Helena said.

"But …"

"Have you used up all your paint, Mercy?" Mother Helena asked. Mercy looked into her bucket and nodded. "Yes."

"There are some rags in a basket in the larder," Mother Helena said. "Why don't you go and get them so we might clean up the spatters on the floor."

Carrying an oil lamp for light, Mercy slipped into the larder behind the large kitchen. She had been inside the place only one other time—when Oona had shown it to her shortly after her arrival. The coolness of the room was an instant pleasure, and she thought how nice it would be if they could all fit inside and take their meals there instead of in the warm kitchen.

She found another lamp and lit it and took a moment to look around. Shelves held glass jars filled with jams, jellies, vegetables, and other kitchen staples. There were bags of coffee beans, containers of lard, and sacks of potatoes stacked in neat rows. Oona had explained that during the war, several of the local families in St. Louis had been generous to a fault with foodstuffs for the nuns. But true to form, Mother Helena had given most of the food away to soldiers passing through town, to prisoners they went to visit, to any young mother looking to feed her hungry family. The nuns were praying for a bountiful harvest from the garden so they would have plenty of food for all the orphans once they arrived.

Mercy held the lamp up as she made her way across the floor. She paused in front of a full-length cheval glass tucked into a corner between two bushels of potatoes. The sight of her own face still took her by surprise, and she took a moment to study her image. Her brown hair had grown since the last time she'd seen herself. The longer it got, the more she noticed the waves that seemed to appear of their own accord. In the heat of summer, her curls stuck to her cheeks and seemed more annoying than anything else, but the sisters assured her that her hair was quite beautiful. She wiggled her eyebrows at herself, then raised one brow the way she'd seen Mother Helena do on occasion. She looked both serious and ridiculous and laughed as she turned to look at her blue dress from all angles. She remembered doing the same thing after she'd first arrived and Oona had taken her into the larder to see her reflection.

"Is this the customary place to keep a mirror?" she'd asked Oona. "Doc keeps his mirror on the wall in the clinic. It seems more useful that way."

"We consider vanity to be a sin," Oona answered with the Irish lilt in her voice that made everything sound pleasant. "'Tis why we keep the lookin' glass in here. In case of an emergency."

Mercy laughed. "What kind of emergency?"

"Let's say you've got a nasty bit of somethin' in your eye and everyone is busy with their chores or they're prayin' or just in the contemplative time of the morn. You can slip in here and take care of your eye yourself."

"Has that ever happened to you?"

Oona looked sheepish. "Once or twice," she admitted. "But not because I feel the need to stare at my reflection. God made me a plain woman, and I'm glad for it. It's just that sometimes, when I'm missin' my family back home, I come in here and look in the glass. I see their faces in mine, and it makes me a wee bit less homesick."

Mercy didn't see any faces but her own. She turned from the mirror and spotted the basket of rags. As she started to lift the basket, something on the floor beside it caught her eye. Her clothes! *Her* clothes. The brown shirt and green pants were lying on top of a heap of rags as if they were waiting to be burned with the rubbish. She remembered Mother Helena saying they would put the clothes away for her. Away in the larder with the rest of the rags is what she meant! The thought was quick and bitter, and Mercy felt a stab of anger that someone had so easily discarded one of the only things she had of her past. She plucked the clothes from the floor.

With her back to the mirror, Mercy dropped her dress to the floor and stepped out of the puddle of blue fabric. She drew her pants up over her slim hips and fastened them. They were snug—but they fit. She shrugged into the shirt and buttoned it over her cotton camisole. When the scratchy wool material settled itself against her skin, she felt inexplicably complete.

Mercy slowly turned to face the mirror. She looked at her reflection—this new reflection in her proper clothes—and willed her mind to find something familiar about the image. But after several seconds of studying herself, the only thing that seemed familiar was her disappointment in her own ability to remember. Her dress still lay in a heap on the larder floor. The blue fabric was so much lighter, prettier, infinitely more feminine than the brown wool of the shirt she had on—so why was she so drawn to these clothes? She shook herself from her pondering and started to unbutton the shirt just as she heard someone coming. Mercy blew out both lamps and ducked around to the back side of the shelves in the dark room.

A circle of light from a lamp floated into the larder. The woman carrying it, Sister Agnes, was cast in a small glow as she headed purposefully toward the shelves that Mercy was tucked behind. Sister Agnes was humming softly—a happy, catchy little tune that put a half smile on her face. Mercy already knew it was too late for her to say anything, so she practically held her breath and hoped that the sister would be quick about her errand and go on her way. Sister Agnes stopped in front of the shelf that held the jellies and jams and all things sweet and moved things around until she finally withdrew one particular jar. As Mercy watched, the nun pulled a spoon from the long sleeve of her habit. Popping the lid of the jar, she dipped in her spoon and moaned in ecstasy with the first taste. Lip-smacking, satisfied sounds followed as she made short work of the contents.

"Maybe just one more wee bite of … something," Sister Agnes muttered, raising her lamp. The light wandered over bags of beans and baskets of potatoes, but they didn't make Agnes pause. She kept shoving things from one side to another. Finally, Mercy saw her smile broadly. "'Twas a good year for raspberries, as I recall." She stretched out a hand toward a small jar right in front of Mercy's face, but then seemed to slip. Agnes caught herself with a hand to the shelf and looked down, then her face dipped out of Mercy's view. When she stood back up, Mercy could see she held a swath of fabric in her arms. Sister Agnes put her lamp down on the shelf at the same time Mercy leaned in from her hiding place to get a better look at the sister's find. Mercy realized her mistake too late. The eyes behind the shelf met the eyes in front of the shelf, and Agnes screamed so loudly it echoed off the larder wall. The nun spun on her heels and ran.

By the time Mercy came to stand at the threshold between the larder and the kitchen, Agnes was already surrounded by concerned nuns. A few of them were consoling her even as they tried to get to the bottom of what had frightened her.

Agnes clutched blue fabric to her bosom and tried to put her fright into words. "An eye … hiding … watching … a sneaky, dreadful demon!" She shuddered.

Mother Helena sailed into the kitchen with Oona and Deirdre on her heels. All three of them were paint splattered. Mother Helena still held her brush in her hand when she crossed to Agnes.

"What's all this, then?" she asked.

"Something in the larder near scared the life out of her," Sister Ruth said.

"What was it, then?"

Mercy stepped all the way through the threshold. "It was me."

All eyes turned on her as she stood barefoot in her shirt and trousers. The sisters parted to give Agnes a better view of her demon in the dark.

"*You?*" Sister Agnes asked. "That was you hiding in the dark?"

"I didn't mean to be hiding," Mercy stammered. "I just didn't want anyone to see me."

"Then that would be hiding, Mercy," Mother Helena said.

"Yes, Mercy." Agnes sniffed. "*That* would be hiding."

"Jelly, jams, marmalade—sugar cubes—have gone missing in recent weeks, Mercy. What were you doing in the larder?" Sister Ruth demanded.

"Mother sent me to find some rags," Mercy said, though she looked at Sister Agnes.

Mother Helena nodded. "That's true. Though I was starting to wonder if you'd lost your way back."

Ruth turned to Agnes. "What were *you* doing in there, Sister?"

Agnes's gaze flew around the room, but before she could answer the question, Sister Margaret pointed a finger at Mercy.

"I have a better question. Mercy, why are you dressed in those dreadful clothes?"

Mercy felt every eye upon her, and she took a step back—away from their accusing stares. "I found them, and I put them on. I would have changed back, but Sister Agnes has my dress."

Agnes looked down at the fabric she held against her chest as if she had never seen it before in her life. "Oh. Um." She thrust the dress out toward Mercy. "Here."

It was Mother Helena who took the dress and then walked toward Mercy.

"You may change now," she said, holding out the dress. "Then we can get back to work."

Mercy looked at the dress, at the sisters with their judging stares—and at Agnes, who couldn't seem to pull her gaze from the floor.

"It makes more sense to clean up paint spatters in these clothes," Mercy said.

Mother Helena raised her brows. "We've discussed this before, Mercy," she said. "Maybe you don't remember ..."

"I remember," Mercy said.

"Then you'll remember that those clothes are inappropriate for a young woman," Mother Helena said.

"Why?" Mercy challenged, powerless to stop the surliness in her voice.

"Because they suggest that the young woman doesn't want to be seen as a young woman. Because they offer a familiar view of your form that should be left behind closed doors. Because I believe the clothes we wear can shape the people we are."

"And if I'm a person who would rather be in this," Mercy said, sweeping her hand down her side, "than that?" She pointed to the dress. "What does that make me?"

Mother Helena held the dress toward her one more time, a look of determination on her face. "It's pointless to speculate," she said. "Let's put this behind us. Just change into your clothes, and we can get back to work."

"*These* are my clothes!" Mercy yelled. "The same clothes someone threw next to the basket of rags in the larder as if they were rubbish."

"There is no need to shout," Mother Helena said crisply.

"I think you need to ask her about the missing food, Mother," Sister Ruth said.

Mother Helena sighed and looked at Mercy. "Is there something you want to tell me, Mercy? Something you need to confess?"

Mercy looked at Sister Agnes, whose fingers were flying over her rosary beads, but then shook her head. "I have never taken any food from the larder. As for other confessions, I have no idea—but I would gladly confess to thievery of any kind if it meant I could remember it!"

"You don't mean that," Mother Helena said.

"And you don't know that! You can't pretend to know me when I don't even know myself. I might be a conniving, sinful, murdering thief who has found shelter with women who have taken a vow not to judge and to always forgive."

"We don't believe you are any of those things, Mercy," Mother Helena said.

"Then stop looking at me as if you do!"

Mercy felt the room grow warmer; the walls crept closer—and her anger edged out her humiliation.

"I know what you all think of me! I see you back up when I come too close. I see how hard it is for you to pray for the sins you think I've committed!"

"We *do* pray for you, Mercy," Mother Helena said.

"I fear that it may be a lost cause, Mother," Mercy said. "I don't hear God, and He doesn't hear me. Save your prayers for those who believe they're doing some good."

She felt as if all the air had been sucked out of the room. She couldn't breathe and couldn't look at the collective group of holy women who all knew exactly who they were and what they wanted to do with their lives.

"I need some air," Mercy finally said in a strangled voice. She turned and ran from the kitchen.

CHAPTER SEVEN

Mercy ran. She ran straight to Lucky without being aware she was doing it.

The horse snorted as she threw open the gate of the corral. As he came closer to investigate, she grabbed a rope hanging from a post, climbed the fence, and threw a leg over his back. He danced anxiously as she settled herself squarely astride, her bare feet dangling at his sides. She made a slipknot in the rope, looped it over his head, leaned forward, and pressed her face close to his neck.

"Go!" She jabbed her heels into his sides, and he took off.

The horse and rider lunged through the gate and galloped past the convent. Mercy was vaguely aware of some of the nuns calling for her to stop. She tightened her legs around Lucky, leaned as close to his body as she could manage, and hung on. He wove in and out of the trees that lined the road to the convent, as if he intended to cam-ouflage their escape. Instinctually, she gave the horse his head and held tight as he thundered across the ground—going from the cover of the trees near the convent to a copse of trees in the distance. Both Lucky's raw power and his speed left her breathless. She closed her eyes and gave in to the feelings—the warm air rushing past her face, the coarse coat of the horse where her cheek skimmed his neck. As Lucky moved deftly through a canopy of gnarled oaks, the landscape became a dappled checkerboard of sun and shadow. She and Lucky were racing toward something indefinable when the sounds around her became a procession of indistinct moments jumbled together. Something hissed past her ear—like an invisible snake slicing the air in half. Bang-whistle-cracks filled the space around her, and she flinched with each new noise. Her eyes flew open, and she ducked even closer to the horse, pressing her face tightly against him. She could feel Lucky's pounding pulse against her own skin and felt her stomach twist with fear for his safety. Booming, thunderous explo-sions and showers of sparks fell like rain. Sounds of panic vibrated against air that smelled of sulfur. Her nose burned from the acrid fumes, and she held her breath. *Don't breathe ... don't breathe. Faster! Go faster!* Her lungs felt as if they might explode as she rode through clouds and clouds of billowing blue smoke. *Don't breathe ... don't breathe.* When she and Lucky finally shot out of the trees into the open, she couldn't wait any longer and sucked in long, even breaths of nothing but the sweet air of the beautiful Missouri countryside.

Mercy's pounding heart matched the horse's cadence across a bucolic meadow. She hadn't consciously given Lucky a single direc-tive, other than the command to go, since climbing on his back. But now, with his flanks lathered with sweat from the long, hard run, she took control. With small, almost imperceptible movements, she slowed him to a trot, then a walk. She had no idea why, but he took her cues without hesitation, and she finally let her guard down long enough to take in the landscape around them. There was no noise other than birdsong; no smoke filtering through the air … just a couple of lazy clouds floating across the perfect summer sky. She looked back over her shoulder at the tree line as if to reassure herself that no nightmare was following her.

She was sweating nearly as much as the horse, and it wasn't entirely because of the heat of the June day. She told herself that everything was fine. Everything was as it should be. She had just had some kind of strange hallucination. At least she hoped it was a hallucination, because if she was actually remembering those things—then maybe she didn't want to know about her past after all.

Lucky abruptly stopped, and she was nudged from her reverie back into the scenery around her. A lovely pond was directly in front of them, edged in cattails and shaded by several big weeping willows. It was so beautiful it looked more like an artist's rendering than an actual, physical thing. Mercy slipped from the horse's back, and her bare feet sank into lush green grass. Free of his rider, Lucky made his way to the pond to drink. Her mind had her so weary she didn't even take the time to contemplate her next move. She stripped off the heavy trousers and peeled the hot shirt from her back, feeling instant relief from the heat in only her white cotton chemise and knickers. After draping her clothes over a low-hanging tree limb, she made her way to the pond and waded right into the cool water. Her swift, efficient strokes did little to disturb the surface of the pond; it looked like she was cutting through a pale-green pane of glass. A light breeze stirred the cattails and sighed through the tall grass of the meadow, and she felt immense relief at being alone. The solitude felt as if an old friend she hadn't realized she missed. She ducked under the water, flipped around, and started back toward the other side of the pond. When she surfaced, the first thing she heard was Lucky snorting indignantly. The horse was standing stock-still, and his ears were pricked at attention. She followed the horse's gaze to an approaching buggy. She uttered a word that would surely make the nuns pray for her salvation and tried to gauge how quickly she could make it from the pond to her clothes, which flapped lazily in the breeze. *I'll never make it*, she thought. *Not without God and everyone else seeing me.* This predicament would certainly have sent the nuns to their knees.

The fancy buggy was driven by a young man with a lovely young woman by his side. They stopped just a few yards from Lucky. For the second time that day, Mercy tried hard to conceal her presence. She was so low in the water her mouth was submerged.

She watched as the young man jumped down from the buggy and offered his companion his hand.

"Beautiful-looking bay, but he's not one of ours," he said.

"Look, Rand. There's a rope around his neck. It looks as if he ran away," she said logically.

In the water, Mercy felt her fingers shrivel and the rest of her body grow cold from not moving. She wanted to yell at them to leave her alone—give her some privacy—but instead, she stayed mute.

"We've picked up strays from the war, of course," Rand said, still surveying Lucky, "but this one looks too well fed and cared for to be a war horse, Cora."

It seemed to Mercy that the woman he called Cora had already grown bored with the conversation about the horse. She popped open a parasol, carefully laid it against her shoulder to shield her from the sun, and gave all her attention to the pond.

"You were right, Rand," she said. "This spot is perfect for a picnic. Absolutely stunning. Are you going to get the hamper?"

Mercy groaned. She would have to make her presence known, but now it seemed awkward that she hadn't spoken up right away. She cursed her own impetuous behavior for the second time that day.

But instead of getting the picnic hamper, Rand was moving closer to the horse. Lucky nickered and whinnied and danced his annoyance at the man's presence.

"Easy, boy, easy there," Rand said in a soothing voice. "I just want to ..."

Mercy knew by the look on his face that he'd spotted her clothes over the limb of the tree. She watched him put it all together when he looked from the rope around Lucky's neck to the clothes on the branch—and then strode closer to the pond.

"You there!" He was walking so quickly toward the water that she backstroked a few feet, being careful to stay fully submerged. "You're trespassing on private property! Come out of there right now."

"Rand! That would be indecent!" Cora protested in a mortified voice.

"Oh," he said. "Right. My apologies for being so insensitive, Cora. Turn around."

Cora spun where she stood so that her back was to the pond. Mercy kept treading water. Rand braced his hands on his hips. "Now get out!"

Her heart hammered in her chest, but she didn't move an inch toward the shore. Would there ever be a time when someone wasn't telling her what to do, what to say, how to dress, or how to feel?

Rand drew a small pistol from the waistband of his pants. "I have no patience for this today," he said. He aimed at the pond. "Out!"

At the sight of the gun, Mercy gasped—and sucked in enough water to make her feel as if her lungs were going to explode.

"Come on now ... don't make me shoot you!"

She was coughing, gagging ... struggling just to keep her chin above the pond while she tried to get some air.

Rand leveled the small pistol in her general direction, then fired off a shot that missed her by a couple of yards. He squeezed off one more shot that zipped into the water behind her.

Still choking, she started swimming hard for the shore until her feet found purchase in the silt. As she rose up out of the water, her cotton chemise and drawers plastered themselves to her body and left nothing to the imagination of the shocked man. Apparently hearing her companion's gasp, the woman looked over her shoulder.

"Oh my good Lord," Cora sang out in a scandalized tone. "Rand! Rand ... are you seeing this?"

Rand was indeed seeing it. The interloper in his pond wasn't a man—but a woman. A woman who stood doubled over in her less-than-modest attire, choking and coughing and sputtering. She shoved her wet hair from around her face and finally straightened up to glare at him.

"I didn't know," Rand said. "You didn't say anything! Why didn't you say anything?!"

The woman took a breath and then coughed as she started toward the horse. "I was choking while you were shooting at me," she said in a scratchy voice. "I couldn't speak!"

He watched her hurry quickly toward the clothes draped over the tree branch and pull them free. Without preamble and without giving him or Cora another glance, she made quick work of stepping into the trousers.

"I swear, Rand, she's nothing but a river urchin who doesn't know enough to dress as a woman!" Cora said snippily. "She probably lives under a bush somewhere."

The young woman threw a bruising glare at Cora.

"I live in a house with the Little Sisters of Hope," she said with a trace of the South in her voice. "*Not* under a bush." She shrugged into the wool shirt, not bothering to even button it before she gathered the horse's rope in her hand.

"I would think an apology would be in order," Cora said loudly. "You were trespassing, and you *did* parade around half-naked in front of complete strangers!"

The young woman seemed to have no intention of apologizing to anyone. She grabbed the mane of the horse and tried to haul herself up onto his back—but couldn't manage it.

Rand started toward her. "Let me ..."

She shot him a look that stopped him in his tracks. "I can manage," she said.

She tried again to hoist herself onto the bare back of her horse but slid off before she had success.

"Oh, for pity's sake," Cora muttered.

Color rose in the woman's cheeks as she led the horse right next to the buggy, climbed onto the frame, and then jumped onto his back.

She looked at Rand and Cora. "I wasn't trespassing. I was swimming," she said. "Good-bye." With a small jab into the horse's side with her bare heels, she was off.

Rand watched her ride away. She sat perfectly on the horse, in command, yet relaxed and natural with his gait.

"I suppose there's one good thing that came out of this very odd encounter," Cora said, tucking her arm through his.

"What might that be?" Rand asked.

"An entertaining story, of course," Cora said.

Rand shook his head and turned from the sight of the girl on the horse to smile at the girl on his arm. "No one would ever believe it."

CHAPTER EIGHT

Mercy saw the cross from a distance—beckoning her back with an indefinable beauty and promises she couldn't quite grasp. Anytime she was outside with Lucky, whitewashing the orphans' house, gardening—her eye was drawn time and time again to the simple cross on the roof. It grew larger against the sky the closer she got to the convent. The thought of facing Mother Helena and the rest of the sisters made her feel weary from the inside out.

She rode Lucky around to the back of the convent, grateful she didn't see a soul. She took him straight to the corral to see to her basic duties for caring for the horse. She took off the rope and set about brushing him. Methodically rubbing him down, she took her time to make sure the horse felt cared for—loved. Finally, she placed a kiss on his nose.

"You have a special bond with that horse," Mother Helena said from somewhere behind her.

Mercy turned to see her standing against the corral fence, but the nun's face masked any emotion she might be feeling.

Mercy nodded. "Yes, Mother. And I'm thankful for it."

Mother Helena walked toward her. "I am thankful for it too, Mercy."

"Do you think it's strange I'm more comfortable spending time with him than with people?"

"I suppose it's because animals seem to have a way of accepting us just as we are."

"Maybe that's it. I don't feel as if I'm disappointing him."

"You're not to live your life looking for approval from others, Mercy. It's only God's approval that matters."

"I'm not having breakfast, lunch, and dinner with God watching me, studying me, commenting on my clothes."

"I beg to differ. He is in every part of our day and night here. It's His approval you must seek—not mine. Not the other sisters'."

Mercy ran her hand along Lucky's nose, then looked at Mother Helena. "I'm sorry I spoke to you the way I did."

"Anger can be a tricky thing," Mother Helena said. "Sometimes it is misplaced, but sometimes it is justified. I'm sorry you felt attacked and judged. That has never been our intention."

"I want to keep these clothes," Mercy said. "But I will put my dress back on."

"All right."

"And I want you to know I haven't been stealing food from the larder."

"I know."

"You do?"

Mother Helena nodded. "I've known for quite some time it's Sister Agnes."

Mercy's mouth dropped open. "Then why did you accuse me?"

"I didn't accuse you, dear. I asked if you had something you wanted to confess. I knew you must have seen Agnes taking the food."

"But if you don't say something to Agnes, she will think she's getting away with it. She'll keep doing it, and more food will be gone!"

"The missing food isn't nearly as important as Agnes coming to me on her own, without the prompting of discovery. It will help both her conscience and her soul."

"What if she doesn't?"

"She will. God is working on her heart. I'll leave the timing of it all to Him."

"Just like you do with everything?"

Mother Helena smiled, and as usual, it took Mercy aback the way it made the nun look so much younger. She could see Helena as a young woman when she smiled. "Yes. Just like I do with everything. 'Tis the only way I can live my life."

"I wish I could do that."

"You can," Mother Helena said. "And I will tell you right now it's not an issue of what you're wearing. It doesn't matter if you are wearing those trousers or a nun's habit or a ball gown for dancing. It's a decision of your soul to trust it all to Him."

Mother Helena took a step back, crossed her arms over her chest, and tucked her hands into her sleeves. "Now, about the way you spoke to me." Her face became stern again. "If you were a sister, I'd be giving you the opportunity to seek penance in the form of many, many prayers, but since you are not in the order, I think being on your knees weeding the garden might offer you the time you need to repent of your anger."

"You mean I can stay?" Mercy asked, even as she was secretly relieved that her punishment was to be outdoors—and not spent in hours upon hours of prayers she had a hard time remembering anyway.

"Have I given you reason to think otherwise?" Mother Helena asked.

Mercy shook her head, relieved that she hadn't completely taken herself out of the nun's good graces. "No, Mother Helena, you haven't. Thank you."

"Good. Now there's something else." Mother Helena looked toward Lucky. "When the time comes to get the children, I have a very important job for you."

"Oh?"

"You must be the one who harnesses Lucky and drives the wagon. That special bond you share will ensure the trip will go smoothly and the children will have safe transportation here."

"Of course, Mother," she said, pleased to be asked. "Lucky will behave perfectly."

"With you—yes. I believe that."

They started to walk toward the house. "You know, Mercy, running from your anger is never the answer," Mother Helena said.

"I don't think I was running from it," Mercy admitted. "I think I was running straight into it."

Mother Helena stopped walking and turned to face her. "And what did you find when you stopped?"

Mercy thought for a second. "I found pond water is very refreshing after a long, hard ride. I found Lucky listens to every move I make and I don't have to say a word. I found a very irritated young man who disapproved of me being on his land and swimming in his pond."

Mother Helena's eyebrows disappeared into the bandeau across her forehead. "Anything else?"

Mercy smiled. "I found out that a handsome man can make it feel as if hundreds of tiny little butterflies are trapped in your stomach when he looks at you a certain way. Even when that man is annoyed."

Mother Helena smiled widely. "Ah. Butterflies."

"Do you think that's a good thing?"

Mother Helena put a hand on Mercy's arm and gave it a squeeze. "I think that is a very good thing." As they started walking again, Mother Helena said, "You may wait until tomorrow to work in the garden, unless you think the punishment is too harsh. I don't want you to think me unfair," she continued. "I suppose I could ask you to finish the needlepoint sampler Sister Gertrude had you start last week."

Mercy shook her head. "Oh, no, please, Mother. Not the needlepoint. It's much too easy—and I don't think I'd learn my lesson if I were to just sit in the chair with the needle and the fabric. I think the garden is a much better proposition for my offense."

Mother Helena pretended to think it over. "Very well. All day tomorrow in the garden, then."

Mercy smiled in relief. "Yes, Mother."

CHAPTER NINE

Running away doesn't solve problems. It only postpones the moment when you have to face them. I can't shake the feeling that this is a lesson I've had to learn before.

Sisters are not perfect. In some strange way, that is a burden lifted from me. If women who devote their lives to God aren't perfect—I guess I can feel better about myself.

Apparently, I have quite a temper. Anger I couldn't stop bubbled up and out of me today (partly because of those imperfect sisters), and I was powerless to stop it. I felt as if I was running down a hill, going faster and faster, and I knew when I got to the bottom I was going to fall and it was going to hurt—but I kept running anyway. The terrible thing is the anger feels good somehow. As if it's a second skin I'm used to wearing. I don't want the thing that makes me feel good to be something so bad. I don't know how to make that part of me disappear like my memory. Mother Helena knows it's there inside me—but like me, she doesn't know why. After the way I behaved today, I had to count on something Oona once told me: nuns are supposed to forgive. It's a commandment, and they have to do it. That is a very good thing for me, or otherwise I may very well have found myself living under a bush.

Deirdre sighs rather loudly when I've spent too much time with the candle burning and she's trying to get to sleep. I shall quit writing for now.

Rand Prescott detested procrastination in others, but he especially despised it in himself. So when he knew it was inevitable he would pay a visit to the Little Sisters of Hope, he set out early in the morning before the heat of the day soaked into his silk shirt and caused him to look like a dripping sop of a human being before he even arrived. He had met most of the sisters during two separate visits with his father to the convent and had on several occasions chatted with the two youngest of the order, Oona and Deirdre, when they made trips to town for supplies. Why young women wanted to be nuns was beyond his understanding, but he did admire their fortitude and faith.

Rand slowed his horse, Sherman, to a trot as the convent came into view. He saw the cross rising out of the roof like an apparition and wondered at the mechanics that must have been involved in getting that heavy piece of wood on the roof.

He turned Sherman onto the road that led straight to the door of the house, then settled his thoughts on his task at hand. He planned to say his piece as quickly and painlessly as possible, have a drink from the well, then put the convent and the sisters out of his mind. He had a dinner engagement with Cora that evening, and it wouldn't do for him to be preoccupied with anything else. Sometimes it was hard enough to give Cora his full attention. Her endless banal statements and predictable replies in conversation sometimes made the time he spent with her drag. He frowned and quickly tamped down such thoughts. Cora was a sweet, beautiful woman—everyone said so. *That* thought made him smile—and he left that smile in place as he rode up to the front of the convent.

It was Mother Helena who opened the door to his knock.

"Rand!" she exclaimed. "What a lovely surprise. Is your father with you?"

He swept off his hat and shook his head. "No, Mother Helena, he's not. I'm here on a solitary errand."

"Is that right?" she asked with a puzzled expression.

"You have a woman staying with you that isn't … like the rest of you. Isn't a sister," he said. "At least that's what she told me."

Her expression remained blank, carefully neutral. He squirmed with the sudden thought that the rogue woman had lied to him. Of all the humiliating, exasperating, time-wasting—

"You mean Mercy," Mother Helena finally said.

"Mercy?"

"Yes. We only have one woman here who isn't of the order, and her name is Mercy."

"Might I have a word with her?" he asked.

"Might I ask why?" Mother Helena countered. "She's a little fragile right now, and I wouldn't want you to upset her."

"I just wanted to apologize to her," he said. "I'm afraid I wasn't much of a gentleman when I encountered her on my property."

"Ah," she said knowingly, "so *you* are the annoyed, handsome man."

He frowned. "Pardon?"

"You may follow me," she said.

He asked no more questions as he followed Mother Helena to the back of the convent. She led him to the large, overgrown garden.

"You'll find her over there," she said succinctly, waving to the tall rows of green.

He squinted. "Are you sure? I don't see anyone at all."

"Mercy?" she called.

"Yes?" a voice answered from somewhere unseen.

"There is someone here to see you," Mother Helena said, then turned to Rand. "Now, if you'll excuse me, I'm writing a letter to the governor. We need money to finish our orphanage, and I'm trying to get him to loosen his grip on some badly needed funds."

As Mother Helena walked away, Rand heard rustling in the garden. *Just hurry up and let me get this over with*, he thought. Apologies had never been his strong suit, and even though he knew it had to be done, he chafed at doing it.

She stepped out of the garden, wearing a yellow dress with spots of dirt around her knees. She stopped when she saw him—her bare feet poking out from the hem of her skirt—her hazel eyes looking both indignant and wary at the same time. She pushed a wayward curl away from her face and left a smudge of dirt across her cheek.

"Are you here for more target practice?" she asked without preamble.

He shook his head, found his voice. "I ... I wasn't expecting you to be ... to look ..."

"Like a girl?"

He had a sudden flash of the way she had looked coming out of his pond the day before and felt his face grow hot in embarrassment.

"Yes," he admitted.

She took a few steps toward him, brushing the loose dirt from her hands across her yellow skirt. He had never in his life seen another woman do that. "Well, I *am* a woman. And I like things women like," she said, tipping her head to the side and pushing again at the hair that was clinging to her cheek. "I like cooking and sewing and needlepoint and singing and ..."

She stopped and looked toward the sky, then sighed and turned her enormous eyes directly at him. "I'm lying to you. I hate doing all those things."

He raised his brows at her bluntness. "Really?"

"I may have liked doing them once," she said, "maybe I was even good at them, but now—now I simply detest doing any of it."

This woman was Mother Helena's idea of fragile? "I believe you are the strangest woman I have ever met," he said.

"Thank you," she said seriously. "Is that what you came here to say?"

"No. I came to apologize for the way I behaved toward you yesterday."

"I didn't know it was your pond," she said. He could hear the defensiveness in her voice.

"I know that now. It's just that with the end of the war and the lingering animosity between the North and the South ... you just can't be too careful when you stumble upon a stranger," he said. "But in all fairness, I should have given you more of a chance to explain yourself."

"Mother Helena and the nuns are commanded to forgive," she said. "I imagine the same commandment applies to river urchins."

Beauty and a quick wit, he decided, could prove to be a lethal combination.

He cleared his throat. "A bit unorthodox in the way of accepting my apology, but I'll take it." He offered a half smile. "And just so the record is accurate, I wasn't the one who called you a river urchin."

"No, you were the one who didn't correct her," she said.

He dipped his head in concession. "Guilty again, I'm afraid."

She made no comment but simply smiled instead. He crossed the few steps between them.

"Let's start over," he said, offering her his hand. "I'm Rand Prescott."

She hesitated, then shook it. "I'm Mercy."

He smiled. "Just—Mercy?"

"Yes. It's what Mother Helena named me."

He frowned, his mind reeling in confusion. "I don't understand …"

"I have no memory of anything that happened to me prior to the last two months," she said succinctly. "I can't recall my name, where I come from, what I was doing, if I have a family … it's called amnesia."

"You're joking."

She shook her head. "I'm not. The sisters were good enough to take me in."

He looked shocked. "Have you seen a doctor?"

"Yes."

"Will your memory ever return?"

"I go to sleep each night hoping to wake up knowing my past. But so far …" She shrugged, then turned her attention to something over his shoulder. He followed her gaze to see one of the young postulants hurrying toward them.

"Hello, Rand!" she called out.

"Miss Deirdre," Rand said. "How nice to see you."

Deirdre smiled. "'Tis nice to see you, too. Mother Helena sent me to see if you were still here. She thought you might be thirsty—and maybe you might like to see our new addition."

"I would appreciate some water," he said, glancing at Mercy. "It's awfully hot out. You must be thirsty too."

"I'll be along soon," she said. "Just a few more weeds to pull." She turned and disappeared back into the overgrown garden, leaving him with little choice but to follow Deirdre inside.

Mercy never appeared inside the convent—much to Rand's disappointment. He was given the grand tour of the impressive addition, built entirely by the nuns themselves. But even he could see that they were far from ready to house any orphans. They still needed beds, linens, rugs, dishes—the list went on and on. Mother Helena told him of her letter-writing campaign asking public officials of the state for monetary help, but she didn't hold out much hope. In the next moment, Rand had an idea he shared with Mother Helena—and the old nun had been delighted. Now that he thought about it, he wondered if he'd been manipulated by a woman of God. The thought that Mother Helena had taken advantage of his visit made him smile. He approached the garden to say his good-bye to Mercy. A visit with Mother Helena had garnered precious little information about their boarder, other than what he'd already learned from the woman herself. As he rounded the corner, he saw his own horse standing in front of her, enjoying a good deal of attention.

"Is he yours?" she asked as she stroked the horse's nose.

"Yes. For some reason, that horse renders any tether useless," Rand said, unable to keep the pride and fondness from his voice.

"He must have been looking for you," she said. "What is he called?"

"Sherman. After General Sherman."

"You are very handsome, Sherman," she said.

Rand was completely shocked to discover he felt a little jealous of Sherman at her light caress and heartfelt compliment.

"I've invited Mother Helena and the rest of the sisters to the theater tomorrow night to see a performance of *Society*," he said casually. "The proceeds of the evening will be donated to a worthy charity, and since I am on the board of trustees, I promised Mother Helena to petition the money be given to the Little Sisters of Hope Orphanage."

"I'm not sure what all that means," she said, "but it sounds like a nice thing to do."

"I hope you'll join them," he said.

"Do you think I'd like the theater?" she asked.

"It's not sewing or cooking. So maybe—yes," he said with a smile. "Now, I really must be getting back." He swung himself into the saddle. She held up a finger at him.

"Wait," she said. She ducked behind some greens and emerged with a fat carrot in hand. She offered up the treat to Sherman, who finished it in two bites. Mercy smiled and, without any complaint or self-consciousness, gathered her skirt to wipe the horse's spit from her hands. And it was that gesture of hers that went straight to Rand's heart.

CHAPTER TEN

I believe Rand Prescott is a man who generally gets his way. I wasn't sure if I liked him or not—until I saw how much he cares for his horse. That settled it for me.

I have never seen Deirdre smile as big as she did when she said hello to Rand. I wonder if he reminds her of the potato farmer she left behind in Ireland.

Oona told me sometimes she misses wearing pretty dresses that are other colors besides black and white. She and Deirdre told me to wear my blue dress to the theater tomorrow night. They said it brings out my eyes. I'm hoping that's a good thing, because the blue dress is the only clean thing I have right now.

After a very earnest prayer from Sister Ruth about the safety of their trip to town the next evening, the sisters climbed into the back of the wagon as if they were about to go apple picking.

St. Louis was bustling with activity—something Mercy still found disconcerting—especially after her quiet time at the convent. Reins held loosely in her hand, Mercy sat between Oona and Mother Helena on the buckboard.

"Mother Helena?" Mercy asked.

"Yes?"

"Do you think that Mr. Prescott knows you tricked him into giving the convent the proceeds from this evening's performance?"

"Mercy!" Oona protested. "That's a terrible thing to say. Mother doesn't trick people into anything!"

"I think he's a smart young man," Mother Helena said, "who didn't know he'd been tricked until he'd already issued the invitation."

"Mother!" Oona gasped. "You *did* trick him?"

"I prefer to think of it as taking advantage of a God-given opportunity." Mother Helena sniffed. "I knew about charity nights at the theater," she continued. "And I also knew Rand's family was on the board of trustees. We have a need. They have the money. And soon—we'll have new beds."

"A few blocks now," Oona assured Mercy. "Turn left there on Eighth."

"You're awfully familiar with the city," Mercy said. "I didn't realize you made so many trips here."

"Not so much now, but we did during the war," Oona said. She pointed out a huge building on the right—an octagonal tower that rose up three stories high between two wings of red brick. "We spent quite a bit of time in that building right there."

"What is it?"

"Gratiot Street Prison," Oona answered. "It was operated by the Union army during the war."

"They put captured Confederate soldiers in there," Mother Helena said. "Horrible conditions. Men dying daily from diseases. Hopeless souls who needed prayer."

"I think I was close to experiencing a wee bit of hell on earth inside the brick walls of Gratiot," Oona said.

Despite the warmth of the early evening, Mercy shivered. The building didn't look nearly as ominous as they made it sound, but just hearing the name of the place made her feel like running away. She glanced around at the neighborhood, which was filled with fine homes. Oona pointed at a two-story colonial house they were passing.

"That was General Frémont's headquarters at one time. President Lincoln himself appointed him to help lead the Union army," she said. Then she pointed at another house at the end of the block. "And that house belongs to Judge Harrison. People say Frémont and Harrison were good friends all through the war, which is a miracle if you'd be askin' me, because Judge Harrison has always been known as a Southern sympathizer—like many families in this area. Everyone knew if a prisoner managed to escape from Gratiot, he could vanish in a flash into any one of these dandy homes."

Mercy glanced over her shoulder at the building as they continued along the street. "I think I'd rather be dead than be held a prisoner in a place like that."

"I spoke to many a man inside who felt just that way, lass," Mother Helena said. "Some of the saddest conversations of my lifetime."

"There's the theater!" Deirdre called out from behind them. "I heard it was built to resemble the Barthelems Theatre in Paris, France! Isn't it a beautiful building?"

The DeBar's Opera House had a unique oval shape. Two stories of vaulted arches spanned the building, with a third story adorned by scores of arched windows. It looked opulent, almost decadent, and was teeming with people moving through the front doors.

Rand, dressed in a tailored black suit with a snow-white handkerchief tucked into his breast pocket, was waiting for them on the steps of the building. Even in her thin cotton dress, Mercy felt wilted from the heat. She marveled at how cool he appeared as he came toward them with a smile.

"If it isn't my favorite sisters!" He directed a quick look at Mercy. "And Miss Mercy, of course." He offered Mother Helena his arm. "Let me show you to your seats," he said as he led the flock of nuns through the theater doors.

The opulent lobby was filled with people who parted as the sea of black habits moved toward the double doors of the auditorium. But as a single woman in a simple, inappropriate day dress, Mercy found she was not afforded the same deferential treatment. She tried to ignore the scornful looks and veiled comments behind the gloved hands of the women she passed as she followed in the wake of the nuns. They followed Rand down the aisle of the theater until he stopped at a long row of empty seats.

"Here we are," he said.

The nuns filled in the seats, causing people around them to nod and smile politely when they made eye contact. Mercy was the last to take her seat and slipped into the velvet-covered chair. Rand sat down right next to her.

"You're sitting here—with us?" she asked.

"How would it seem for your host to abandon you in favor of his family's box seats in the balcony?" he asked in a teasing tone.

"I would imagine it would be considered rude," Mercy said.

"Indeed it would."

"But I'm sure the view from up there is wonderful," she said, looking to the side at the reserved seats in the balcony.

Rand smiled. "I'm perfectly happy to sit right here beside you— and the nuns, of course."

The houselights dimmed just as the color in Mercy's cheeks rose.

CHAPTER ELEVEN

I am at a complete loss as to how I am supposed to act around Rand Prescott. He has come to the convent several times since that night at the theater. He always has a reason for his visit—and the reason is never me—but I can see something in his eyes that makes me think he wants me to be the reason. Mother Helena told me to be myself—nothing more. The trouble, as it has been since the minute I woke with my cuts and contusions and bullet wound, is that I don't know who I am. I find myself daydreaming about a past I can't remember—missing a family I don't even know.

Tonight, while Oona slept, Deirdre told me stories about her potato farmer in whispered words that painted a picture of her lost love and of Ireland. Rolling green pastures, fields of wildflowers—shamrocks and moss and thatched roof cottages with a view of water as far as the eye can see. I asked Deirdre if she was sorry she joined the church and came to America, but she said no. She's living the life that was planned for her since she was just a child. Nothing is ever going to change that. Not even the potato farmer. Her family is very proud of the daughter they gave to God. There is no greater sacrifice or anything more pleasing this side of heaven.

Deirdre's stories wore her out, and she dropped off to sleep before I could even pick up my quill and begin to write. Sometimes I envy Deirdre and Oona. I envy their memories of the past—and the neat, tidy path of their future. They are already on their journey, but I have yet to find my path. And I'm afraid to let someone journey with me. It seems like a selfish thing to give my heart to someone—when it might not even be mine to give.

A loud clap of thunder brought with it the first fat drops of rain just as Rand came into view, riding Sherman with two loaded wagons behind him.

Mercy ran outside, feeling ridiculously happy. Despite the rain on her face, she smiled up at him.

"What are you doing here?" she asked.

He grinned back. "I brought beds for the orphans."

The rain fell in fits and starts. "Let me go get the sisters so we can carry them inside," she said. "Bring the wagon around back."

The sisters were a force to be reckoned with when they put their collective minds and bodies into a task. With help from Rand and the wagon drivers, the women thrummed along together, lifted the wooden framed beds from the wagons, and hurried them into the addition of the convent—and out of the rain pelting everything in sight. Rand and Mother Helena received the last of the beds that Sister Ruth was pushing toward them from the back end of the wagon. Rand looked over at the old nun as she blinked against the rain, water soaking the band across her forehead.

"I'm sorry about this, Mother Helena," he said. "I had completely forgotten what day it was when I went to pick up the beds."

Mother Helena laughed. "Don't be ridiculous, Rand! This is a wonderful surprise and an absolute answer to prayer. Sunday makes it all the more perfect, dear boy!"

Between them, they hefted the bed through the doors of the orphanage and placed it beside a dozen others already on the floor. Mother Helena looked around at the room, and her eyes filled with tears.

"Sisters … a prayer."

The nuns all obediently stopped what they were doing and bowed their heads. With a synchronized sign of the cross from the women, Mother Helena spoke up in her musical brogue and offered simple, heartfelt words.

"Heavenly Father, You know our needs before we do. And You answer our prayers in Your most perfect timing. Thank You for these beds, this place, and the children I know will be arriving."

While the women had their heads down in supplication, Rand took the opportunity to study Mercy. She was wearing the same yellow dress he'd seen her wearing in the garden, and it was a beautiful splash of color in the room. She stood with her head dutifully bowed and her hands clasped.

"We thank You for the generosity of a man like Rand, who has proven to be Your loving servant. Amen."

Rand heard his name, registered the *amen* that had just been uttered, but still couldn't take his eyes from Mercy. When she raised her head, her gaze went straight to his—but then she quickly glanced away. The conflict he saw in her eyes disappointed him. He was sure they'd made some kind of a connection on his visits, but he never could seem to break through the polite reserve she kept in place. He was running out of excuses to visit the convent. This bed delivery was the last of the plans he'd made for the sisters, and the thought made him feel as gloomy as the rainy day.

"Sister Constance?" Mother Helena said. "Maybe this morning we will end our fast and have some of your delicious soup?"

Constance bobbed her head. "Yes, Mother. I will have it ready posthaste."

Mother Helena looked at Rand. "It's coming down in sheets out there. You must stay."

"Thank you, Mother," he said.

"And let Mercy help you see to your horses. They can be tucked into the barn with Lucky," she finished.

Rand thought the horse was aptly named. He was a lucky horse indeed to have Mercy as his mistress.

The wagon drivers made quick work of unhitching the horses and led the animals into the dry barn, just behind Mercy and Rand, who attended to Sherman.

Mercy had worn a shawl around her shoulders to ward off the rain, but the two of them were soaked through by the time Sherman was settled.

His horse nickered his appreciation and shivered as Mercy ran her hand over his flanks and down his nose. "There now," she said. "Much better in here, isn't it?"

Rand looked around the small barn and thought how much bigger Sherman appeared in here than in the large stables at his home. For a flash of a second, he imagined Lucky standing in a stall in his stable, right next to Sherman.

Lucky snorted and pushed his chest against the stall. Mercy laughed, pulled the wet shawl from her shoulders and shook it out as she approached him. She kissed his nose. "Big baby," she said affectionately. "Big, jealous baby."

She turned from the horses to look out the big barn door where a waterfall of rain cascaded off the roof. "It's raining even harder now," she said. "I think we missed our opportunity to run back into the convent without drowning."

"I don't mind if you don't," he said boldly.

"It *is* nice and dry," she responded. "And I'm sure the horses like the company."

"I like *your* company," he told her.

A moment of conflict in her eyes was replaced by a smile. "Always a gentleman, aren't you?"

"Except for the times I'm aiming a gun at beautiful young women," he said, returning her smile.

"In your defense," she said, "you didn't know I was a woman."

His smile dropped, and his expression turned serious. "To this day, I can't imagine how I made that mistake."

He watched her cheeks flush with color before she turned to look back out the barn door. He wished the rain would continue for hours so he could stay in the barn with her. He moved to stand beside her—so close their arms touched.

"Mercy," he began, "I'd like to spend some time with you."

"Isn't that what we're doing right now?" she asked.

"No. Well, yes. But that's not what I'm talking about."

Mercy turned and looked up into his eyes. "Oh? What are you talking about, then?"

"How about a picnic?" he asked. "Just the two of us."

"I don't know if Mother Helena will allow it," she said. "I'm quite sure she would say we need chaperones."

He sighed. "You're right, of course. I will extend the invitation to Deirdre and Oona as well, as long as you say yes."

"You don't want to take me on a picnic, Rand."

"I do. Yes, yes, I do."

"And if we go on this picnic and have a lovely time and plan for more picnics, and I wake up one morning and remember all my picnics have been promised to someone else—a young man—maybe even a husband I have not remembered? What then?"

"It's just a picnic, Mercy," he said. "Just fried chicken and potatoes and maybe some spice cake on a blanket under a tree. I'm not suggesting it is anything more, so we needn't worry about what is past or what is in the future."

When she still didn't answer him, he continued. "It's *just* a picnic."

"All right then," she said. "As long as we're clear that that's all it can be."

"We're clear," he said.

She nodded, then turned her attention back outside.

"The rain is stopping," she said.

"Yes, I suppose we should go inside before Mother Helena sends out a battalion of nuns to rescue me," he said with a straight face.

Mercy stepped out of the barn and smiled over her shoulder at him. "She *is* a force to be reckoned with."

"I'd wager that she has met her match in you."

Chapter Twelve

At supper tonight, Sister Ruth laughed at something Sister Marie said and told her it reminded her of the time they all got poison ivy last year. The mention of the malaise had the entire table of nuns nodding and smiling and remembering the same event. It was a shared experience then—and the memory a shared experience now. Of course it happens all the time—the question that is asked based on something that has happened. An opinion of an event that everyone remembers but me. A book, a play, a president— a war. All things I can't speak to because I don't remember them.

Every day, the magnitude of what I've lost hits me just a little bit harder.

All the more important that I make new memories. Maybe next year the sisters will say, "Remember when we had the cabbage soup that came straight from the garden, Mercy?" And I will be able to say yes!

I will admit here to you, my dear journal, that I enjoy Rand Prescott's company. I don't know what a man is supposed to be like—or how he is supposed to treat a woman—but I am supposing Rand is exactly how a man should be.

Deirdre and Oona have become my chaperones. Mother says it is necessary, and I don't know why she would make them come along if it wasn't. Rand seems to accept that where I go, they go. I think that's very nice of him.

There had been great anticipation on Mercy's part at the thought of spending the afternoon with Rand, but that lovely feeling of excitement had quickly been replaced by a deepening sense of dread. She sat on the picnic blanket, feeling as if her only purpose for the moment was to hold down a corner of the quilt to keep the slight breeze from catching it and messing up the puddle of blue lying over grass that was too long to be kept but too kept to be wild. She eyed the others on their respective corners of the blanket—Oona and Deirdre in their ever-present role as chaperones—and Rand. He was reclining on his side, elbow bent to prop up his head, eyes glazed over in that way she knew hers did when someone forced her to sew. *He's bored*, she realized with a start. *Bored to death and probably wondering why in the world he asked me to yet another picnic with him in the first place.* A question for which she had no answer, because his interest in her was a constant puzzle. But now, watching him hide a yawn behind his hand, she understood that his interest seemed to be waning—thus the dread she was feeling. She had enjoyed the attention, the compliments; sometimes she caught him looking at her in such a way that it made joy rush right over her and she couldn't stop a smile to save her life. When she thought about losing Rand's attention, she knew her feelings for him had slipped beyond safe, despite her worry over her mysterious past. She was going to miss him.

"Shall we say a prayer and then open the hamper?" Oona suggested into what had been prolonged silence.

Rand pushed himself into a sitting position and frowned. "I'm not especially hungry right now, but by all means, you go ahead."

"Are you all right, then, Rand?" Deirdre asked. "You seem a little preoccupied."

With Deirdre's observation, Mercy fretted even more. If Deirdre and Oona had noticed Rand's mood, then it wasn't her imagination. It must be signaling the demise of their short relationship.

He leaned forward as if he was about to share an intimate secret. "The truth of the matter is I feel I've let you all down today, and I'm a little embarrassed by that."

"What in the world are you talking about?" Oona asked.

Mercy wasn't sure she wanted to hear Rand's explanation.

Rand looked sheepish. "While I believe I brought some delectable food, I completely overlooked planning an activity we could do during our afternoon. And now we're left with nothing to do but eat."

The rush of relief Mercy felt was quick and surprisingly physical. She couldn't help but laugh. "But isn't that the whole idea of a picnic?"

"Of course it is," Deirdre offered.

Rand shrugged. "A truly memorable picnic is one where there are games and such. I should have brought along my croquet mallets, or maybe we could have played running hoops. Even cards would have been—"

Oona quickly jumped in. "We can't play cards."

"Anymore," Deirdre amended. "But, oh, how I loved a good card game when I was younger."

Rand laughed. "You're hardly ancient now, Deirdre."

Deirdre smiled. "I meant before I joined the order. My brothers and sisters and I used to play card games all the time."

"We used to spend hours out of doors," Oona said. "I remember my mama practically sweeping us out with the dust in the morning and telling us to stay in the fresh air till supper."

"What about you, Mercy?" Deirdre asked.

Mercy opened her mouth to speak but didn't get a word out before Deirdre realized her error. "I'm sorry, Mercy. I forgot."

Mercy smiled. "Me, too."

"I remember loving to play hide-and-seek when I was a boy," Rand offered. "I recall being quite good at it."

"I loved that one too," Deirdre said.

"Let's play," Rand said, grinning. "It will make up for my lack of foresight into having a planned activity."

"Don't be silly, Rand. We're grown adults," Oona said.

"Oh, don't be a spoilsport, Oona," Deirdre said. "We can teach it to Mercy, and then she'll have a memory of a game. Right, Mercy?"

Mercy saw the hopeful look on Rand's face and smiled. "What are the rules?"

"Well," Rand started, "one person counts to thirty while the others hurry to hide. The counting person then tries to find the hiding places of the others."

"I'll count," Deirdre said.

Rand looked at Deirdre. "Close your eyes when you count, and no peeking."

"Don't worry. I won't have to peek. I recall being quite good at this game too," she said, moving off the quilt and going to stand with her face toward a tree. "I'll even face this direction and shut my eyes while you hide."

As Deirdre started to count, Rand crossed to Oona and whispered in her ear, "There is a great little tangle of bushes over that way." He pointed in a direction opposite Deirdre, and as Oona nodded, he added, "She'll have a hard time finding you."

Oona hurried off, and Rand took hold of Mercy's hand and pointed another direction. She nodded, and they made a quick dash across the grass.

"… eight … nine … ten," Deirdre sang out.

Though she relished holding Rand's warm hand, Mercy had to ask. "Aren't we supposed to hide in different places?"

Rand was leading her along a ten-foot wall of manicured hedges. Obviously looking for something, he kept going. "Yes."

"So are you going to show me a good place to hide?" she asked, a little breathless with the pace he was setting.

"We're going to hide together," he said, now trailing his hand over the hedge as they hurried along.

"Isn't that cheating?"

He looked over at her and grinned. "Probably." And then he finally found what he was looking for and stopped.

"Here we are," he said, pulling her through a hidden space in the wall of greenery.

Mercy heard Deirdre call out, "Ready or not, here I come." But she was too astonished at the sight before her to give Deirdre a second thought. An elaborately staged picnic for two was set on an ivory brocade quilt under the shade of a magnificent oak. Silver ribbons cascaded down from the low-hanging branches of the tree and created a shimmering curtain.

"Oh, Rand. How beautiful."

Rand slipped an arm around her waist, led her to the quilt, then settled her by a silver platter laden with fat purple grapes and assorted cheeses.

"Hide-and-seek?" she asked.

"A ruse," he confessed as he sat down right next to her and pulled a bottle from a bucket. He didn't look the least bit sorry he'd tricked the others, and she realized she wasn't the least bit sorry either. She glanced around at the beautiful scenery; the wall of hedges they'd managed to slip through created a perfect backdrop for the acres of manicured grounds around them. They sat atop a small rise that looked down on a sprawling estate. She pointed. "Is that …?"

"Home? Yes," he said, popping the cork on the bottle. He poured the liquid into one of the flutes and handed it to her.

"Champagne," he explained.

She sipped, wrinkled her nose, and swallowed. "It's … good."

He chuckled. "You'll get used to it."

Mercy studied him. "Ten minutes ago I would have sworn you were bored to tears and wishing the day away."

"I promise I could never be bored with you, Mercy."

She took another sip of her champagne. "Why go to all the trouble of two picnics?"

"Why do you think?"

"Because Oona and Deirdre probably won't approve of champagne?" She said it with a small smile, knowing the answer but wanting to hear it anyway.

"Yes," he said, surprising her. "That's it exactly."

"Oh," she said, her smile disappearing.

Rand took her glass, put it down on the silver tray, and reached for her hand. "I am teasing you," he said. "Of course the reason for two picnics—the reason for the silly game, and the reason I found myself anticipating today so much—was because I wanted to be alone with you. A few stolen moments without the prying eyes of the Little Sisters of Hope."

CHAPTER THIRTEEN

Deirdre had dutifully counted to thirty before she opened her eyes and looked around. She stood still for a few minutes, studying the landscape before setting off to find her hiding companions. In just minutes, she found Oona hiding behind some shrubs.

"Well, that didn't take too long," Oona said. "I've already lost the game, and we've barely begun."

"Did you happen to see which way Mercy went? Or Rand?" Deirdre asked. Oona shook her head.

"No. Rand gave me the tip about hiding behind the bushes, though," Oona answered. "He may have given Mercy some pointers on a good hiding place too."

"Is that right, now?" Deirdre mused. "Why don't you help me find them, Oona? It will be much quicker with the two of us looking."

Oona crossed her arms over her chest and shook her head. "That would be cheating. 'Tis up to you to find them."

"I have a feeling it's not going to be as easy to find them as it was for me to find you."

"I'll admit that Rand knows the lay of the land well, but Mercy won't. She should be easy to find."

Deirdre shook her head. "I'm quite sure that where we find one—we'll find the other."

Understanding dawned on Oona's face. She lowered her voice and looked around. "What are you saying? That they purposefully snuck off to be together?"

Deirdre shrugged. "I would."

Oona's mouth fell open. "Deirdre!"

"Well, not now. But once upon a time—I would definitely have snuck off together."

Oona pointed. "I'll go this way—you go that way."

When Deirdre came upon the tall, thick hedge, she took one look and started to turn back—until she heard soft voices. She stopped and listened and was rewarded by a low chuckle from the other side of the tall wall. Deirdre moved closer to the hedge, and her foot found a dried tree limb that snapped. She froze.

Rand and Mercy both looked toward the sound. Mercy started to say something, but Rand put his finger to his lips and shook his head.

Though she didn't want their private picnic to end, Mercy knew that Deirdre and Oona would be tolerant only for so long.

"She'll never find us," Mercy whispered. "We need to give up."

Rand frowned as if he couldn't hear her and moved closer. He was so close she could see gold flecks in his eyes before he dropped his gaze to her mouth. She felt the lightest touch of his hand under her chin before he leaned in and covered her lips with his own. She felt herself give in; it was as if her bones had become liquefied—she could barely remain sitting there as the kiss deepened.

"Deirdre! There you are! Did you find them?" Oona's voice on the other side of the hedge brought Mercy quickly back to reality. She pulled back from Rand and started to say something, but he put his finger against her just-kissed lips and shook his head with a small smile. "Wait," he whispered. "They'll go away."

"Mercy? Rand? I give up," Deirdre said loudly through the hedge. "Did you hear me? You win!"

Moments later, they heard the muted sounds of conversation as Deirdre and Oona walked away.

"We need to get back," Mercy said. "I don't want them to be mad. The sisters have been so good to me. If I spoil things, they might not let me live with them anymore."

"At least it would mean the end of chaperones," Rand said.

"Don't tease about that, Rand. I'd be homeless without them."

"I would never let that happen to you."

Mercy watched his gaze travel to her mouth again, and she blushed. "We need to go." She started to get to her feet, but he pulled her back down beside him.

"Mercy, it's time you met my parents," Rand said.

"No, it isn't."

He studied her in the way that made her feel light-headed and filled with anticipation. "Yes. It is. That kiss meant something to me. And I'm quite sure it meant something to you too, didn't it?"

She hesitated. "It shouldn't have, but ... yes."

He looked both relieved and victorious at her admission.

"My mother is insisting on meeting the young woman I have been going on and on about," he said.

She felt a kind of panic seize her. "What have you told them about me?"

"Enough to pique their curiosity," he said evasively. "Please. Just agree to one small dinner party, and if you never want to see them again after that, so be it."

"Dinner party?" she asked with alarm.

"Mother, Father, and a few of their close friends get together every few weeks."

"That sounds worse than dinner with just your parents," she said bluntly.

He smiled. "It will actually be easier for you. My mother won't exclude all her other guests by peppering you with personal questions."

She sighed. "You aren't going to let this go, are you?"

He shook his head. "You'll find once I set my mind on something, it's almost impossible for me to let go."

Deirdre dropped the unopened picnic hamper into the back of the carriage. "They were on the other side of the hedges, Oona. I heard them!"

"They would have said something if they were," Oona said. "Mercy wouldn't keep hiding if she knew we were looking for her."

"That's the point of the game!" Deirdre sounded exasperated. "To hide!"

"Do you suppose that Rand and Mercy planned this whole thing?"

"Yes, Oona. That *is* what I suppose."

Oona folded her hands. "We need to pray." She bowed her head. "Heavenly Father, forgive us for failing at the task of keeping watch over our sister Mercy. Please keep her safe from harm—and, Lord, please spare us from Mother Helena's wrath if we return to the convent alone."

"Amen," Deirdre muttered.

"Deirdre! Oona!" Mercy's voice preceded her appearance into the small clearing where they stood.

Oona hurried toward Mercy when she saw her. "There you are! Are you all right?"

Rand came up right behind her and exchanged a glance with Deirdre. "She's fine. Just fine."

"Yes," Mercy agreed. "I'm fine."

"What happened to the two of you?" Deirdre asked, crossing her arms over her chest.

Rand cleared his throat. "The truth is …"

"The truth is that Rand was going to show me a good hiding place, but I got distracted when I saw his house in the distance, and I really wanted a look at it—and he took me to a spot where I could see just how lovely it is from way up high, and we forgot about the game …" Mercy's voice trailed off. "I'm sorry if I worried you. I guess I lost track of time."

"We both did," Rand said. "Can you forgive us for ruining the game?"

Oona exhaled. "Of course. There's nothing to forgive. Isn't that right, Deirdre?"

Mercy felt the blush creeping up her neck and knew that Deirdre saw it. The young woman was staring hard at her, but then she smiled.

"That's right, Oona. Nothing at all to forgive."

Chapter Fourteen

I have had my first kiss. At least the first kiss that I can remember. And the most glorious part of the whole thing is that at any given time, if I want to, I can call up the exact moment when Rand leaned over and kissed me—and relive every second of it. What an amazing thing. This must be how it is for everyone else—think of something pleasant that has happened, and voilà, you can make it happen again by memory.

We didn't fool Deirdre one little bit at the picnic—she knows. I'm sure of it. Just as I'm sure she won't outright ask me. Instead, she'll wait for me to confess and then get me to tell her the details. But the only place I do my confessing is here, dear journal. You can't judge—you can't comment. You only take note.

I told Mother Helena about Rand's insistence that I meet his parents and how much I don't want to do that—but she was unsympathetic.

"Don't build mountains out of molehills, Mercy," she told me. "Whatever you imagine might go wrong, most likely won't." I'll never know for sure until I have the courage to go through with it—so I accepted Rand's invitation.

Deirdre is upset she won't be joining us for dinner. She didn't say so—but I can see it on her face and in her eyes when she looks at me. I wonder if she's thinking again of her potato farmer and dinners with his family.

According to God (and Mother Helena), the children will be arriving soon. We won't know the exact day or hour, but we are to be ready.

Sister Martha said Mother has a heart for children nearly as big as her heart for God. It makes me wonder again how these women can give their lives away in an act of faith before some of them even had enough time to really live. Does Mother Helena ever mourn the loss of the children she never got to have? Does Oona want to have one more dance with her father on this earth instead of saving all her dances for her Father in heaven? Sister Rebecca can play the piano as if it was the only thing she was born to do—and Sister Gertrude is so skilled with a needle and thread, the other sisters say she could be making clothing fit for a queen. Sister Marie must have been very beautiful as a young woman with many husband prospects, and Sister Rachel has a voice like an angel. Their faith is staggering to me. How I wish I had just an ounce of what they have—but I don't. I don't have the same faith in God, and I certainly don't have faith I can sit at a dinner table with Rand and his parents tomorrow evening without stumbling over my missing past.

Mercy shifted uncomfortably under the scrutiny of several nuns. After Mercy turned one way and then the other in her pale-green taffeta dress, Sister Gertrude finally smiled.

"I know it's boastful," she said, "but I believe 'tis the finest-looking frock I've ever made."

Oona, Deirdre, Ruth, Rachel, and Marie murmured and nodded in agreement with her.

"It *is* beautiful, Sister. Thank you so much," Mercy said sincerely.

"You look just perfect. He'll be so enamored with you."

"She's not worried about Rand, Sister," Deirdre said. "It's the parents she's hoping to win over, isn't that right, Mercy?"

"Yes. No. I don't know," Mercy said with a worried shake of the head. "I just don't want them to think I'm not fit to shine their son's shoes."

"Well, now, if that is their attitude, it's them who aren't fit to sit at the same table as you." Oona sniffed.

"Just mind your manners and see to it that you don't make any big blunders, and you'll be fine," Sister Ruth chimed in.

"If it were me, I'd not be knowin' what piece of cutlery to use at a big, fancy table such as the Prescotts might have," Sister Rachel said.

Mercy's eyes widened. "I hadn't thought of that."

Sister Gertrude threw a sidelong glance at Rachel before turning back to Mercy. "'Tisn't so hard to know. You use the flatware farthest to the left and just work your way in."

"But don't be reaching for your fork until your hostess does," Oona said.

"And if they serve a piece of fruit, for goodness' sake don't just pick it up. You should eat it elegantly," Sister Marie said.

"Elegantly?"

"Yes. Peel it with your knife and cut it into small pieces," she answered. "Likewise with bread or rolls. Small, manageable pieces, or you'll look like a cow chewing its cud."

"Don't monopolize the conversation," Oona said. "A lady always listens more than she speaks."

"When you are introduced to the guests, never offer your hand to a man," Sister Marie said. "Just bow politely and say, 'I am happy to make your acquaintance.'"

Deirdre puffed out a breath. "I say be yourself, Mercy. Rand is smitten with you as you are—he isn't looking for some stiff-mannered woman who doesn't have a thing to say."

"I'd be sick with worry if I were you," Sister Rachel said, eliciting another glare from Sister Gertrude. "Aren't you just the tiniest bit nervous?"

"I'm shaking in my borrowed shoes," Mercy said.

"You look calm as the day is long," Sister Ruth said.

Mercy swallowed. "Say a prayer that I can keep up that charade, will you, Sisters?"

Mother Helena approached the group. "I imagine this little meeting means everyone has finished with her tasks for the day?"

The nuns scattered like leaves on the wind, leaving Mercy alone with the older nun.

"You look lovely," Mother Helena said.

"Thank you. And thank you for allowing me to go unchaperoned."

Mother Helena raised a brow. "I'm trusting that Rand's parents will act as chaperones," she said, "and I'm also trusting that you won't give them the slip as easily as you did Oona and Deirdre."

Mercy's cheeks colored. "But that was all a mistake, Mother. We didn't actually mean to …"

"I live separate from the world, but I am not ignorant of it, Mercy," she said. "So please don't insult my intelligence with excuses. And please remember our curfew. I'll expect you back by then."

"Yes, Mother, I'll remember."

Mother Helena crossed her arms over her chest and slipped her hands into the bells of her sleeves. She looked out the window of the common room and then smiled, the lines in her face softening. "Your escort is here."

As Rand led her up the wide stairs of the Prescott mansion, Mercy couldn't help but admire how handsome he looked. Dressed in a black waistcoat with velvet lapels, he looked every inch a well-to-do gentleman. She tried to tamp down her nerves as he looked over at her with a reassuring smile.

"Ready?" he asked.

She shook her head but answered in the affirmative. He laughed. "You truly don't know how charming you are, do you?"

He opened the door before she could answer, and they stepped into a huge foyer handsomely furnished with side tables and arrangements of freshly cut flowers. From another room, voices carried on the floral-scented air, and an ornate pendulum clock ticked off the seconds like a metronome. As Rand closed the door, the clock chimed loudly—then once again. Mercy felt the world tilt, felt her heart stutter in her chest, then on the third chime, saw a face as black as night magically appear in the foyer. She slammed her hand over her mouth to stifle a scream, and her knees buckled. Rand slipped an arm around her. "Mercy! What is it?"

She looked pointedly at the black man standing a few feet away. "Who is that?"

"Ellis, our butler," Rand said.

Ellis offered a small, puzzled smile. "Good evening, sir. I am sorry I didn't hear the bell on the door."

"I didn't ring it, Ellis," Rand said, his eyes still on Mercy. She didn't move, just stood there staring at Ellis.

"Is everything all right, sir?" Ellis asked.

"I … don't know. Mercy?"

"I'm … fine. Sorry," she stammered, averting her eyes from the butler. "I don't know what came over me."

Rand took her hand and tucked her arm through his. "Steady. The evening won't be nearly as bad as you're imagining."

She nodded. "I'm fine now. Truly."

"Everyone is in the drawing room, sir," Ellis said.

Rand led her into a large, handsomely appointed room where eight people sat and chatted, though their faces swiveled at Rand and Mercy's appearance. Mercy immediately realized she was woefully underdressed. Her high neckline and long sleeves were the antithesis of the other women's elaborate gowns. She had a moment when she wondered if Mother Helena, in her separateness, would have been shocked by the amount of décolletage in the room.

Rand's mother came forward with a smile. Ilene Prescott was effortlessly elegant, Mercy decided. One of those women others would compare themselves to and probably fail miserably in that comparison. Ilene stopped in front of them and presented her cheek to Rand, who gave it a perfunctory kiss. Ilene turned her attention to Mercy, and Mercy felt the woman's veiled scrutiny as clear, alert eyes skimmed over her dress.

"You must be Mercy," Ilene said. "Rand's new friend he keeps talking about."

"Yes, Mother. This is Mercy," Rand said. "Mercy, may I present my mother, Ilene Prescott."

"I am … pleased to make your acquaintance, Mrs. Prescott," Mercy said.

"Please. Call me Ilene. We don't stand on ceremony here," she said, glancing over her shoulder and gesturing to an older man who looked so much like Rand, Mercy had to do a double take. He was at their side in a moment.

"Charles, this is Rand's guest Mercy," Ilene said. "Mercy, my husband, Charles Prescott."

"Welcome, Mercy. Happy to meet you," Charles said, and Mercy was overcome by the thought that she knew exactly what Rand would look like in twenty years. "Rand has told us about your unique circumstance. Must be dreadful not knowing who you are or where you come from."

The statement was so frank and forthright that it caught her off guard. "Um, well … yes. That's a good word for it. Dreadful."

"No need to get into all that right now," Ilene said with a slight shade of reproach in her voice that Mercy knew was intended for Charles. "Come and meet our friends."

By the end of the introductions, Mercy reminded herself again of everyone's name. Frederick and Ava Klein were polar opposites of each other—Frederick, a serious stick-thin man with a timid little mustache, and Ava, a plump woman with a generous smile. On the other hand, Howard and Betsy Vaughn looked like bookends. Two halves to one whole, and Mercy wondered how two people could look so much alike and not be related by blood. Betsy raked her eyes coolly over Mercy, giving her the distinct feeling that the woman disliked her before she even opened her mouth. Leon and Anna Zimmerman were the oldest of the group and seemed to Mercy to be the least pretentious of the dinner guests. Leon pumped her hand enthusiastically (apparently he didn't know etiquette any more than she did), and Anna leaned toward her with a wink. "No wonder you're here on Rand's arm, my dear. You are simply stunning."

Mercy allowed a moment of hope to creep in. Maybe the evening wouldn't be so taxing after all. And then the carefully built wall of confidence came crashing down around her as the woman from the pond breezed into the room as if she owned it.

CHAPTER FIFTEEN

Cora swept across the drawing room toward them.

"Charles. Ilene," Cora said, kissing Ilene on both cheeks. Mercy saw Rand's jaw tighten. Then Cora turned to Betsy Vaughn. "Mother. I *do* love that gown on you."

The chill Mercy had felt from Betsy Vaughn suddenly made sense. She was used to seeing her daughter on Rand's arm, not some interloper.

Ilene made her way to Rand's side. He gave her a long look and said quietly, "What is Cora doing here, Mother?"

"I am as surprised as you are, darling," she replied in the same low voice.

Cora herself answered the question as she boldly approached Mercy. "I am sorry to show up uninvited, Ilene, but I need to make amends for the sake of my own conscience."

"What the devil are you talking about, Cora?" Howard Vaughn demanded of his daughter.

"Mother mentioned that Mercy was going to be here, and I owe her a long-overdue apology," Cora said. She turned to Mercy. "I just had to come and tell you in person how sorry I am about my rudeness the day we met."

Mercy shook her head. "No need."

"No, honestly, it was reprehensible of me to call attention to the state of your dress or intimate that you were immodest," Cora said sweetly. "After all, if a woman doesn't have her modesty in this day and age, then I ask you, what does she have?"

Mercy forced her mouth into a smile. "What indeed?"

"Do you forgive me?"

"Yes, of course."

Cora smiled. "Wonderful. I feel so much better now. I can go home with a lighter step."

"So you and Mercy know each other?" Ava Klein asked.

"No, they don't," Rand said.

"I met Mercy the same day that Rand did," Cora said. "It's a lovely story."

"It's time we all moved into the dining room," Ilene announced. "Cora, will you stay and join us for dinner?"

Cora smiled prettily. "If you're sure I'm not intruding."

Ilene smiled and pulled a long velvet rope suspended by the fireplace. In seconds, Ellis appeared.

"There will be one more for dinner, Ellis. Please tell Marjorie that Miss Vaughn will be joining us," Ilene said.

"Yes, Mrs. Prescott," he said, then quickly took his leave.

As they started toward the dining room, Charles looked at Rand. "I managed to speak to Governor Fletcher today when he was in town."

Rand raised his brows and stopped. "And the outcome?"

Cora came up beside Mercy and took her arm, leading her toward the dining room and away from Rand.

"Tell me, Mercy, what have you and Rand been up to today?" Cora asked.

"Up to?" Mercy asked, throwing a glance over her shoulder at Rand.

"Yes. A picnic? Shopping in town, maybe?" she asked.

"He picked me up, and we came straight here," Mercy said.

"Oh. I only supposed by your dress that you didn't have time to change into suitable evening attire before arriving," Cora said. "My mistake."

The insult stung, but before Mercy could reply, Rand materialized on her other side and drew her arm through his. "Sorry. Just a quick bit of business."

"Cora kept me company," Mercy said as she forced a smile at the other woman.

"Yes. Lovely to have a moment alone," Cora quipped. She called out to Ava Klein, who was a few steps in front of them.

"Ava!" Cora said, hurrying up to the other woman. "You were absolutely right about the new seamstress you sent me to. She was wonderful."

Rand covered Mercy's hand with his own as he led her into an elegant dining room. The twelve-foot-high ceiling had gold stenciling around a chandelier that illuminated the room with twinkling gaslight. The table setting alone was a feast for the eyes, even without the food—ivory damask linens, crystal glasses, heavy silver sat on either side of ornate china plates.

Guests located place cards, and the fact that Cora had been a late addition to the beautifully set table didn't so much as create a hiccup in the presentation. Mercy found herself seated between Leon Zimmerman and Betsy Vaughn, and directly across the table from Rand—and Cora.

Under the watchful eye of Ellis, Marjorie, the downstairs maid, served the first course of the meal. Ava Klein watched her for a moment, then asked, "What happened to your girl Cecilia?"

"Had to let her go," Charles said. "Caught her stealing food. Intolerable—especially since she was given three meals a day like every other servant."

"I never did care for Cecilia," Ava said. "I think she forgot her place one day and complimented my shoes. Imagine."

The food on her plate should have made Mercy's mouth water, but she couldn't eat a bite because of her nerves. Sure she was going to do or say something to embarrass Rand, she found herself sipping so much wine she actually grew to like it.

On the brighter side, Charles Prescott was an excellent host. He kept the conversation flowing with small talk even Mercy could follow—the unusually wet summer, rising produce prices, the intersection in midtown St. Louis that had become a giant sinkhole of mud. Marjorie hovered anxiously near the sideboard, set at a moment's notice to refill water glasses, pour more wine, whisk away dirty plates, and replace them with china that gleamed in the gaslight of the chandelier that had been lit against the darkening day.

With the arrival of the second course, Mercy started to relax. So far, she had managed to nod at the right times, laugh at the right times, and use the silverware in the correct order. And despite Cora's unwelcome presence, Mercy decided that maybe the evening wasn't such a mistake after all. She took another sip of wine, relaxed just enough to start enjoying her food, and listened with half an ear to the shift in conversation.

"They were talking about you the other day in the mayor's office, Charles," Frederick Klein said.

"What did they say?" Ilene asked.

Charles grinned. "Nothing that can be repeated in mixed company, I'm sure."

"It was about that senate run," Frederick said. "They think they'll talk you into it by the next election."

Howard looked at Mercy. "Did Rand tell you Charles was instrumental in the Union's victory over the Confederacy?"

"No, he didn't," Mercy said.

Charles held up his hand. "Now, Howard, there's no need …"

But Howard wouldn't be dissuaded. He plunged ahead. "Charles used his railroad to provide strategic support for the Union. They figured out that they could use the locomotives in such a way that they were invaluable. They helped deliver supplies to the troops, and the Federals were able to gain information on the location of the Confederates. It got real dangerous for the engineers of those locomotives, though. Scoundrel rebel sharpshooters would lay in wait and try to get a bullet inside that cab. Union engineers put armor around those cars, but they soon figured out a crack shot's bullet that pierced the boiler was a bad deal. That ruptured boiler could scald a crew in their iron cab like lobsters in a pot."

"Father! This is hardly dinner conversation!" Cora objected.

"Talking about a hero is always dinner conversation, young lady, and that is exactly what Charles is, considering he was the one who figured out where to put the armor so those engineers could get their trains through safely."

Mercy knew he expected her to make some kind of comment, but she had no idea what to say.

"Fact of the matter is that Charles helped win the war as sure as we're all sitting here," Howard said.

"That's—good," Mercy finally said. She looked at Rand, who smiled his encouragement. The food on her plate became tasteless again.

Leon, on Mercy's left, leaned over his plate and fixed Charles with a serious look. "What's your opinion about Drake's proposed addendum to the state's constitution, Charles?"

"He might be a member of the Radical Party, but I'm inclined to agree with his idea on the Ironclad Oath."

"You're agreeing with a Radical?" Howard asked in an incredulous voice.

"In this case—yes," Charles said. "It seems to me if an individual isn't willing to attest to his innocence of acts of disloyalty against the state of Missouri and the Union, he doesn't deserve to be licensed as a lawyer or a teacher."

"The way I understand it, even an expression of sympathy for the Southern cause could keep a man from holding public office—or even voting in an election," Frederick said.

"Doesn't that seem a little … severe?" Anna asked.

"Absolutely not," Rand said. "Someone has to take a firm hand with those who went against the Union, and it certainly doesn't seem like it's going to be President Johnson."

"You're right, Son," Charles said. "His plan for reconstruction for the South is so lenient toward the Confederacy, it's going to allow those who dominated Southern politics before the war to return to power."

"Where do you stand on the issue, Mercy?" Cora asked.

Mercy swallowed. "The—issue?"

"Yes. Do you believe in the Ironclad Oath?"

"I, um, I suppose, that is, I'm not …"

"Boring, boring, boring," Ava said. "I'm sick to death of talking about the nasty war and reconstruction! Let's talk instead about how Rand and Mercy met."

Cora beamed. "A wonderful idea."

Mercy reached for her glass of wine and marveled that it never seemed to empty no matter how much she drank. She heard Rand launch into a quick narrative about the first time they'd met. She waited for all the terrible details to materialize, but they never did.

"So after I fired a couple shots at her, she scrambled out of the pond, got on her horse, and rode away," Rand said.

"And I made him go apologize to her the next morning," Ilene said.

"And apparently you accepted his apology, eh, Mercy?" Leon asked.

She nodded, feeling hot and flush and a little bit nauseous. "I could see he loved his horse," she said. "You can't stay mad at a man who loves his horse like that."

Everyone laughed, and Mercy felt a small thrill of satisfaction that she'd said something amusing.

"It seems to me you skipped over some details about that day, Rand," Cora said.

"Unimportant details," Rand said.

"Oh, I don't think so," Cora said smugly. "For instance, you forgot to tell everyone that the reason you shot at her is because she was wearing men's clothing."

"Cora …"

"Actually, I'm not entirely correct," Cora continued, looking straight at Mercy. "You weren't actually wearing the shirt and trousers. You weren't really dressed at all."

"Well, this certainly isn't boring conversation," Anna said. "Where exactly did you say you hail from, Mercy?"

"Mercy has amnesia, Anna," Ilene said. "It's a clinical condition …"

"I know what it is," Anna said, keeping her eyes on Mercy. "Poor girl. I can't imagine how awful that must be."

"Where do you live?" Ava asked.

"At the Little Sisters of Hope Convent," Mercy answered.

"You live with … nuns?"

Mercy nodded. "For as long as I can remember."

Leon looked very uncomfortable. "You should have said something. I hope I didn't use vulgar language or say something offensive to you."

"She's not a nun, Leon. She just lives with them," Rand said. "And besides, nuns are like regular people, you know."

"Rand has been spending a lot of time at the convent," Ilene said dryly. "He does odd jobs, brings supplies. Why, he even arranged for an evening's theater profits to be given to the Little Sisters of Hope."

"Well, that explains it, then," Frederick said.

"Explains what?" Charles asked.

"Honestly, I've been wondering all evening how Mercy came to be at this dinner table—and now I know. It's awfully nice of you to do charity work at home, too, Rand."

Mercy didn't immediately understand Frederick's implication, but everyone else did. Cora smiled triumphantly.

"Mercy isn't a charity case, Fred," Rand said, not bothering to hide the anger in his voice. "She is the woman I love, and she has every right to be at this dinner table."

Mercy's eyes widened in surprise, and Cora's smile died. Ilene laughed nervously. "Young people! So dramatic!"

Rand pushed back his chair. "If you will excuse us, I believe it's time I got Mercy back to the convent."

Mercy had drained her wine glass by the time Rand came around the table to pull out her chair. She stood, looked at the group staring at her, and hiccuped.

"Thank you for dinner."

They rode in silence for the first few minutes under a full moon. Finally, Rand brought the carriage to a stop. He shifted so he could look at her.

"I am so sorry about what was said tonight, Mercy."

She studied him. "Sorry you said you loved me?"

He smiled and reached for her hand. "No. I meant that, though I'll admit it's not the way I wanted to tell you. I'm sorry about Frederick's thoughtless comment, and Cora's veiled barbs, and my mother's not-so-subtle way of reminding me that I come from a wealthy family."

Mercy looked down at her hand clasped tightly in Rand's, then raised her eyes to his. "I saw your home, Rand. You *do* come from a wealthy family. And I don't blame Mr. Klein for wondering what I was doing there." She paused. "I have to admit, I was wondering the same thing."

He leaned closer to her. "I want you there, Mercy. I want you with me. Now, tomorrow … next week …" His voice trailed off. "My father convinced me that working with the railroad was how I helped fight the war. I lived with them for the duration, but now that it's over, I'm thinking about leaving. I have the means to build a very nice home."

When she didn't answer, he slipped his arm across her shoulders. After a moment, she relaxed against him and looked up at the sky. "Look how beautiful the stars are tonight," she said softly.

"You can change the subject, but you won't change my feelings about you," he said. There was a smile in his voice … a tenderness that made her snuggle even closer.

"I could stay like this forever," she said wistfully.

"That would be nice, but unfortunately, you have a curfew," he told her. "We need to get you back soon."

"Just a little while longer," she said. "The sisters will be long asleep by now anyway. They won't even miss me."

"It does seem like a shame to waste a moon like this one," he said, tightening his arm around her shoulder. "A little while longer, then."

Deirdre was pacing back and forth in front of the window in the common room of the convent when she finally heard Rand's carriage pull into the yard. She watched Rand jump off the carriage and come around to help Mercy down as if she were a princess.

She started to go out the door to tell Mercy she better hurry herself inside but stopped short when she saw Rand lean in to kiss Mercy good night. And Mercy kissed him back! Deirdre could see it plain as day even in the dark of night. It was a lover's kiss. One that made her burn with the memory of her own stolen kisses under full moons and scattered stars.

Mercy was humming softly when she entered the convent. Deirdre stepped out to confront her.

"Mercy! Do you know what time it is?"

Mercy's hand flew to her chest. "Deirdre, you scared the life out of me!"

"You're two hours past curfew!" Deirdre said.

"Oh. Oh, I'm sorry. I completely lost track of time," Mercy said.

Deirdre moved closer. "Is that alcohol I'm smelling on your breath?"

Mercy smiled but shook her head. "No. It's only wine."

Deirdre shook her head. "Coming home in the wee hours of the morning, smelling of alcohol, and stealing kisses in the dark!"

"You were watching me?" Mercy asked.

"Mother was looking for you," Deirdre said. "She's gone to get the orphans."

Mercy frowned. "It happened tonight?"

"She waited and waited for you to get back, but when your curfew came and went, she convinced Oona to harness Lucky and try to tame that horse into an easy ride to the city."

Mercy's eyes filled with tears. "It's the only thing she wanted from me."

"She wasn't angry," Deirdre said.

"She wasn't?"

Deirdre shook her head. "Mother rarely gets angry. For her it's disappointment, but believe me when I say, anger is quicker and over in a flash. Disappointment seems like it settles in and takes its own sweet time to go away."

CHAPTER SIXTEEN

The evening with Rand's parents is done. I went. I met them. I survived. But just barely.

My head feels foggy. And my heart feels heavy that I managed to miss the one opportunity I had to really help Mother Helena. The orphans arrived, and I was not there. Why didn't You tell me, God? Why am I always the last one to know of Your plans? Am I paying the price for something I did but can't remember?

Tomorrow I will try and make things right with Mother. I'm counting on the forgiveness commandment for this one.

The first glass of wine isn't very good, but the taste seems to improve the more you drink.

Rand said he loves me.

I can't keep my eyes open.

Mercy heard the sound of laughter through the haze of sleep and groaned. On some level it registered that the sun was up and she should get out of bed, but on another level, she wanted to sink back into the depths of her dreams and forget about her pounding head.

Oona took the choice away by entering the room and announcing, "Mother would like to see you, Mercy."

She sat up and squinted at Oona. "Now?"

Oona nodded grimly. "Yes. Right now."

Mercy went in search of Mother Helena, weaving her way around children of various ages and sizes and wincing at noise that seemed to reverberate off the walls. Some of the children smiled when they saw her; some regarded her with solemn eyes. She wondered what it would be like to be that age and find yourself in a strange house, maybe hundreds of miles from home, surrounded by nuns. And then it dawned on her—she needn't wonder at all. She knew.

She had been told Mother was outside and found her near the garden, humming softly to a baby girl asleep in her arms. It wasn't until Mercy was almost upon her that the nun looked up from the baby's face and registered her presence.

"Oona said you wanted to see me?" Mercy said.

"Yes."

A fat cloud passed in front of the sun, and Mother Helena glanced up. "I think it may rain," she said. "Always good for the garden."

Mercy nodded but stopped when her head swam with the motion. She stepped closer to get a look at the baby. "She's beautiful."

"She is called Amelia. I think it suits her."

"I saw the children," Mercy said.

"It would be hard to miss them."

"But I *did* miss them last night," Mercy said, ready to get her scolding over with and move on with the day.

When Mother looked past her, Mercy turned to see Sister Ruth coming toward them. Ruth looked at the sleeping baby and smiled. "The wee one is all tuckered out," she said, then raised an eyebrow. "But I can't say the same for the children inside the house. I've never seen so much energy in my life."

"Children being children. Such joy," Mother said. "Turn them out for a while and let them run."

Ruth looked at Amelia. "Shall I take her inside for you, Mother?"

Mother Helena hesitated, then said, "Thank you, Sister."

As Ruth left with Amelia, Mother looked at Mercy. "Walk with me."

They walked toward the barn behind the convent, where Lucky stood munching on a bucket of oats.

Mercy walked gingerly, as if the jarring action of putting foot to ground was too much. Mother Helena looked at her.

"How are you feeling this morning?"

"My head feels as if someone is pounding on the inside and trying to get out."

"I was told that you arrived back here last night with alcohol on your breath," Mother said. Though there was no discernible reproach or judgment in her voice, Mercy felt both.

"I just had a little wine at the Prescotts' house," Mercy said.

"And now you have a headache as a parting gift."

"Oh. I didn't know one had anything to do with the other," Mercy said. "But if this is the price to pay for drinking wine, I don't think I'll have it again."

They stopped at the corral fence, and Lucky looked up. His ears pricked up as he seemed to register Mercy's presence, but then he went back to eating his oats.

"I am giving Lucky to you," Mother Helena said without preamble.

Mercy's jaw dropped, and she stared at the diminutive nun. "I'm sorry? What?"

"I said I am making you a gift of that horse. When anyone but you tries to coax anything out of him, his behavior is unpredictable and erratic, and I can't have that around the sisters or the children."

"Yes, of course, I'll always make sure the children are safe," Mercy said.

"You won't be here to worry about that. That is why I'm giving him to you."

Mercy's mouth went dry. "But I live here."

Mother Helena looked at her and shook her head. "You need to find another place to live." Her tone was gentle but firm.

"You're making me leave the convent?" Mercy's voice rose. "Just because I came home late for curfew once?"

"We have provided you with clothes, food, and a roof over your head. And in return, I made only one request. That I could count on you to help me bring the children safely here."

"Mother, I …"

"Oona tried. She did. But that horse has a mind of his own when you aren't around, and he got away from her three times. Once, we almost went off the road and into a ravine *with* the children. They were already frightened enough at their new situation. They didn't need to hear the terrified bantering of their new caretakers."

"I am so sorry, Mother," Mercy said sincerely. "I promise I won't be late again. Please don't turn me out. I don't have anywhere else to go."

Mother sighed. "The tardiness is not the only issue. And last night isn't the first time you've come back to the convent after drinking alcohol. Deirdre said—"

"Deirdre is jealous! Jealous that I get to be with Rand and she can't have a man! She's never gotten over that potato farmer back in Ireland, and now she's going to ruin things for me!"

"That is enough," Mother said sternly. "Deirdre only answered the questions I asked her."

But Mercy was fuming. "I see how she looks at Rand. How she looks at me when I'm wearing pretty dresses and she's—"

"I would be extremely careful about your next words," Mother Helena said. "Because whatever you say about Deirdre, you are saying about the rest of us."

Mercy's eyes filled with tears, and she gripped the fence as Mother continued.

"We are women, Mercy. Women who have hopes, dreams, needs, frustrations, and yes, even passions—just like other women. The difference is what we have chosen to do with all those emotions and how we choose to avoid temptation. We live separate, dress separate, *are separate* from the world on purpose. Whether you realize it or not, you are falling in love and want to experience all that goes along with that. What you are doing is not wrong—but *where* you are doing it is."

"So I'm the outsider, and the outsider has to leave; is that it?"

"Yes, child. That's it."

"I'll tell Rand I can't see him anymore," Mercy said, her voice rising in panic. "I'll dress in black and do the chores and even learn to sew—just don't make me leave, Mother."

"You can't deny who you are," Mother said.

"Who am I? *Who?* How can I deny what I don't know?" Mercy practically yelled.

"I can't have the distractions that accompany your presence here any longer. I can't have sisters worrying about your dinner parties and fancy dresses and the latest style in hair bows. I have children to think about now, and I need everyone to focus on their emotional, physical, and spiritual needs."

"You have all told me, time and time again, that nuns have been called by God to this life. If that's true, how can all of you be so easily distracted by temptations? Are you sure your calling is truly from God?"

The look on Mother Helena's face was enough to make Mercy regret her sarcastic tone.

"From the time I was a wee girl, I planned to marry the church. To give myself to Christ and live my life in service," Mother Helena said. "I knew it as sure as I knew my own name. God called me. And I would answer when I was of age. No questions. No hesitations. Until I was careless with where I went and who I met, and I fell in love with a fisherman named Padraig O'Brien. He became all I wanted, and because the heart wants what the heart wants, I turned my back on God and who I really was—and married Padraig. We had a son together. A beautiful little boy named Aidan, who was the best parts of both of us.

"I know what romantic love is, Mercy. How it feels. How it fills up every space in you until you are ready to burst with happiness that someone cherishes you that way. It's the way a nun is supposed to feel about God's holy love. But in the life of a religious, there is no room for both."

"Where are they now? Your husband and your son?"

"Padraig and Aidan drowned in a boating accident," Mother said in a carefully modulated voice. "I allowed myself to be distracted by the world. I took my eyes off God and turned my back on my true path in life, and because of that a wonderful man and an innocent little boy died."

"But you can't think it was your fault ..."

"I have a house filled with children who have lived through the hell of losing one or both of their parents, and I won't rest until every one of them has a safe and loving home," Mother said. "I've grown very fond of you, Mercy, but every time you leave and come back, the world comes back with you, and I can't allow that to continue. I'll give you a few days to find other arrangements."

"Lucky is truly mine now?" Mercy asked, the hurt on her face turning to hard lines of anger.

"Yes."

"Then I'll be on my way as soon as I can collect my belongings," Mercy said. "I wouldn't want to stay here one more night and risk being the cause of someone's fall from grace."

"I had prayed we could part in a civil manner," Mother Helena said quietly, "and that you wouldn't leave angry."

"You told me God answers all our prayers, Mother. But I can tell you for certain, He won't answer this one the way you want Him to."

Before Mother Helena could say another word, Mercy ran for the house, resisting the hot tears she felt burning behind her eyes, and quickly gathered the few things in the world that were truly hers. With all the nuns preoccupied with their new boarders, Mercy slipped out the back of the house and made her way toward her horse.

Riding bareback on Lucky, Mercy nursed the flame of anger that had steadily grown since she'd left the convent. Better to stew in rage than allow any other emotions into her head—hurt, embarrassment, fear. She was the woman without a past. The outsider. The interloper who had been accused of corrupting God's holy women by her mere presence. She had one moment of thankfulness when it came back to her how in tune she was with Lucky. The horse seemed to feel her every move—responded to the way she shifted on his back or leaned a forearm near his neck. They flew across the countryside, trampling shadows stretched across the ground as heavy clouds puckered with rain hung overhead.

Mercy came onto the property from the back, riding alongside the tall hedges that served as a barrier just days ago between a lovely summer picnic and two nuns who would unwittingly cause her to lose her place to live.

The Prescott estate looked to be sleeping in the small valley below—no one out and about under the timpani thunder that was a prelude to the first fat drops of rain. Instinctively, Mercy kept Lucky close to trees and bushes as they approached the back of the house. She slid from Lucky's back, looped the reins over a low-hanging tree branch, and waited.

Mercy was soaked to the skin by the time the rain stopped and she saw Rand come out of the house. His father was with him, and Mercy shrank back farther into the shadows of the landscape. She watched Charles and Rand speak for a few moments, and then a carriage came from the direction of the stable and stopped. She felt her heart sink with the lost opportunity to speak to Rand alone—until the carriage pulled away and she could see that although Charles was gone, Rand remained. He started to go back into the house—but then he turned, and she felt as if he looked straight at her. It was the moment she had waited for, and she couldn't move. Could a man still love a woman he pitied? He hesitated a second longer, and her fear and desperation won out over her pride.

"Rand!" she called out, stepping out of the shadows.

She was close enough to see his surprised expression and then the frown as he saw the state she was in. He quickly started to cross the space between them, and she moved to meet him, her wet dress heavy around her ankles.

"Mercy!" he said, finally getting so close he could see that the wet on her cheeks wasn't from the rain. "What is it? What's wrong?"

"I don't know what to do," she said, all anger dissipating into helplessness and fear, "or where to go."

"I don't understand," Rand said, confused. "What are you telling me?"

"I'm telling you that I need help," she said. "I need … you."

Chapter Seventeen

Mercy and Rand rode side by side, and with each mile they went, she felt the weight of her dilemma lighten. She had gone to ask for a loan. Enough money to get her a room at a boardinghouse until she could find something more suitable, but Rand had a better idea.

He told her of a modest cottage his family owned on the lake. He'd spent summers there when he was a boy, and the family kept it for sentimental reasons. The place stayed empty except for a bare-bones staff. She could stay as long as she needed to. She'd made a few cursory, weak objections. "Your parents won't like it."

"They're reasonable people," he said. "And they know how much I care about you. I've not kept it a secret from them."

"Still, maybe you should speak to them first."

"Father just left for the day, and Mother has retired with a head-ache," he said. "I'll speak to them about it later."

Less than an hour later, they brought the horses around a sharp bend in the landscape.

"There it is," Rand said.

She stared at the home about a hundred yards in front of her—the manicured lawn and hedges, the gorgeous birch trees and meticulously planned flower beds. The house itself was a long, ram-bling one story with a shake-shingled roof that pitched out over a sweeping front porch with strategically placed rocking chairs. Acting as a perfect backdrop for the whole thing was a sparkling lake that went on as far as her eye could see.

"*That* is not a modest cottage!" she said.

"Of course it is."

"No. It's too much. I can't stay there."

"You can—and you will," he said firmly.

"I … I will find another solution quickly," she said. "This will just be temporary, until I can find some kind of employment and earn my own way."

"Let's just get you settled and then think about our future."

She cast a quick, sidelong glance at him. "You mean *my* future."

He smiled but kept his eyes on the cottage in front of them. "Same thing."

"Why do I get the feeling that you were the one who put Mother Helena up to throwing me out of the convent?" she asked.

He turned to her with wide eyes. "I'm shocked you would sug-gest such a thing," he said, feigning hurt feelings. "And I'm actually sorry I wasn't the one who thought of it."

They stopped in front of the porch. Rand dismounted, then held up his arms for Mercy. She slid from the horse, her small bundle of possessions in hand.

"Welcome to Ruby's Cottage," Rand said.

A screen door pushed open, and a black woman in her midfifties stepped outside. She fisted her hands on generous hips and grinned. "I sure is happy to see you, lil' mister," she said.

Mercy unconsciously crossed her arms over her chest at the woman's appearance.

"I'm happy to see you, too, Kizzy," Rand said. He sniffed at the air. "Do I smell shortbread cookies?"

Kizzy chuckled. "I swear to da good Lord, you gots a nose like a bloodhound, Mr. Rand. I just did up a batch. It be Isaac's birthday, and I aim to give him a treat."

"Isaac's birthday? Today?"

Kizzy nodded, kept her shoulder against the screen, and shoved her big, padded hands into the pockets of a flowered apron. "Mmm, hmmm, it shore is. I hope you ain't minding me baking somethin' for the boy in the cottage. The stove in da quarters ain't as good ..."

"It's fine, Kizzy. Cookies are a nice gesture," Rand said. "Now, I want you to meet Miss Mercy. She will be staying here indefinitely."

He ushered Mercy forward and up the steps of the porch. "I want you to afford her all the hospitality you can muster up."

Kizzy's chocolate-brown eyes did a quick sweep up and down Mercy, then she nodded graciously. "Welcome to Ruby's Cottage, Miss Mercy. We'll do ever'thing we can ta make you feel at home."

Mercy stopped short inside the door of the cottage and let her eyes wander around the comfortable yet expensively furnished room.

The green velvet chairs and sofa were high backed, with deep cushions and cabriole legs. Parlor tables were polished mahogany and boasted carvings of fruit, flowers, and leaves. Mercy knew nothing—or at least *remembered* nothing—about art, but even she could see that the oil paintings on the walls were of the highest quality.

"It's ... beautiful," she said, not moving from her spot near the door.

Rand put a hand on the small of her back to gently urge her forward.

"I want you to consider this your home for now," he said.

She had barely moved into the room when the screen door banged open and a gangly black boy charged inside. He was halfway across the floor before he realized he wasn't the only one in the room. Stopping as if he'd seen a ghost, his eyes widened in worry, and he looked around as if to see who else had witnessed his entry to the house.

"'Scuze me, Mr. Rand! I ain't had no idea you was here!"

"It's all right, Isaac. We just arrived." He gestured to Mercy. "This is Miss Mercy. She will be staying here for a while, and I know you'll do everything and more that she asks of you."

Isaac nodded. "Yassuh. I will. Yes, I will. Everything and more, suh."

Rand nodded. "Good. I'll need you to see to Sherman—and to Miss Mercy's horse, Lucky. In fact, I'll expect you to see to Lucky's needs every day."

Isaac nodded solemnly. "Yassuh."

"Where is Ezra?" Rand asked.

"He be cuttin' wood down by the lake. Letty be with him, harvesting some berries for Kizzy."

Rand arched a brow. "Berries? Maybe for one of Kizzy's special pies?"

"I ain't sure, suh, but I s'pect so."

"Could be that special pie is actually a birthday pie? Maybe for you?"

Isaac ducked his head in embarrassment but grinned. "Yassuh, but I think I's s'posed to be surprised."

"How old are you today?"

"'Bout thirteen."

Rand pulled his hand out of his pocket and walked over to Isaac. He pressed a dime into the stunned boy's hand. "Happy birthday, Isaac."

Isaac stared down at the coin in his palm, then wrapped his fingers around it. "Thanks be to you, Mr. Rand! Thanks be to you. I be seein' to the horses now."

"Wait a minute, Isaac. You were in an awful hurry when you came through that door. What were you after?"

Isaac glanced toward the kitchen. "I smelled me some shortbread cookies, and I was gonna talk Kizzy out a' one or two."

"I don't blame you a bit," Rand said. "Get your cookies, and then look after the horses."

Isaac grinned. "Yassuh."

As soon as Isaac was out of earshot, Rand turned to Mercy. "Isaac will be told to come through the back door from now on, and only when summoned. I don't want you to be uncomfortable," he said.

"How many of them are there?"

"Them?" he asked.

"Colored people. Blacks," she said bluntly.

"There are four *servants* at the cottage," Rand said, gently correcting her. "You've met Kizzy and Isaac, and there are Letty and Ezra. They're a married couple who have worked for my family for two decades."

"And they all live here? In the house?"

"No, of course not. There are servants' quarters behind the cottage," Rand said.

"Oh. Of course."

"Kizzy does all the cooking, Letty does the housekeeping, and Ezra handles the maintenance and the grounds."

"And Isaac? Is he Letty and Ezra's son?"

"Letty's cousin's boy. His parents are dead, and she's his only kin. He does odd jobs, runs errands for Kizzy and Letty. Ezra makes sure he doesn't just laze around all day long."

"So ... he's an orphan?"

Rand nodded. "I suppose so." He held out his hand. "Come on. I want to show you the rest of the place."

She put her hand in his. "You're sure your parents aren't going to be angry about this?"

"I promise it will be fine." He said it with so much conviction, it had the opposite effect on Mercy. She didn't believe him for a second.

Given my history and my luck, she thought, *I had best enjoy this cottage while I have the chance.*

Chapter Eighteen

When I got up this morning I had no idea things would change so drastically for me. When Mother Helena made me leave the convent, I went straight to Rand. I knew he would help me, but I had no idea I would end up in such a beautiful place. By going to him as I did—by accepting his help and living in his house—what am I saying to him? Have I accepted that my past is just that—the past? Is it time for me to get on with my life without the weight of what might have been? I'm growing tired of worrying about people I can't even remember—people who may have gone on with their lives without me.

There are blacks here. Servants who live on the property and take care of the house and the grounds. I don't know why that bothers me—but it does. I tried not to let it show, but I think Rand noticed my aversion to them. Where does that come from? Why do I feel the way I do?

Tonight, I will sleep in a real bed with soft sheets and a beautiful quilt in a room all to myself. If I want to keep the lamp lit and write the night away, I can do it without fear of bothering Oona and Deirdre.

I wonder if they will miss me.

I wonder what Rand's parents will say when he tells them I am living in the cottage.

I wonder if the morning will have me moving on again.

Please God—just let me stay.

"Have you lost your mind?" Ilene Prescott said, keeping her voice low enough so that the nosy servants wouldn't overhear. She sat on the edge of an ivory-draped sofa in her formal living room and fingered the strand of pearls around her neck. The gaslight in the room made everything in the room seem soft—except for the hard lines of Ilene's annoyed face.

Rand paced in front of the fireplace with a drink in his hand. "No, Mother, I haven't lost my mind."

"Don't you think this is something you should have discussed with us first, Rand?" Charles asked. He lit a pipe, then flicked the match into an ashtray on an ornately carved table.

"I like to believe that you trust my judgment, Father," Rand said.

"I just cannot reconcile Mother Helena asking the girl to leave the convent," Ilene ruminated. "There must have been a reason, Rand. What did she do?"

"Believe me when I say the infraction was so minor, it boggles the mind."

"Well?" Ilene lifted a brow.

"She was late for her curfew last night," Rand said.

"I thought you left in plenty of time to get her back to the convent."

"I misjudged the time," Rand said. "In any event, Mercy believes, and I concur, that it was time for her to go. She didn't really belong with the nuns."

"I still don't understand why this *girl's* unfortunate circumstance has become your dilemma," Ilene said. "I know you were just peeved with the notion that Mercy was a charity case, so you made your big declaration of love, but for goodness' sake, Rand, we all know you cannot possibly entertain the idea of a future with her."

Rand dropped his eyes to his drink. When he failed to look his mother in the eye, she audibly gasped.

"You are! You *are* thinking about a future with her!" she said accusingly, stabbing a finger in the air at him. "I was right—you *have* lost your mind!" She turned to Charles, who sat stoically puffing away on his pipe. "Well, Charles. Don't just sit there. Don't you have something to say about this?"

"Look, Son, you *are* putting us in an untenable situation here," Charles said. "We know nothing about this young woman except for some very unusual details. It was fine you brought her home to dinner, took her to a few plays, and had a picnic or two—just like you've done with more young women than I can begin to count. But that's where it needs to end."

"Amen to that," Ilene said succinctly. "Tomorrow you will help her find another living arrangement."

Rand shook his head. "No, ma'am, I won't. Ruby's Cottage is partially mine, and I want her to stay."

"Your grandmother is probably spinning in her grave to think of a complete stranger in her cottage," Ilene said.

"Grandma Ruby had a bigger heart than the three of us combined," Rand said, "and you know it, Mother. She would have been the first to take in a stranger if there was a need."

"There are other women far more suitable for you, Rand. Cora, for instance ..."

"I don't want any other woman," Rand said. "I want Mercy."

"I forbid it," Ilene said. "I forbid you to marry her."

"Good heavens ... what if she's already married?" Charles mused. "She would be a bigamist! You cannot move forward with this relationship until her memory returns, Rand. You have to wait!"

"For how long, Father? How long is long enough for you to believe her memory is never coming back? One year? Two? Five? Because I will wait if I have to—but not because you want me to," Rand said. "I'll wait because Mercy won't even discuss marriage with me. She doesn't want to see me hurt—nor hurt anyone she doesn't remember from her past."

"Well, thank God for small favors," Ilene muttered. "At least she has a brain."

"Yes, Mother, she has a brain. She's also funny, courageous, sweet, and beautiful ..."

Ilene held up her hand. "Stop. Just stop extolling her virtues, because it doesn't change anything."

"I never dreamed you would be so narrow-minded," Rand said.

"We have worked very hard to get what we have, Rand. Your father's reputation is sterling—his work ethic incomparable. The Prescott name is synonymous with patriotism and the cause your father worked so hard to preserve. That young woman would embarrass you at every social occasion. She wore a common day dress to a dinner party, for heaven's sake. She has no idea how to be the perfect companion to a successful young man."

"Then help her," Rand pleaded. "Who better to teach her how to be everything she is expected to be than you, Mother? Everyone in St. Louis admires your style, your grace—your eloquence when speaking. If you want to see me make a good match, then help Mercy become a proper lady!"

"And if she happens to wake up one morning and remember that she has a husband and a child or two tucked away somewhere? What then?"

"I don't believe that is going to happen, but if it does, I will bow out gracefully," Rand declared.

"And if I refuse to help?" Ilene asked.

"Then I will find someone else who will," Rand said. "Mercy won't have the benefit of the very best instruction, but at least she will learn the basic social graces. Maybe Ava Klein might help."

"Ava Klein? Be serious, Rand," Ilene scoffed. "Unless of course we are talking about Mercy entering a pie-eating contest."

And with that statement, Rand relaxed. They spoke of logistics and a shopping trip, and he assured them again that he wasn't going to rush into anything. His only intention was for Mercy to have a roof over her head in a safe place and for her to have the instruction of a cultured woman such as his mother. As he watched his parents retire to their respective bedrooms, Rand congratulated himself on winning the first round in his quest to make Mercy his bride. Now all he had to do was convince the girl.

CHAPTER NINETEEN

There was a sickle moon in the autumn sky tonight that appeared to be hanging by a thread. I noticed it after I made my trip to give Lucky his evening carrot. Then as the sky darkened, stars emerged in handfuls at a time—twinkling, sparkling—reflecting off the lake and teasing me into believing my past and future don't matter, that only the moment I'm living in is important.

There are still things that bother me that I haven't told Rand.

I hate a chiming clock. Hate it with a passion that makes no sense.

Sometimes Ezra rounds a corner and I have to bite back a scream.

I had to get rid of the silver-handled brush Rand gave me as a gift. It felt like a hot poker in my hand.

Still, I am happy. Happy to be living in this cottage, happy to have a bed to call my own at night, and happy to have Lucky to ride

*whenever the spirit moves me. I want to give in to it—the happiness—
but there is something that lingers at the edges of my mind, and it
tells me to be careful. That I've been happy before only to have it all
come crashing down on me. It scares me more than I want to admit—
because there is something else that I have to contend with now, and it
makes things so much more complicated. Despite all my concerns and
worries about the damage it could cause me, Rand, and people I don't
even remember—I've gone ahead and done what I said I wouldn't do.
I have fallen in love.*

Mercy sat in the bow of the fishing boat and watched the muscles
in Rand's arms tense and relax as he rowed them farther and farther
away from the shoreline. She snuggled into the shawl across her
shoulders, and he stopped rowing for a moment. A crease of concern
crossed his forehead.

"Too cold?" he asked.

She shook her head, causing the natural curls in her hair to dance
with the motion. "No. I'm just perfect."

He gave her a look that sent sweet chills up her spine. "That's
what I was going to say."

She blushed at her choice of words. "I meant to say that the
weather is just perfect—and I'm not too cold."

Rand smiled, then found the familiar rhythm of rowing again.
She tipped her head back to admire the steel-blue October sky.

"I think Mother Helena was right," she said.

"About?"

"She said autumn would be beautiful. So far, it's my favorite
time of year."

"Maybe you'll say that about winter," he said, securing the oars on the sides of the boat. She looked at him and smiled. "Maybe I will."

"On the other hand, winters can be long and tiresome," he opined. "Unless of course you have a project to keep you occupied."

She felt the boat glide to a gentle stop and then held tightly to the sides as Rand carefully moved to sit on the seat directly in front of her. They swayed for a second before he reached out and enclosed both of her hands in his.

"Don't you want to know what kind of project I'm talking about?" he asked.

She shook her head and tried to stifle her smile while she teased him. "No, since I'm fairly sure it involves some kind of sewing—quilting—needlepoint. Things I am terrible at and don't particularly enjoy."

"What if I promised you it doesn't involve sewing needles of any kind but is something you can do during the long, dreary cold months? Something that will keep you busy—and before you know it, spring will be here."

"I don't need that kind of work, Rand. What I need is to find a way to make money. I can't keep living off your family's charity forever," she said.

"It's not charity," he said.

She raised a brow. "Really? Maybe I don't remember what the word *charity* means … is that what you're telling me?"

"Mercy. Stop. We've been through this a hundred times."

"I can see it all over your mother's face," Mercy argued. "The few times we've been together since I moved into Ruby's Cottage, she looks at me as if I'm—I'm—a thief who has come into her life and stolen from her."

He smiled. "The only thing you've stolen is her son's heart."

"Rand ..."

"You can't argue with the truth," he said. "And it's rude if you won't even let me tell you about this project I'm so excited about."

He was so handsome and so earnest looking; she couldn't help it. She squeezed his hands. "Fine. What's the project?"

Rand kept a grip on her hands. "I want you to take the winter to plan a spring wedding."

It took a moment for what he was saying to sink in. She tried to pull her hands away, but he held on.

"I love you, Mercy. You know I do. Marry me, and make me the happiest man in the whole world."

Quick tears filled her eyes, and she whispered her reply. "You can't ask me that."

"I just did," he said. "Don't you love me?"

She sighed and looked down at their hands, then nodded. "You know I do. Though I don't have any right to."

He reached over, tipped her chin up, and leaned closer. "You have every right to be happy. Every right to go on with your life. You don't know if there is someone else or not."

"But if there is ..."

"There isn't."

"We don't know that," she said.

"But I *do* know. Because any man worthy of your love would never have let you go."

He pulled a ring from his pocket, and she was helpless to stop him as he slid it onto her left hand. She looked down at the ruby surrounded by a ring of diamonds.

"It belonged to my grandmother Ruby," he said.

Mercy couldn't take her eyes off the ring. "It's the most beautiful thing I've ever seen."

"Ruby was my father's mother, Mercy. It was her cottage that you're living in. She was strong willed and tender and energetic and courageous and very, very beautiful at one time. She married my grandfather when she was only sixteen, and they lived happily together for forty-five years until his death. Family meant everything to her. Everything. There is nothing she wouldn't have done for us, and even now, five years after her death, there isn't a day that goes by that I don't think about her."

Mercy looked from the ring to Rand's face. "She sounds like she was a remarkable woman."

"She was. But then, so are you. That's why I'm asking you to be my wife."

"Wouldn't you rather have someone like Cora? Someone with a pedigree, an old family name, and a—a memory?"

"Marry me."

"Rand."

"Marry me."

"But your parents …"

"Marry me, Mercy. Please."

Mercy couldn't help herself. She wanted him—marriage—children. A life where she wouldn't constantly be looking back at the black hole of her past. Her memory seemed as gone as the day before—never to return—and there was nothing she could do about that. She did deserve some happiness … didn't she?

"Well, I guess I *could* use a project to keep me busy during the long winter months that are coming up," she said. Her face radiated joy. "I wouldn't want to sit idly by the fireplace while the winds howl."

He stared at her. "Does all that mean you're saying yes?"

She smiled at the tremble of emotion in his voice. "Yes, Rand. I would love to marry you."

He leaned forward and tenderly touched his lips to hers. When the kiss ended, he cupped her cheek and gazed intently into her eyes.

"I promise you won't regret marrying me, Mercy."

"I know I won't."

She held up her hand to watch the sun glint off the ruby in the ring. "I only hope Ruby approves," she said. "And that someday *you* don't regret it."

"Never."

She looked at Rand, watching the way he turned the boat around and headed it back toward shore—and Ruby's Cottage. She gave in to the happiness that consumed her. She was young and in love, and in a few months she was going to marry a wonderful man. Then something dawned on her.

"Rand? You know what this means?"

"What?"

"I'm finally going to get a last name."

CHAPTER TWENTY

It is nearly Christmas. There are beautiful decorations at the cottage and at the Prescott mansion. Lovely greenery that fills the house with the smell of pine. Twenty-foot trees brought in and decorated with candles, bows, and expensive glass ornaments that shimmer against the branches. Rand has told me stories of his childhood Christmases, and they sound wonderful. I am excited that next year I will be able to look back at this Christmas and remember it.

Charles and Ilene are hosting an engagement party for us. Ilene told me that only Missouri's finest citizens are on the guest list. I asked if she invited the sisters from the convent, but she told me that wouldn't be appropriate. I don't know why—but I've learned it's best not to argue with my future mother-in-law. As long as I see things the way she does, we get along just fine. She has made it her mission to turn me into someone who is socially acceptable. Even my past—or lack of one—has become a nonissue, thanks to an article that appeared on the society page of the St. Louis Daily Press. The editor of the paper is a good friend of Charles and Ilene, which is why, I suppose, the reporter was able to write a story that glossed over my amnesia and focused instead on how Rand Prescott fell in love with a lovely young woman who was working alongside the nuns at the Little Sisters of Hope Convent. His glowing article went on to list my many charitable contributions to the community, the impressive list of classics I've read, my remarkable skill with a paintbrush, and my fondness for writing poetry. None of it is true, of course, but I quite liked the young woman in the piece. She was very interesting—and doesn't seem to need a past at all. Her present is quite compelling.

Mercy stood in the guest suite of the Prescott mansion and tried to be still as Sally, one of the housemaids, fluffed out the skirt of her dress. Ilene entered the room and stopped to smile at the picture Mercy made.

"I was right," she said. "That dress is perfect on you."

Mercy smiled. "Thank you."

Sally moved around the dress, fussing, pulling, smoothing it perfectly over the hoop. Mercy looked at her future mother-in-law. "You look beautiful, Ilene."

Ilene glanced at herself in the cheval glass, touching a hand to the back of her upswept hair. "I had a new girl do my hair tonight. I think I'll keep her on."

Sally stepped back from Mercy and looked at Ilene. "There be anything else, Mrs. Prescott?"

"Not here, Sally. Check to see what Ellis may need help with," Ilene said.

Sally slipped out of the room, and Ilene crossed to Mercy. "Just a reminder, my dear. Not only will our closest friends be here this evening, but some of Missouri's elected officials. I don't think I've made a secret of the fact that Charles is an influential man in this state, Mercy, and I hope you will always remember to act with the decorum that's appropriate for this family."

"Of course, Ilene," Mercy said. "I have nothing but the highest admiration for you and Charles and for Rand. I would never do anything to embarrass you."

"I know that. It just needed to be said," Ilene said. "And it's something that Rand has heard since he was a little boy—it's only fitting his future wife hears it too."

Ilene ran a finger under a pearl choker at her neck, prompting a comment from Mercy.

"The choker is lovely," she said.

Ilene smiled absently. "An early Christmas gift from Charles," she said, then touched the pearls hanging from her ears. "These too."

"He has good taste," Mercy said.

"He's been trained well all these years," Ilene said with a smile. "You must do the same with Rand. Then maybe he will get you a more … suitable piece of jewelry to wear around your neck."

Mercy's hand went to the medallion. The décolletage of her dress was just low enough to showcase the medal against her ivory skin. "He knows I always wear this," she said. "I have no need of other jewelry."

Mercy watched Ilene's smile freeze in place, as it always did when any mention of Mercy's past—or more to the point, lack of a past—was brought up. But then her smile softened.

"I understand your attachment to your necklace. I have similar pieces that I am attached to, but not wearing them doesn't diminish their sentimental value."

Mercy frowned. "I'm not sure what you mean."

"If you take the medallion off this evening, it won't lessen what it means to you, Mercy," Ilene said.

In the past few weeks, she had gotten used to Ilene's strong opinions about everything from politics to social graces and, for the most part, always felt as if the life instruction she was receiving from her future mother-in-law was to her benefit. She couldn't remember a time when she hadn't deferred to the older woman, and because of that she felt as if Ilene had grown to not only tolerate her but like her. The medallion, though, was another thing altogether.

"I don't see what possible difference it makes to anyone but me if I wear it or not," Mercy said.

"You know I've missed having a daughter all these years," Ilene said. "Rand and his father and all that maleness around my house, and now you come into our lives, and I get to speak to you as a mother."

"And I appreciate that more than I can say," Mercy told her, "especially since I don't remember my mother. But I still don't understand ..."

"The dress is simply better without any jewelry at all," Ilene said. "The deep neckline that draws the eye to the delicate lace over the bosom; the silver sash that gives your waist an impossibly small appearance. Those are the details that we want to appear in the article on the society page of the paper tomorrow. Not that the look was spoiled by a medallion that had no place in your ensemble."

Ilene softened the speech with a smile and tilted her head to the side. "It really is the only thing that is keeping you from being a perfect picture. That dark green is divine on you—and Sally dressed your hair to perfection. I love the little sprigs of holly she's tucked into the curls. Very festive, yet elegant."

Mercy hesitated. Her hand went to close around the medallion. Ilene waited, but then added, "It's only advice, dear. As with everything else I tell you, it's entirely up to you whether or not you adhere."

Slowly and carefully, so as not to muss her hair, Mercy drew the chain of the medallion up and over her head. "If not for you, I wouldn't be standing here looking like this," she said.

Ilene smiled her approval. "The trappings that you're wearing may have come from me, my dear, but the beauty is all yours. You should carry yourself proudly—as the woman who will become the wife of Rand Prescott, heir to a railroad empire."

Mercy nodded. "I know this hasn't been easy for you. Our engagement, I mean."

"I'll admit I had my reservations in the beginning about you and Rand," Ilene said, "but as time has gone on, I can see how much he loves you—and you him. As long as your past stays in the past, I think the two of you can be very happy together."

Mercy smiled. "I think so too."

"Now. An engagement party can't start without the bride-to-be. There are over a hundred guests downstairs waiting to get their first glimpse of the future Mrs. Rand Prescott."

Mercy and Rand stood next to Charles and Ilene just inside the arched doorway of the drawing room. A fire burned cheerily in a massive hearth, and a string quartet tucked away in a corner played Christmas carols. The room was decked out with wreaths and ever-green boughs, and Mercy had counted no less than five servants circulating with trays of hors d'oeuvres and cocktails. The line for introductions snaked back through the foyer to the front door and was moving so slowly, she wondered if the entire evening would consist of polite nods and banal chitchat. Her cheeks ached from the constant smile she wore as she greeted one person after another.

"Mercy, may I present Mr. and Mrs. Andrews," Ilene said.

"I'm pleased to meet you," Mercy said to the next couple in line.

"It's our pleasure," Mrs. Andrews said.

"You wear love's glow like a candle in the window," Mr. Andrews said to Mercy.

"Ah, thank you," Mercy uttered as Mr. Andrews shook Rand's hand and said, "Congratulations, Rand."

Rand waited until the couple was barely out of earshot to lean toward Mercy. "He fancies himself a poet, though he's never been published, and she will have had one too many glasses of champagne and will glow like a candle by evening's end."

Mercy pressed her lips together to keep from laughing and heard Ilene greeting the next guest in line.

"Francis," Ilene said. "How good of you to come. May I present my future daughter-in-law. Mercy, this is Francis Fontaine, one of the elected officials here in St. Louis."

"You are marrying into a fine family, young lady. One of the finest in St. Louis," Fontaine said.

"I feel very fortunate," Mercy said humbly.

"Rand, I'll admit I'm shocked you're settling down," Fontaine continued, pumping Rand's hand.

"I was just waiting for the right woman, Francis," Rand said with a stiff smile that dropped as soon as Fontaine made his way toward another group of guests. "Surprised he still has a job," he said into Mercy's ear. "Rumor has it he's a Copperhead."

"What's a Copperhead?"

But Ilene interrupted Rand's explanation with a touch to Mercy's arm. "Mercy, may I introduce our very good friends John and Mary Henderson." John was tall and distinguished with just a touch of gray at the temples; Mary was more handsome than beautiful, but striking in her own way. "John is a superb congressman and represents the interests of the great state of Missouri."

John Henderson laughed. "Maybe I should have you write my next speech, Ilene." He bowed slightly to Mercy. "It's a pleasure, Mercy."

"Your dress is stunning," Mary said. "Simply perfect on you."

Mercy flushed with pleasure. "Thank you. The credit goes to Ilene, of course. She helped me choose it."

"And speaking of choices," John said to Rand, "it seems you have chosen well, Rand."

"Thank you, John. I think so," Rand said.

Mercy was aware of a man in a military uniform immediately to Mary's left. He seemed to hang back just a little—as if not wanting to intrude on the Hendersons' introduction, but then Mary reached over and tugged on his arm.

"Mercy, Rand ... I'd like to introduce our good friend Captain Elijah Hale of the former army of the Potomac," Mary said. "Captain Hale is staying with us while he awaits his next assignment."

Captain Hale moved a few steps to stop in front of Mercy. Though his shoulders were squared and he looked every inch a military man, his eyes were sad, and she had the fleeting thought that he would rather be anywhere else than in a room filled with people.

"I hope you enjoy your stay in St. Louis, Captain Hale," Mercy said politely.

"I'm sure I will," he said, studying her intently with a distracted frown. "John and Mary are perfect hosts."

"How long have you known the Hendersons?" Rand asked Captain Hale. But the captain seemed unaware of the question. He continued to stare at Mercy while John Henderson jumped in to field Rand's question.

"It's been ten years or more, am I right, Elijah?" John said, deferring to the captain. But the question went unanswered. Mercy was aware that Rand had moved a few inches closer to her so that their shoulders were touching.

Mercy wanted the captain to move on, but he hadn't moved a muscle. She felt scrutinized to the point that she smiled uncomfortably.

"Well, it was a pleasure to meet—" Mercy started to say, hoping he would take the hint, but he interrupted her with a single sentence that sent her heart racing.

"I'm sorry," Captain Hale said, "but have we met before?"

"What?" Rand's voice sounded strained.

"Elijah, remember I told you Mercy has amnesia?" Mary said in a stilted voice.

Ilene and Charles were both looking their way. For a stunned moment, Mercy just stared at him, her mouth open. After what seemed like an eternity, but in reality was mere seconds, she felt the world tilt as she took a step toward him. "Are you saying you *know* me?"

Captain Hale continued to look at her as if he'd seen a ghost, but then, abruptly, it seemed as though the ghost disappeared. "No. I mean, I don't think so. My apologies if I upset you."

"Are you sure?" she asked, aware that her voice had risen just a bit and that Rand had taken hold of her arm. "Because if there is any chance that you might … I need to know. Please."

John Henderson leaned over and put a hand on Captain Hale's shoulder. "Yours is a memorable, beautiful face, Mercy. I would highly doubt a man would ever forget meeting you."

"He's right, of course," Captain Hale said. "I misspoke. Again, I'm sorry."

Ilene turned to the next person in line, and Mercy heard her laugh. She felt Rand's tension radiating through his shoulder as Captain Hale stared a moment longer.

"You should join us for our annual pheasant hunt on New Year's Eve, Captain Hale," Rand said, a little too loudly. Mercy heard the false cheerfulness in his voice. "John is a good shot, but I imagine that you, being a military man and all, can show us all a thing or two about taking aim."

To Mercy's relief, Captain Hale finally pulled his eyes from her and looked at Rand. "Thank you for the invitation."

"We'll bring him along if we have to hog-tie him," John said.

"Splendid," Rand said halfheartedly.

"Congratulations," Captain Hale said.

"Thank you," Mercy said.

John and Mary had already moved out of the line by the time Captain Hale followed after them. Rand watched them go and then leaned toward Mercy, and she heard him try to recapture the cozy, conspiratorial tone he'd used all evening long.

"I think the war has made the good captain a little daft," he whispered into her ear.

She smiled and nodded, even as she watched the retreating form of Captain Hale turn back and give her one last searching look before joining his friends.

"Mercy," she heard Ilene say, "you remember Leon and Anna Zimmerman."

And it was with great relief that Mercy could turn and say, "Yes, of course, I remember."

CHAPTER TWENTY-ONE

Tomorrow there is to be a pheasant hunt on the property adjacent to the cottage. Though it's been an annual event with the Prescotts, Rand said they didn't have the hunt the last few years because of the war. He's anxious to return to the tradition and, in a rare moment of bragging, told me he's an excellent shot. He even showed me a cabinet filled with rifles at the cottage. They are all in good working order, and there is enough ammunition to have been able to hold off the rebel army if it had come to that.

I can't help but wonder if Captain Hale will attend with the Hendersons. He looked at me so strangely the night of the engagement party. I'll admit I felt a moment of excitement coupled with dread when he asked if we'd met. But then when he changed his mind, all I felt was relief. I keep telling myself I want to know my past, but I'm not sure that's *true. There is always the fear that my past will completely upend my life with Rand, and I know I don't want that. I suppose what I'm admitting to you, my dear journal, is simply that I'm willing to live without my memory—so I can live with Rand.*

Mercy would be the first to admit that she had no idea what to expect from a pheasant hunt, but she was surprised it was such a spectator event—albeit a quiet one. Rand and Ilene had both advised her that all conversation would be in hushed voices so the quarry wouldn't be spooked.

As the hunt was to take place in close proximity to the cottage, Ezra, Letty, Kizzy and even Isaac were there to see to the needs of the women who were piling out of buggies and carriages with thick woolen blankets in tow. Mercy and Ilene settled themselves on a blanket that soon became the centerpiece for all the other guests who vied for a spot near the hostess and her future daughter-in-law. Cora and her mother arrived, instructing Letty to place their blanket right beside Ilene's. Mercy supposed that Cora would be a permanent fixture in her life at social occasions, and the thought both depressed and annoyed her.

She turned her attention to the men and watched them go through their hunting rituals. It seemed as if the hunters preened more than the quail she'd seen on the fringe of the cottage grounds. There was plenty of chest puffing and strategy talking in quiet voices so as not to alert the pheasants loafing in the tall grasses about fifty yards from the hunters. The bird dogs sat anxiously at their masters' feet, tails barely sweeping back and forth in anticipation of flushing and pointing out the quarry.

Captain Hale stood slightly apart from the others—surveying and watching just as Mercy was doing. His rifle was secured under his arm, his expression one of almost sardonic amusement. Mercy had the impression that the sole reason he was there was out of respect to his hosts, the Hendersons. He didn't have the same eager air of anticipation as the others—wasn't jockeying for position with the men who were spreading out and getting ready. He had greeted Mercy politely, and she was relieved when no mention was made of his mistake the night of the engagement party.

Ilene leaned closer to Mercy. "Rand has been shooting since he was five years old," she said proudly. "He got his first rifle from my father that Christmas and has proven himself to be an accomplished hunter ever since."

Mercy watched as Rand adjusted a Henry rifle on his hip and then lifted his eyes to the grasses in the distance.

Mercy smiled. "He looks very handsome in his hunting clothes."

"Yes, he does," Ilene agreed. "You know, I have always found it amusing that the male pheasants—the roosters—are the beautiful birds. The white ring around their necks, their lovely copper breast and sides. Even the blue patch on their back end is decorative."

"And the females?" Mercy asked.

Ilene chuckled. "The hens are plain as plain can be. They're a dull beige. Mottled from head to toe. Smaller, of course, than their male counterparts."

Mercy smiled. "Am I the dull hen compared to the brilliant rooster, Ilene?"

"No," Ilene said quickly. "Of course not. I was simply making an observation about nature." They both watched Rand a moment more, then Ilene continued. "But you are very blessed, my dear. He is simply *the* most eligible bachelor in St. Louis, you know."

"*Was* the most eligible bachelor in St. Louis," Mercy answered.

Ilene raised her brows and then smiled. "You are quite right. I stand corrected."

Mercy sensed the change in the hunters, the dogs—the general air of anticipation that settled over everyone as the men lined up.

"What now?" she asked quietly.

"Now they send in the dogs to flush out the birds. Pheasants prefer to run but can fly quite quickly if they lose ground cover."

"And then it's over? Just like that?"

"No—they'll keep hunting until the dogs can't find another bird to flush."

Rand glanced over his shoulder and caught Mercy's eye for just a moment. Ilene smiled. "Men love to be watched when they are doing something well." She nodded toward the group of men. "Here we go."

All eyes were on Charles, the host of the hunt, as he leaned down and gave Beau, his dog, a tap on the rump. Beau and the other dogs took off for the tall grass, barking, baying—hurtling toward the hidden prey.

Mercy heard the first panicked cries from the pheasants—a loud, raspy *kok, kok, kok, kaw-kok*—just before they scattered from their cover in a dead run. Some burst into the air at speeds far greater than she would have imagined possible.

With the sound of the repeating rifles echoing in her ears, Mercy watched the first round of the hunt come to a close in less than a minute. Dogs trotted after their prizes, returning with pheasants hanging gingerly from their jowls.

She heard pleased exclamations from the women around her. Cora leaned over toward Ilene to confide in her.

"I plan to try my hand at shooting this year," she said.

"Really?" Ilene said. "I didn't think you had an affinity for hunting, Cora."

"I don't. But I do have an affinity for something else. I thought I'd ask Captain Hale for some pointers."

Ilene and Mercy glanced over at Captain Hale as he reloaded his gun. The Hendersons' dog sat at his feet next to two large roosters laid out on the ground. "I will admit that Captain Hale would be a very handsome instructor, Cora," Ilene said with a small smile.

Cora cast a quick look at Mercy. "I think he'll do just fine, since Rand is otherwise engaged."

Mercy smiled. "Yes. He is."

Cora got to her feet as the hunters repositioned themselves by turning toward the south. She crossed the space between spectators and the men and walked boldly up to Captain Hale.

"I have a feeling she always gets what she wants," Mercy said quietly to Ilene as they watched Cora make her case to the captain.

"Not always," Ilene said. "She didn't get Rand."

The hunters were positioned to shoot again, their dogs obediently waiting for the signal to charge.

This time, Rand was the one who set Beau in motion, and the dog sprinted toward a new fringe of wild grass—other dogs baying right on his heels. The birds took flight quickly now, leaving behind only a handful who tried to stay the course and outrun their predators.

Again the whole thing was over in less than a minute, and dogs returned with roosters and hens and placed them with pride at their masters' feet.

Mercy looked over and saw a look of mild irritation on the face of Captain Hale. He had missed the second round of the hunt because of his instruction to Cora. She played the part of the helpless female perfectly; even Mercy could see that.

"She's an excellent shot," Ilene said. "Her father taught her when she was just a little girl."

"Really? Then why …?" But as Captain Hale leaned a little closer around Cora, Mercy knew exactly why she was pretending to be a novice with a gun. Cora smiled, then leaned over and said something to Rand.

Rand looked from Cora to Mercy, then frowned. Mercy could see that Cora was trying hard to make a point—but just what that point was, she didn't know. Until Rand headed right for her.

"What are you doing, Rand?" Ilene asked.

"Cora suggested that maybe Mercy might want to try and shoot," Rand said. Mercy wanted to strangle Cora. She had no interest in getting up in front of everyone to make a fool of herself.

"How about it, Mercy? Want to give it a try?" Rand asked.

Mercy shook her head. "No. I'm fine just watching." But even as she said it, she looked past Rand and saw the smug look of satisfaction on Cora's face.

"I didn't think you'd want to," Rand said. "But …"

Mercy held out her hand. "I changed my mind."

Rand helped her up. "Are you sure?"

"I'm sure I don't want Cora to think I'm afraid to try," Mercy said through gritted teeth.

Rand chuckled softly and led her back to the spot where Beau was waiting. He wrapped his arms around her and gave her a quick lesson on how to hold the Henry rifle.

"Keep the butt of the gun braced hard against your shoulder," he advised her in a low voice. "This rifle has quite a kick that can leave a bruise if you're not careful."

She nodded. "All right. Anything else?"

"Just remember to stay composed and not rush the shot," Rand said. "And make sure you aren't aiming at anything but the birds. We don't want any dead dogs or hunters out here today."

Mercy felt her heart start to race. "Maybe this is a bad idea."

"You'll be fine," Rand assured her.

"What if I miss?"

Rand smiled. "You *will* miss. It takes skill and practice with a rifle to be able to hit anything—let alone a flying or running bird."

Mercy nodded and expelled a pent-up breath. "All right."

She raised the rifle and adjusted the position until it felt comfortable. She cocked her head to the side and felt the wood against her cheek. She could smell the earthy residue of spent gunpowder. From the corner of her eye she was aware of Charles getting ready to turn the dogs loose. She cocked back the hammer, instinctually lowered her shoulder, and widened her stance to brace for the recoil. The dogs were sent flushing—birds shot skyward from the last stand of tall grass. Mercy felt the pressure of the trigger under her finger and squeezed, dropping a pheasant in an instant. She cocked the gun again, led with the barrel of the rifle, aimed at another large rooster, and fired. Not even breathing, she repeated the process, tracked a hen gaining height, and fired. The loud noise from the barrage of bullets ceased, and she took a deep breath as she lowered the rifle. It was only then she became aware that every pair of eyes in the field was trained directly on her.

"I don't believe it." Rand's voice was stunned as he came up beside her. "You shot three before Cora even fired once," he said. "Three shots—three kills."

Mercy's knees felt weak; her stomach knotted into a cold ball of nerves over what she'd just done. A group of hunters was gathering around them.

Mercy smiled weakly at Rand. "Must be beginner's luck."

Cora and a very intense-looking Elijah Hale joined the group, along with Charles, who gave her an awkward pat on the back.

"Nice shooting," Charles said.

"Thank you," she said, wishing the ground would open up and swallow her whole.

"You better watch yourself, Rand!"

"Got yourself quite a shot there, Prescott!"

"Maybe you can send the little woman out in the field and you can cook the birds," someone else called out.

Mercy could see the color starting to rise in Rand's cheeks, but he grinned good-naturedly. "I think a better idea is that I make sure to keep her happy," Rand quipped. "For all I know, she's a trained assassin who might dispatch me in my sleep after we marry."

Mercy was relieved to see that everyone laughed. Everyone that is, except for Elijah Hale.

Chapter Twenty-Two

The leather wing-back chairs were deep, comfortable, and at the perfect angle for conversation in front of the fire crackling in the hearth of Congressman John Henderson's study. Elijah Hale and John were savoring their brandies when Mary entered the study and positioned herself directly in front of them.

"Gentlemen, I'm turning in," she said, stifling a yawn.

"It's still the shank of the evening, darling," John replied with a small smile. "Are you getting so old and decrepit you are bounding into bed before nine?"

Elijah lifted his brows at his host's teasing. "My, my, what a brave man you are."

Mary also lifted a brow at her husband. "Or a very foolish one."

John chuckled. "I'd say I'm a little of each."

"And I'd say that I've been up since long before sunrise, and unless you want a very grumpy, cantankerous, and decrepit old wife, you'll bid me good night and good sleep right now," Mary said, moving to kiss her husband's cheek.

"Good night and good sleep," John said with affection.

"Good night, Mary," Elijah said.

"Don't keep him up too late, Eli," Mary said with a smile. "He's the one whose knees creak when he stands."

"You have my word," Elijah promised.

Mary headed out the study door.

"Speaking of looking foolish," Elijah ventured, "what do you make of Rand Prescott's girl putting us all to shame on the hunt line today?"

John took a sip of his brandy and stared into the fire. "I don't suppose you would say it was beginner's luck?"

Elijah shook his head. "Not a chance. It was out-and-out skill that bagged those birds."

John nodded, thoughtful. "It's fairly obvious she's had some kind of training. I'll admit some people are natural-born hunters, but it's rare to see a woman take to it so spectacularly."

"What do you know about her?"

"Only what I'm sure my wife has already told you," John said. "I do have to take my hat off to her, though. All the women that I've seen Rand with in the past couple of years—and she's the one who got him to propose. That, in itself, speaks volumes."

"He's been a bit of a ladies' man, eh?"

John lifted a corner of his mouth in a half smile. "He does have the pedigree to make a good catch. Family money, respectability, good looks, charm when he wants to use it. His father will undoubtedly hand down the reins of the railroad empire he's built someday—and Rand will go on to follow in Charles's substantial footprints."

"So for a girl with no memory, she's done all right for herself."

"I'd say so."

"And no one seems to question the validity of her claim," Elijah said.

"What do you mean?"

Elijah leaned forward, his forearms resting on his knees, his eyes filled with speculation. "I'm not exactly sure—it just seems so risky for someone of Prescott's affluence to take a chance on someone with no past. Added to that is the fact he can't know for sure if she's telling the truth about her amnesia—or has just concocted the whole story."

"Charles told me the young lady had been left at a clinic across town. It was the doctor who treated her that offered the amnesia diagnosis," John said, "and frankly, Eli, unless you've had your judgment clouded during the war, surely you've noticed that Mercy is a true beauty. I would think someone like that would have dozens of young men swooning at her feet. Why hide who she is to capture Rand's attention?"

"Unless if who she *really* is … would prohibit the relationship?"

Intrigued, John frowned. "To what purpose?"

"I haven't the slightest idea. But it would be interesting to find out."

Elijah went back to the beginning of Mercy's time in St. Louis. At least the beginning anyone knew about. He walked through the door of Abe Johnson's clinic and found the older man with his eye pressed to a microscope.

"Hello? Doctor Johnson?"

Abe didn't immediately look up. Instead, he raised a finger in the air, keeping his eye on the lens.

"One minute," Abe said.

"All right," Elijah said, unsure if he should venture farther into the room or just stay put. Seconds ticked away, then a full minute, and still the doctor stayed bent over his microscope.

"Ah, maybe I should come back another time?" Elijah said.

Abe jerked, then straightened and looked at Elijah. "Forgive me. I completely forgot you were there." He rubbed his eyes. "Fascinating, fascinating things to be seen on the slide under magnification," he said. "You wouldn't believe how one single drop of blood can keep me spellbound."

Elijah smiled. "I might."

"What may I do for you, Captain?" Abe asked, after taking note of the rank on his uniform.

"I'm Elijah Hale," he said. "I'm looking for some information about a former patient of yours."

Abe went to a washstand and dipped his hands in the water. "What patient would that be?"

"A young woman with amnesia," Elijah said. "Do you remember her?"

Abe wiped his hands off on a towel and turned to look at his visitor. "Of course I remember her. A most fascinating case."

"I have a few questions about her," Elijah said.

Doc frowned. "It's one thing to say I know her, but quite another to discuss her with you. Can you tell me what this is about?"

"Mostly it's about satisfying my own curiosity," Elijah admitted. "I met the young lady at her engagement party …"

Abe smiled broadly. "Yes, yes. I heard she'd gotten engaged to Rand Prescott. Fine young man. Fine family."

Elijah nodded. "I heard her … story … and naturally I found it compelling, as I'm sure so many others have."

Abe narrowed his eyes. "Yet no one else has come here to talk to me about her. Not even her intended. Is this a military matter?"

Elijah shook his head. "No, sir. As I said, I'm here strictly out of curiosity. I've never met someone who claims to have amnesia."

Abe raised his brows. "Claims? You speak as if you don't believe her."

"You do?"

Abe rubbed absently at one of his eyebrows. "Unequivocally."

"So you've seen cases of this condition before?"

"No. Not personally. But I will tell you that I've done thorough research on the subject, and Mercy is a textbook case." The doctor shook his head. "If you could have seen the panic on her face that day she woke up and realized she had no idea what her name was … where she came from … anything in her past. She was scared to death. Afraid to even glance in a mirror. The poor girl had no inkling what she looked like."

"Beautiful."

Abe nodded. "Yes—even then with a man's haircut."

Elijah felt a twinge of unease. "Is that right?"

"Yes, sir. Cut just as short as mine. In fact, the fellows who brought her into my place here thought she *was* a man."

"Not to be indelicate," Elijah said slowly, "but the woman in question looks nothing like a man."

"She was dressed as a man. Even had her, ah, attributes hidden by some heavy binding," Abe said. "Of course, the reason for that was as elusive to her as the rest of her history."

"May I ask what you treated her for? Besides the amnesia?"

"Bumps, bruises, contusions," Abe said, "and a gunshot wound to the back of her leg."

"Don't you find the whole thing odd?"

"I find a great many things odd, Captain. I find it odd that we just finished a bloody war that sometimes pitted brother against brother. That I live in a land where the president was shot while attending the theater. That I can look at a drop of blood under a microscope and tell a great many things about the person it came from." Abe sighed. "Is her situation odd? Yes, I suppose it is. But it doesn't stop me from wishing her well and hoping she has a wonderful life despite her handicapped memory."

"I was told she only spent a couple of weeks with you," Elijah said.

"That's correct. When she was well enough, I brought her to the Little Sisters of Hope. Mother Helena and the sisters took her in and helped give her a fresh start at life."

Elijah thanked him for his time and headed for the door.

"Captain?"

Elijah turned. "Yes?"

"I hope that this curiosity of yours won't lead to a disruption of the life that Mercy is trying to forge for herself."

"I hope not either."

The Little Sisters of Hope Convent was not at all what Elijah expected. The only thing that did seem to fit was the large wooden cross on the roof of a building that looked more like a farmhouse than the home of an order of nuns. In the back of his mind he had expected the place to be quiet, orderly, maybe even with a reverent air about it. But after he had knocked several times, the nun who opened the door looked more disheveled than holy—more irritated than welcoming.

"Yes?" the woman asked. "May I help you?"

Elijah slipped the hat from his head. "I'm Captain Hale, Sister …"

"Sister Agnes."

"Pleased to meet you, Sister Agnes. I wonder if I may speak to the … nun in charge. Uh, Sister …"

"That would be Mother Helena," she said.

"That's right," he said, more to himself than to her. "May I please speak to Mother Helena?"

"She's a little busy right now," Sister Agnes said.

"It's important," he insisted.

She nodded. "Come in. Follow me."

He entered the austere common room and felt for a moment as though something finally fit his imagination. Then he heard the noise coming from the back of the place and lifted his brows.

"We've recently become an orphanage," Sister Agnes explained as they made their way toward a definite ruckus. "And we've yet to find the fine line between letting children express themselves and letting children run rampant. Right now they are having a lesson in bed making."

"Sounds like a noisy lesson," he observed.

Sister Agnes nodded, her jowly cheeks bouncing a little with the effort. "Mother Helena believes in fun with the lessons. She's made a contest of it. The little mites are competitive, I'll give them that."

They entered the back of the house, a seemingly new addition where all the beds were set up in neat rows and the children were in some form or another rushing to pull sheets taut, spread quilts just so. The bigger ones helped the littles. And in the center of the room stood a diminutive nun who was calling out instruction like a coach at a game.

"That's the way, Frankie! Pull it up—smooth the corner! No, no, no, Matilda! You have a lumpy middle there! See it?"

"Mother?" Sister Agnes said over the children's squealing. "This is Captain Hale. He'd like to speak to you."

Mother Helena turned and swept her eyes over Captain Hale. "Captain Hale? What might I do for you?"

"I'm here to inquire about a young woman you had staying here," he said. "Her name is Mercy."

A little boy jumped up onto his bed, and Mother Helena shook her head. "Thomas! Off the bed, child! That won't do at all!" She looked at Elijah. "Are you someone from Mercy's past?"

"No. I am a friend of a friend of her future husband's family."

Mother Helena frowned. "And they asked you to speak to me about her?"

"No. I'm here on my own."

A feather pillow slammed into Elijah. He snagged it, and Mother Helena fixed a stern look on the young girl who had pitched it like a ball.

"Marie. We don't throw things indoors." But when she turned back to Elijah, he could see a twinkle in her eye. "I am not in the habit of discussing others, Captain Hale. I suggest if you have questions, you go straight to the source. Go see Mercy."

Her eyes swept around the room. "Stop!" she said loudly, holding up her hand. The children all froze in place. She held the suspense for a moment, then said, "Kathryn is the winner this time."

A little girl in braids grinned broadly, and the other children groaned. "Let us start again!" Mother Helena said.

The kids gleefully ripped the covers back off their beds and began a new race to make the perfect bed.

"It seems to be the general consensus that the amnesia Mercy is suffering from is real," Elijah said over the din of the children, trying to bring the nun's attention back to the topic.

Mother Helena looked at him. "I wasn't aware that it was a question."

"So you believed her?"

"Haven't I made that clear?"

"I don't believe anything about her is clear," he said with a touch of frustration in his voice. "I was told she lived here but then was asked to leave."

"Tuck the sheet in at the bottom, Lois," Mother said. "Martha—help Lois, please!"

Mother Helena looked at Elijah. "For a man who claims to need answers, Captain, you seem to be very well-informed. I'm afraid you wasted your time with this visit. I'm sorry."

He understood he was being dismissed. "I'll let you get back to your ... lessons."

"I know it seems chaotic, but trust me, it will be effective. These children will be able to turn out a bed like a soldier. You should be able to appreciate that."

He nodded. "Well, thank you for your time." Elijah started to turn to leave, but then as the noise in the room diminished with the efforts of the children, he thought of one more question.

"Her name?" he asked. "I don't know how she came to be called Mercy."

"She was wearing an Our Lady of Mercy medallion when she came to us," the nun said. "I thought it only fitting to call her Mercy."

Elijah's mind filled with the image of a ragged Confederate sergeant holding a knife while his brother, Jed, lay dead not ten feet behind him. He remembered that exact moment when he slipped his own mercy medallion over the sergeant's knife.

My mother gave me this. She said it would keep me safe.

"Captain?" Mother Helena's voice brought his thoughts back to the present. "Do you need someone to show you out?"

Elijah hesitated just for a second, then gave her a sad smile. "No, thank you. I know exactly where I have to go."

Chapter Twenty-Three

I am missing Rand. Though he's only been gone a short time, the business trip with his father seems as if it's gone on forever, and there are still a few weeks left to go. On the good side, Ilene has left me blissfully alone these past few days.

I spent today watching the snow fall. So beautiful as it hits the lake and disappears. The ground is covered, and I watched as Isaac tried to make a snowman in the yard. He didn't know I was there—it was just a boy having some fun in the snow until Ezra came and caught him at it. I couldn't hear what he was saying, but I saw the look of fear on Isaac's face when Ezra knocked the snowman over and lifted his hand as if to hit the boy. I didn't even think about how Ezra makes me feel sometimes, I just flew to the door and called for Isaac. Ezra turned with his hand still poised to strike Isaac and saw me. He dropped his hand and tried to wipe the scowl from his face. But it was there. I saw it plain as day. I asked Isaac to go and check on Lucky—and then maybe get some more wood for the fire. I could tell by the look on his face that he was happy to be scampering away from Ezra. I need to remember to tell Rand about Ezra. I get the feeling this isn't the first time he's raised his hand to that boy.

The cottage is so quiet at night when I'm in here all alone and writing down my thoughts. Will I still write in you, dear journal, when I am a married woman? Or will I be so willing to share all my rambling thoughts with my husband that I won't need you anymore? Only time will tell, I suppose. But tonight, my secret is that I am happy. So blissfully happy that some days I can go for hours before I remember that I still can't remember my own real name.

Mercy opened the door to find a man on her porch. His brown leather jacket was dotted with snow, and his hat perched so low on his head that it shadowed his face.

"May I help you?"

He swept the hat from his head, and though she had only seen him in his army uniform, she instantly recognized him by those piercing eyes of his.

"Sorry for the intrusion, ma'am," he said.

"Captain Hale?" She couldn't mask the surprise in her voice.

"Yes. I wonder if I might have a few minutes of your time?" he asked in a tone that made her wonder what he'd say if she refused. But there was no reason for her to refuse. He was a vetted friend of the Hendersons, an officer in the army—and she had the protection of Ezra and Isaac should she feel the need. She felt a ripple of unease at the thought of inviting in the man who'd made the remark about possibly knowing her. She stepped out of his way.

"Please, come in."

He stepped through the door and glanced around the room. "You have a very nice home," he said. Letty appeared and took his hat and jacket, and he thanked her.

"My pleasure, suh," she said. Turning to Mercy, she asked, "Tea, Miss Mercy?"

Mercy looked at her guest. "I'm afraid I don't have anything stronger in the house."

"Tea would be appreciated," he said.

"And, Letty, would you please ask Isaac to see to Captain Hale's horse?"

"I don't plan a lengthy visit, ma'am," he said.

"Still, the horse deserves a respite from the cold just like you—don't you agree?"

He acquiesced. "Yes. Thank you."

Letty hurried from the room.

"I hope you haven't misunderstood homesteads." Mercy looked puzzled. "The cottage belongs to the Prescott family, but they don't live here. It's only me right now. Rand isn't even here visiting at the moment. He's out of town with his father."

"I didn't come to see any of the Prescotts," he said. "I came to speak with you."

Mercy considered it, then smiled and gestured to chairs in front of a fireplace. "Please. Have a seat."

His large frame almost seemed to overwhelm the parlor chair. He was taller than Rand—broader in the shoulders and chest. His dark hair was thick and trimmed so it just touched the collar of his white shirt. Mercy had to admit he was just as handsome as Rand—but in a different way. He was more rugged—his features not so refined and chiseled as her intended. He looked every inch as a composed officer in the military must look, she decided. Even without his uniform. It occurred to her that she was staring at him—and he was staring back.

She smiled self-consciously. "I don't mean to be rude, Captain Hale, but I can't imagine what you would need to speak to me about."

Mercy watched him hesitate for a moment; his carefully arranged composure looked as if it might fail him. Letty reappeared with tea and gave them each a cup. The china was nearly dwarfed in his hand, and Mercy could see his discomfort in handling it. He took a sip of the warm liquid and then put it down on a table beside the chair.

"It's about the war," he finally said.

She smiled politely. "I don't know how much you know about me, Captain, but I feel I must be frank and tell you I know nothing about the war other than what others have told me."

"I'll be frank as well and tell you I know your story."

She tried not to look as confused as she felt. "Excuse me?"

"If you'll indulge me, I'll explain," he said. She felt a surge of unease. What could she possibly have to worry about from this man—this stranger she had met on only a handful of occasions? He'd assured her he'd been mistaken about knowing her—so it couldn't be about that. Or could it? Despite the misgivings about his visit that were surfacing faster than she could squelch them, she looked him in the eye.

"Go on, please," she said.

He drew in a deep breath. She could see that he was trying to form his words carefully, and she felt a new wash of nerves. What could he possibly have to say that was so difficult? She had a moment of regret that she'd ever opened the door at all.

Even though he'd rehearsed his words and his story several times over the course of the last couple of days, now that he was sitting in the presence of the woman, Elijah's carefully constructed monologue failed him. She *was* beautiful—poised, self-possessed. She was dressed in a wool skirt and a silk blouse, and her hair hung in loose ringlets around her face. He nearly abandoned his plan ... until he looked into her dark-brown eyes and thought about all that was at stake if he didn't say something.

"If you'll permit, I will start with a little of my background," he finally said. "Some context for the rest of the story."

She nodded patiently. If she had any inkling of what he was going to say, then Elijah was impressed at how well she was hiding it. By all appearances, the woman truly didn't know what was coming.

"I'm from Pennsylvania," he said, "and I answered the call for men to join the Union cause in the summer of '62. I firmly believed secession would ruin the country—weaken us irrevocably—and wasn't in the best interest of either the Northern or Southern states."

"And of course, there was the issue of slavery," she offered.

He nodded. "Yes. Ethically wrong. Morally wrong. But not the original reason I joined up." He looked into the fire, away from her face. "My father passed away in '55 when I was sixteen years old— leaving my mother with me and my younger brother. When the first drums of war sounded, she begged me not to go. I resisted as long as I could, but ultimately, I knew I couldn't live with myself if I didn't fight for the country to stay intact. Though she was proud of me, my mother was very unhappy when I was given my commission in the cavalry. Her only consolation was that my brother would stay home and look after her.

"Then—in the summer of 1863, Philadelphia began the practice of conscription for young men. The war had gone on longer than anyone had thought—and there was no end in sight. My brother, Jedidiah, went into the infantry."

"Your poor mother," Mercy said quietly. "She must have been sick with worry."

He nodded. "Just like thousands of mothers during the campaign—waiting and worrying and wondering when they'd get the news their son had perished on some bloody battlefield." He stopped, reached for his cup, let the tea slide down his throat and moisten the dryness of his mouth. It wasn't every day he went to make threats and accusations against a beautiful woman. It was, in fact, a first for him.

"When I heard that Jed had been called to serve, I procured a transfer to serve in a cavalry regiment that accompanied the infantry company he was in. I spent the last two years of the war under the command of General Sheridan."

"So you could protect your brother?"

"I had promised my mother I would," he said. "I swore to her I wouldn't let anything happen to him on my watch. She even gave me a piece of jewelry that she said would keep me safe. I asked her why she hadn't given it to Jedidiah, but she told me he didn't need it. As long as *I* was safe, she knew I would protect him. 'He has you and God, Elijah,' she told me. 'And I know neither of you will let me down.'"

The day had grown progressively darker as he spoke—the light draining from the room as the firelight glowed orange.

"I broke my promise to my mother and wasn't able to protect my brother, and that's something I live with every single day. I had the horror of watching my younger brother get shot on a field in Tennessee during what was to be one of the last battles of the war. I was able to get to him and take him to a private spot near a stream to say our good-byes—and to pray with him as he was dying."

"I'm so sorry," Mercy said. "But I'm sure you treasure that time you had alone with him."

"I *thought* we were alone—but it turned out we weren't," he said. "A Confederate sergeant appeared out of nowhere—had followed us to the bank of that river. His objective, as with any soldier, was single-minded in purpose. He was there to kill his enemy. He was there to kill me."

Her eyes widened, but she remained silent.

"Even though the sergeant was behind me, I knew he was there. He could have shot me in the name of the war we were both fighting. We don't call killing a man in a war murder. We call it victory."

"But as you are clearly alive—he didn't claim his victory," she observed.

"No. In a moment of humanity that I will never forget, he allowed me to be with my brother in the last seconds of his life."

He heard the clock ticking in the room, the crackle of the fire; the smell of stew filled his nose, but his stomach recoiled at the thought of food. He wasn't sure how to say the next few words out loud, but then she unwittingly helped him out.

"That's a touching story, Captain," Mercy said. "But I still don't understand why you wanted me to hear it."

"That day, I gave the Confederate sergeant the silver medallion that my mother had given me to keep me safe. It had done what she promised—but I had failed to do the same for my brother. It was called a mercy medallion," he said. "And *you* were the Confederate sergeant that I gave it to."

Mercy's mouth dropped open, and she fought to keep the dull roar she heard from completely overwhelming her. She shook her head.

"That is the most ridiculous thing I've ever heard," she said when she could finally speak.

"It's the truth," he said. "It was you. You were disguised as a man; your hair was cut short, you were wearing a dark-brown wool shirt and a pair of green pants. You followed us from the battlefield to the stream so you could do your duty and kill me—but you didn't. I hung that medal on the end of your knife, collected my brother's body, and didn't look back. I never expected to see you again, but then in the receiving line at the Prescotts' that night—there was something about you. Something familiar that I couldn't place."

She was shaking her head so hard now that the curls moved like springs around her face. "You're lying! I don't know why you would make up such a cruel story and lie about me, but it stops now! Do you hear me? It stops right now!"

He stared evenly at her. "What possible reason would I have to lie about this?"

"You hate the Prescotts! You have an agenda to sully their name with this fabrication!"

Elijah set his jaw, and she could see the muscles in his neck as he strained to be still. "I wish to God I didn't know this about you—but I do. And because I value the truth above all else, I had to come to you with it."

"I don't believe a word of this," she said in a voice husky with fear and emotion, "but even if I did, what would you propose I do with this information?"

"Rand deserves to know the truth. He needs to know who he is about to marry," Elijah said.

Mercy choked out a nervous laugh. "Tell one of the biggest supporters of the Union cause that he's about to marry a rebel soldier?"

"Yes," he said. "You owe him that."

"He won't believe it. He loves me," she said. "He knows I could never hurt anyone. Just last week he was laughing at me because I couldn't step on a spider."

"And yet you dispatched three pheasants that day at the hunt like the skilled marksman that you obviously are," he said bluntly.

"That was an accident!"

"That was your training as a soldier in the Confederate army, whether you will admit it or not," he said.

"No," she said flatly. "I'm not telling him this wild theory of yours. I've already lost my past—I do not intend to lose my future as well."

"Although I didn't believe in your amnesia at first," he said, "I've come to the conclusion that you're telling the truth."

"How noble of you." Her voice dripped with sarcasm.

"What happens someday when your memory returns—and along with it, all the hatred that you felt for the North? For the believers in the Union? For people like Charles Prescott and his son, who not only championed the cause with their railroad but almost certainly had a hand in obtaining victories against the South? *Your* South."

"Other people have made peace since the war ended. Other people are able to have civil, cordial relationships despite their political differences," she said.

"Those people have had months and months since the war ended to come to terms with their emotions. It's possible if your memory returns you will be in the thick of the emotions that propelled you to fight for the South. You could wake up one morning and literally be sleeping with your enemy. He has to be told before you marry him," he said. "Because you spared my life that day, I will give you the time to tell him yourself. But if you don't—then I will."

Her eyes filled with angry tears. "How do I know this is true? It could have been someone else."

He stood. "The mercy medallion."

"What about it?"

"You didn't deny that you have one."

"It proves nothing. Someone could have told you I wear one. There are probably hundreds that look just like it."

"I'll admit Mother Helena told me you have a medallion," he said. "But I promise you—it's the same I wore until I gave it to you."

"There is no way to prove that." Her voice had taken on a higher pitch, and she knew that the rising hysteria she felt was too close to the surface to stop.

"There is a letter that is missing from my medal," he said. "On the bottom are the words *pray for us.* If you look closely—you'll see the *y* is missing from the word *pray.*"

She stood on legs she wasn't sure would support her. "I think you should go now." She rang a silver bell on a table beside her, and almost immediately, Letty appeared.

"Captain Hale is leaving. He'll need his jacket and hat."

Letty nodded and hurried from the room.

Captain Hale studied her. "I'll wait to hear what you decide to do with the information I just gave you."

When Letty came back, he shrugged into his jacket, settled his hat on his head, and walked out into the snowstorm.

With arms that felt like lead, Mercy withdrew the medallion from underneath her dress and lifted it over her head. She stared at the silver medallion and felt her world crack when she spotted the space where the *y* should have been. The flames in the fireplace had turned into nothing more than burning embers. She started to cry.

Chapter Twenty-Four

I haven't had a full night's sleep since that awful man came here and demanded the impossible from me. I can't think of anything else—can't eat, can't sleep, can't imagine a way out of this nightmare.

I don't want to believe it—but I do. I fought for the Confederacy in the war.

Why? What could have possibly driven me to dress as a man and take up arms? How did I get away with that? I have most likely killed men in the heat of battle.

I look in the mirror and search my eyes for hints that I have seen death up close. But all I see is confusion and worry. What to do with this information?

This whole thing is so unfair. That one man—one stranger—should have so much control over my life. My future. My happiness.

I have tried to come up with a solution—a plan to circumvent what he's asking of me. I think the best approach is to tackle the issue head-on. I can say that my memory has partially returned and I remember being west of the Mississippi at the same time I was supposedly in Tennessee. Though the flaw in my plan is that I don't have a single person to substantiate my claim. Would Rand believe me over someone else with convincing evidence?

Or I could claim the Yankee is a liar and a rabble-rouser who just wants to cause me harm. The logical question from Rand—or anyone for that matter—would have to be why. Why would someone make up such terrible lies about me? Maybe he is a man who I have scorned. He approached me one day when I was riding Lucky in the woods and professed his interest in me. I, of course, rebuffed any advances he tried to make, and he vowed to get even. Can I get Rand to believe I am the victim here?

I don't want to believe anything he said is true, but I do.

I wish we had never met—again. I wish I didn't believe he will make good on his threat and tell Rand the truth if I don't—but I trust that he's a man of his word and he will.

There is only one logical way for me to fight to have the life with Rand that I want: I must tell him the truth and pray that he finds my admission brave. Maybe his love for me will be stronger than any of his political feelings about the war. If courage can be stockpiled, then I'm praying to have a good bit of it laid in before Rand's return tomorrow so I can do what I must do.

Mercy stood in front of the cheval glass in her bedroom and studied her own reflection. It had been three weeks since Elijah Hale had come to turn her world upside down. During those weeks, she thanked God that Rand had been traveling with Charles, that Ilene had been down with a cold, and that social engagements had all but been abandoned due to the bitterly cold February weather. She had spent her days with open books—but could honestly not remember reading a single page. The only thing that had been on her mind was Elijah Hale's declaration about her—and Rand's possible reaction when he heard the truth. The fact that she was so close to finding out how it would all play out made her heart clutch in her chest.

She made a graceful turn in front of the mirror and looked over her shoulder at the deep-blue satin gown she wore. The ribbons cascading from her waist went to the floor, and the hoop under the skirt was just wide enough to be at the height of style—at least, that was what Ilene had said when she'd had the dress made for Mercy. Mercy crossed to the vanity and swept aside her skirt so she could sit and touch up her hair. Drawing the brush through her curls, she stared at the reflection of her necklace in the mirror. Then, as Mercy drew her brush through her hair again, Letty's dark face bent into the mirror beside her.

"He's here, Miss Mercy," she said, smiling so wide that it seemed to Mercy she was all teeth. For just a fraction of a second, Mercy had a flash of another dark face beside hers—and then it was gone.

"Thank you, Letty," Mercy said. "I'll be right along."

Letty disappeared from the mirror. Mercy took a moment to collect the composure she so desperately needed to do what she must. Leaning toward her reflection, she whispered to herself, "He loves you. He loves you, and nothing you say will change that."

Rand beamed a smile at her as he crossed the room to take her hands. "Being away from you was intolerable," he said. He bent to kiss her cheek.

She smiled. "I missed you, too."

He stepped back but kept one of her hands and twirled her as if they were on a dance floor. Her dress belled out around her and swished over the hardwood. She felt her heart rip in two with the worry it would be the last time he ever looked at her in the admiring way that made her feel treasured.

"Missing me has agreed with you," he teased. "You look stunning."

"I could hear that every day," she said. "Maybe we should incorporate compliments to each other in our wedding vows."

It was his turn to laugh. "I don't need to swear in front of church and family that I'll tell you you're beautiful. It's as natural as breathing to me."

In the next moment, he turned serious as he stared at her.

"You're wearing it," he said. "All by itself."

Mercy knew instantly what he was talking about, and her hand went to the ruby necklace around her neck. The one he'd given her weeks ago, which had been in a box ever since.

"It's time I put the past away," Mercy said. "And the medallion is just that—my past."

"You don't know how happy that makes me," Rand said. "The necklace looks beautiful on you. Much more suitable than the medal."

"Thank you for being so patient with me," she said, hoping to set the tone for the coming conversation. "I told Kizzy we would have dinner at six. I hope that's all right. I wasn't sure what time you were arriving."

"Perfect. Gives us a chance to talk without the distraction of Kizzy's …" He paused and sniffed at the air. "Roast beef?"

Mercy forced another smile. "Yes."

They made their way to the very same chairs Mercy had sat in with the army captain to hear the horrible truth from his lips. Ezra materialized with a brandy for Rand, and Mercy wondered briefly where it came from. She had thought she was telling Captain Hale the truth when she said there was nothing stronger than tea in the house. Rand waited for Mercy to sit, then accepted the drink from Ezra.

"Thank you, Ezra," he said as he lowered himself into the chair. "Just what I need to warm me from the inside out."

"Tea for you, Miss Mercy?" Ezra asked.

Mercy nodded, her mouth dry with the thought of what lay in front of her. The curiosity about the liquor swept away.

Rand took a drink of his brandy, then issued a contented sigh. "Ah. I've been waiting all day to sit here with you like this." He smiled. "Actually, I've been waiting for weeks. I started to miss you the day we left."

"How was your trip?" she asked, trying hard to keep the trembling from her voice.

"Exhausting," he answered. "My father is a force to be reckoned with when he's got his mind set on something. Meetings morning, noon, and even during dinner to try and secure promises from elected officials for future railroad contracts. I don't think the man ever gets tired."

"I suppose that's why he's been so successful," Mercy observed, trying to delay the turn she knew she must make in the conversation.

Rand lifted the corner of his mouth. "Yes. One of the reasons. He gets what he wants—always has. I've seen very few obstacles thwart him."

"Not even the war?"

"Especially not the war," Rand told her. "The Missouri Pacific is a stronger entity now because of the way my father used the railroad during the war. After a serious attack on the tracks and several engines by Sterling Price in the fall of '64, Father helped finance the repairs so future construction could take place. It's the wave of the future, Mercy. The mode of transportation that makes the most sense. Did you know you can leave Kansas City at three in the morning and be here in St. Louis by five that same evening?"

Rand took another drink of his brandy, then swirled it around in the snifter in his hand. He stared into the amber liquid. "The country is years away from healing. All the way to the Carolinas, land has been destroyed, homes have been burned. Confederate money is worthless. According to Southern sympathizers, scalawags and carpetbaggers have taken Sherman's place as the source of all evil. The Thirteenth Amendment to the Constitution that was passed in December has incited fury in the South. It's an absolute mess. One I'm glad you don't have to witness."

"But you must have seen evidence the colored people are happy now that they are free?"

He frowned. "I'd say more like liberty has become anarchy. President Johnson's administration has done little, if anything, to promote the Freedmen's Bureau, and he's allowed Southern states to implement their own black codes."

"What does that mean?"

He offered a small shrug. "In essence, it makes the Freedmen's Bureau null and void. If the blacks can't vote or hold any public office, then there's no social equality." He shook his head. "The president is in quite a pickle. Johnson and the Congress are at odds—the Republicans are furious with him, and the Radicals are ready to storm the White House because of his lenient policies toward the South."

"What do *you* think? Are his policies too lenient toward the South?"

The Rand Prescott she had come to know would be fair, she decided. He would be open-minded and logical about his response. Still, she felt a round stone of dread form in her gut.

"He's a fool to think the feelings that drove the Southern states to try and secede have changed just because they lost the war," Rand said succinctly. "Nothing has changed for them except for the level of their bitterness."

She hated that Rand seemed to echo Elijah Hale's sentiments. "Don't you believe that people can change?"

Rand paused, swirling the brandy up the sides of the snifter. "I don't believe they can change that much—that fast—just because one side surrendered. We've been looking to hire workmen for the railroad, and Father thought it prudent to show good faith and hire some rebels."

"So did you? Hire former Confederates?"

"Only those who had signed the oath, seeking a presidential pardon for their support of the Confederate cause."

She felt some measure of relief. "That's good, then. Everyone can forgive and forget and move forward."

Rand tossed down the rest of his brandy, and his features hardened. "I don't see much forgiveness happening in our lifetime," he said. "I don't see how you look at people and forget they tried to tear the country apart. Lincoln claimed that the Southerners didn't commit treason because they never actually seceded—but to me, they all committed treason in their hearts. They killed my friends, put my mother in harm's way by marching so close to the house that we had to put up a defensive wall … other people may claim they can forgive and forget and move forward. But I'm not one of them."

Mercy knew that the only opening she'd ever have to tell Rand the truth about herself had just closed. She felt physically sick and took a deep breath to calm her nerves

Rand frowned. "I'm sorry, darling. All this time apart, and now I've spent the last few minutes running on and on about business and politics. Let's talk about something else."

"Dinner is on the table, Miss Mercy, Mr. Rand," Kizzy announced from the threshold of the dining room.

Rand got to his feet and held out a hand to Mercy. Dazed over her own predicament, she felt her head spin as she allowed him to take her into the dining room.

Mercy didn't realize she wasn't eating anything until Rand finally pointed it out. "I thought you loved Kizzy's roast beef," he said, more as a statement than a question. "You haven't touched a bite."

She looked down at her plate. "Oh. I suppose I've just been too caught up in our conversation to eat." She forced a smile.

"Wedding plans have you excited, do they?" he asked.

"Yes."

"You still need to eat. I think you've gotten even thinner since I've been gone. I don't want to see you get so caught up in my mother's mania for the wedding that you neglect yourself."

How could she tell him it wasn't the wedding plans that had her losing sleep and losing weight? It had been the thought of telling him the truth about her past. A truth, she now knew, that could never come out. She had seen the look on his face when he spoke of the Southern sympathizers and the Confederate soldiers. She couldn't bear to think of him looking at her that way. She had to think of another way to stop Elijah Hale from ruining her future. How ironic that she had spared his life in an act of compassion and charity, and now it had come back to be her undoing. *No good deed goes unpunished*, she thought.

"You know, darling, if you don't eat Kizzy's cooking, you are taking away her purpose."

She saw Captain Hale's face that night of his visit. *His objective, as with any soldier, was single-minded in purpose. He was there to kill his enemy. He was there to kill me.*

Mercy forked a beef into her mouth and saw Rand smile with approval. The food was tasteless to her, but she swallowed it.

"You know, I nearly brought you a little kitten today," Rand said. "It was loose on the edge of the property. I followed it, but it slipped away before I could catch it."

Mercy smiled. "It was thoughtful of you to try," she said, but her mind was on Hale's words. *You followed us so you could do your duty and kill me—but you didn't.*

She picked up her fork and cut her food into dainty little bites. *I hung that medal on the end of your knife.*

She was that person he spoke of. That soldier who was derelict in completing her mission. That rebel who denied herself victory.

If she was still that person—then he was still her enemy. She knew what she had to do. Victory would be hers. Captain Hale must die.

Chapter Twenty-Five

I am building a fortress of lies. The worries involved with this are so great I can't list them all; suffice it to say I will spend the rest of my life living with guilt that can be buried only by time—and more lies.

I wish only to fulfill my duty. Finish my task. End the battle with a different outcome. Construct a plan so carefully thought through that there is no chance of error.

It is my only chance at happiness with Rand.

For a few days Mercy went about her business even though her nerves were stretched to the breaking point. She feigned interest when Ilene had a flower arrangement to show her or a morsel of food that needed tasting, or when she wanted to celebrate the growing list of important guests who would attend the nuptials. The daily checklist of wedding tasks had started to weigh her down so much that it began to feel like an anvil on her back. As the list grew, her weight dropped, and Ilene began to study her in a way that made her feel as if she could never let down her guard. She must smile. She must eat. She must be excited.

The time spent with Rand was the worst. The ever-present knowledge in her head of what she intended to do made every moment between them feel like a lie; time had become her enemy. If only she could stop it from moving forward—freeze it and keep the glow of Rand's love alive and her past at bay.

The careful balancing act kept her on the precipice of panic during the days—and at night, either she did not sleep at all, or when she did, she had a recurring nightmare:

Elijah Hale's face is in shadow.

He steps into the sunshine.

She raises a rifle to her shoulder and catches his chest in her sight.

Her finger trembles against the trigger as she squeezes it.

Hale falls.

Then Rand is behind her. He knows! He saw!

He walks away and won't come back no matter how loudly she screams his name.

She woke every morning in the same drenched despair. Who would she become if she actually took the life of another human being? But just as quickly, the sobering thought would occur that nothing would change. *She* would not change. If Elijah Hale was to be believed about her past, then she was *already* a person who could kill another. She even had the proper clothes to wear for the job.

In the beginning, she had no plan. Just scattered images of what she must do. Then she saw Ezra one day, doing nothing more than a routine task—but to Mercy it was filled with possibilities. Her remark to him was casual but brought about enough information to move forward with her task.

Ezra, Letty, Kizzy, and Isaac were fairly predictable—up by dawn and back in bed by nine. Lamps were extinguished in the servants' quarters at the same time every night. She had a few hours in the darkness in which she could disappear and not be missed.

"Letty?" she said one afternoon. "I'm thinking of tying my hair in rags for extra curl. Do you have some put aside I might have?"

"Shore thing, Miss Mercy," Letty said, obliging her with a bag of torn rags that could have easily serviced ten women who wanted curls.

There were thick matches and pieces of flint above the fireplace.

Kerosene was plentiful and easily carried in a jar meant for preserves.

A history of the war had been unwittingly preserved in the stacks of newspapers Kizzy had saved to "catch the guts of the fish I hafta clean."

There were rifles and ammunition in a cabinet in the cottage study. Rand told her that during the war it had been locked in the event rebel scum might have broken in and stolen them; but with the hostilities over, the lock had been removed. Rand didn't know that rebel scum lived in the cottage now. She recognized the irony of the situation and, at another time, might have even smiled.

With ammunition safely tucked in a leather pouch, she sneaked a rifle out the door during a midday meal when the servants were eating in their quarters. She stashed the Springfield muzzle-loading gun and pouch in some bushes a hundred yards or so from the cottage. As the weather had improved over the winter, she had taken to afternoon rides on Lucky, and now she felt as if fate had finally slipped her some luck. She could sashay up to Isaac and ask him to saddle the horse for her daily jaunt, and no one would think anything of it.

She took a ride to the Hendersons' house. It was a small country estate—small in comparison to the Prescotts', but still stately and relatively remote. Other buildings on the property included a barn, servants' quarters, and a shed close to the house itself. The landscaping was minimal—a few trees and shrubs. John and Mary would see anyone approaching their house from quite a distance, Mercy decided. Unless, of course, the visitor didn't want to be seen.

Mercy fished the rifle and the leather pouch from the bushes the next afternoon. She rode for several miles in the hopes no one would hear her practice shots, dismounted, and paced off fifty yards. She loaded the rifle with a .58 caliber minié ball; her target was a broken tree limb. The gun felt comfortable and eerily familiar. She took aim, fired, and the tree limb fell.

She paced off a hundred yards and fired.

Paced off three hundred yards and fired.

She never missed.

The rifle and pouch went back into the bushes before she handed Isaac the reins of her horse when she returned to the cottage. Mercy confessed to Letty that evening that she had a headache and asked for some tea. Letty fussed and carried on and heated a brick to tuck under the covers for her feet in case she started to feel a chill and was getting sick. Now that she thought about it, Letty said, Miss Mercy had been looking mighty peaked lately. Mercy assured her that all she needed was some uninterrupted rest. She was sure a good night's sleep would do the trick. She asked Letty to put out all the lamps on her way to the servants' quarters and said she'd see her in the morning.

It had all been carefully arranged when she slipped out the door in the dead of night with a small satchel in hand—wearing her brown wool shirt and green pants. Her hair was in a single braid she had pinned up in back. She told herself she'd try to forget the moment she had looked into her mirror at the familiar stranger who stared back at her.

Mercy fetched Lucky and wondered if the crescent moon was a curse or blessing for her mission. She led the horse away from the cottage, not wanting to rouse anyone in the servants' quarters— worrying that a midnight ride might prove to make Lucky giddy and loud. She stopped and collected the hidden rifle and ammunition in the pouch, then mounted Lucky and spurred him into a gallop.

She was relieved that the waiting was over and it was finally time to act. She had a mission to complete, and that was the only thought she allowed herself to have as she rode across the sleeping landscape.

The Hendersons' place was still. No lamps shone from the windows. No noise crept from the house. She had two things to accomplish—well, three, actually, if she was going to count a murder. Lucky was tied a good distance from the house, and she looked around for a spot to place a note she pulled from her satchel. A black lawn jockey was positioned on the edge of the gravel drive that led to the house, and Mercy speared the paper over the dark hand held up in a perpetual wave of greeting for all visitors. One down. Two to go. She squatted on the ground and took out the second thing she had brought along, courtesy of Ezra.

"What are you doing, Ezra?" Mercy had asked.

"We's got some fierce-looking rats in the barn, Miss Mercy, and I is flushing 'em out with the smoke," he'd told her as he tended a small fire in front of the barn door.

It was simple, really. Make a ball of tightly bound strips of fabric, or some curling rags, and soak the whole thing in a healthy dose of kerosene. A match to the whole lot, and you'd get yourself a dandy fire that would create as much smoke as it would flame.

Ezra had unwittingly been the impetus of her plan. She'd flush out her target; as they'd used dogs to drive the birds into the open, she'd use smoke to drive out her prey.

She lit the fat match in her satchel and touched it to the longest tail end of the rag ball she carried before tossing it at the ground near a shed close enough to the house to provide her smoke but far enough away to spare the home. For a heart-stopping minute, she was sure the thing was going to burn itself right out. And then a spark caught on the wood. Two down—one to go. She dashed for Lucky, and they galloped into the darkness while Mercy calculated three hundred yards. She slipped out of the saddle, pulling the rifle along with her. She found a V in the branches of a tree and used it to brace the long barrel of her gun. Flipping up the sight, she let her eyes adjust to the high-powered scope.

In less than ten minutes, she saw John Henderson sprint outside in his bathrobe. A large black man followed right behind him, and Mercy could see John gesturing for him to go to the well in the yard. John took off his robe and tried to beat back the flames. His face glowed in the firelight, and she could see him coughing in the thick smoke.

Mercy's heart rate quickened when Captain Hale stepped into her sight and pulled the congressman away from the building flames.

She tracked him with the scope.

The noise of the fire roared in the quiet night.

Captain Hale grabbed the bucket from the servant and pointed for him to go back for another.

Shoot him.

He turned and threw water on the fire.

Shoot him.

Back to the well with the empty bucket, John on his heels.

Her finger hovered over the trigger; she felt it start to give.

Orange sparks spiraled into the sky.

Hale doused the fire again and turned as if to face her.

Shoot him. End it.

A cornet played in her head; the loneliness of it shattered her.

Her knees hit the ground as she realized she was going to fail—but then the butt of the rifle jammed into the dirt behind her, and the finger still hovering on the trigger actually squeezed it. The shot rang out over the sound of the fire. She looked up to see Captain Hale look toward the darkness. Toward her. Into the worn shallows of ground where she kneeled. She saw rather than heard him yell to the others, gesturing at the distance between them.

Scrambling onto Lucky's back, she spurred him hard, and he broke into a full gallop. She was reeling from her failure when she misjudged a tree, and the branch not only tore into her right shoulder but tore her from the saddle as well. She felt the searing heat of the pain from her ripped skin and the warmth of the blood that immediately ran down her side. Lucky whirled around and came back for her as she pushed herself to stand. She could hear Hale yelling in the darkness behind her—he was getting closer. He was going to catch her. She scrambled into the saddle when he was almost upon her and leaned low over Lucky's neck. She pressed her knees tight against the horse's side, and they galloped hard away from the fire.

Everything was going to change now. Everything had to change. She had failed at her mission.

He wasn't dead.

Fear of discovery was greater for the moment than the pain she felt from her shoulder. Mercy managed to get Lucky back into the barn at the cottage and stifled a scream of pain with a rag in her mouth as she lifted the saddle from his back. She told herself not to hurry, not to rush—not to make a mistake that would bring one of the servants running outside to check on them. She forced herself to go through the motions of Lucky's care, then made her way to the cottage with the rifle under her good arm.

Mercy put the Springfield back in the cabinet with all the other guns and shut the door with a firm click. Moving carefully, slowly, quietly through the dark cottage, she made her way to her room and dropped her clothes on the floor. She winced when she saw the bloody mess that was her shoulder and found some of the unused rags from Letty. She did the best she could with her wound, crawled under the quilt, and started to shake.

Then the tears came—and along with them, a prayer that morning would never come.

CHAPTER TWENTY-SIX

In the predawn hour, Mercy wrapped herself in a quilt from the bed and dipped her quill into the inkwell. She was anxious to get the dreaded note to Rand composed before she lost her nerve or—at this point—her mind. By candlelight, she scratched the nib of the pen across the linen paper.

Dear Rand: I hope someday you'll be able to forgive me for ending our relationship this way, but believe me when I say it's for the best. I cannot marry you. The decision has been painful and not without considerable thought—but it's the right thing for me to do. I cannot be the wife you deserve. I cannot be the woman you need by your side in the future you will have in your father's business ...

This was the last glancing blow to what had promised to be a happy future. She had been a fool to think she could lose so much of her past—herself—and still skip happily on as if it didn't matter. What else lurked in the dark corners of a mind that couldn't remember? What would have driven a woman to war?

She found she had a talent for lying, and she called on it now to finish her good-bye to Rand. She ended the note with words like *resolute* and *unyielding* and begged him to accept her decision. She didn't even realize she was sobbing, weeping so hard her throbbing shoulder shook from the effort.

There was a sudden knock on her bedroom door.

"Miss Mercy?" Letty's worried voice boomed through the wood. "Is you all right?"

Mercy's eyes flew to the window, where she could just make out the earliest dawn light. She forced her voice to sound normal and called back, "Yes, Letty. I was having a terrible nightmare. Thank you for waking me from it."

"Would you be wantin' some tea now?" Letty wondered. Mercy couldn't tell from her voice if she had believed her story or not.

"No, thank you," Mercy said. "I think I'll try and sleep a little longer."

"Yassum," Letty said.

Mercy heard her footsteps retreat and then used her quilt to wipe her face. She folded the note for Rand and sealed it with the wax Ilene had given her for the purpose of correspondence. For a brief moment, she allowed herself to imagine Ilene's face when she heard the news that her beautifully planned wedding was off. Mercy trembled at the thought.

She dropped the quilt from her shoulder and studied the wound in the mirror. There was a gaping three-inch gash, and the skin around it was bruised blue and purple. She tried to rotate it and bit down on her lip to keep from crying out. The wound needed to be tended to, wrapped and bound with something clean. No one could see it; no one could know. The basin of water on the washstand would suffice. She could stuff her bloodied shirt into the satchel she would take when she left. She looked for any evidence of blood on her sheets and saw traces of red. *With any luck, I'll be able to wash them out—and Letty will never be the wiser.* She nearly laughed at her use of the phrase. *With any luck* her body would do her a favor and her heart would simply stop after she rode away from the cottage.

It was midmorning by the time Mercy came out of her room. She hoped she looked no worse for the wear—other than the dark circles under her eyes—after her eventful night. Kizzy, in the kitchen, looked at her with a small frown. "Mornin', Miss Mercy," she said. "You be ready for yo' breakfast now?"

Mercy shook her head. "I'm not hungry, Kizzy."

"'Scuze me fo' sayin' so, ma'am, but you look mighty tired. Letty tol' me 'bout your pain."

Mercy was aware that she was holding herself very still. She purposefully relaxed her painful shoulder. "What are you talking about?"

"She said you had a bad headache," Kizzy continued. "Ain't it better?"

"Oh, yes. It's better, thank you," Mercy said.

Kizzy turned to leave the room, but Mercy stopped her. "Kizzy? I may not be hungry this morning, but I want you to know I think you are a wonderful cook."

Kizzy looked both surprised and pleased at the unexpected compliment. "Thank you, Miss Mercy. I try."

"And please tell Letty that I appreciate how well she took care of me."

"She be pleased you say that, Miss Mercy."

With her satchel in hand, Mercy found Ezra in the barn, giving Isaac an earful about his lackadaisical ways. Isaac was actually cowering in the corner, his eyes wide and scared as Ezra continued his tirade. But when Ezra raised his hand to hit Isaac, Mercy, despite the pain in her shoulder, grabbed his arm.

"Don't!" she said with as much force as she could muster.

Ezra spun around. "'Scuze me, Miss Mercy, but this here business be between me and the boy."

"It will be between you and Mr. Rand if I tell him that you've been abusing this poor boy," Mercy said. "There is no excuse for hitting him, Ezra, and it needs to stop."

Isaac's eyes widened at her words, and he scrambled out of the corner of the barn. Mercy could see Ezra trying to control his anger. "Yassum."

"I'd like your promise that you won't hit Isaac anymore," she said.

"Boys gots to be taught ..."

"Ezra ..."

"All right, Miss Mercy," Ezra said, even as he glanced at Isaac. "No more hitting on the boy."

Mercy didn't believe him, but she nodded. "Fine. Now, I have something for you to do."

She handed him the wax-sealed note. "I need you to see that Mr. Rand receives this."

He nodded. "I'll leave directly."

"No. I want you to wait until nearly sundown before you deliver it," she said.

Ezra's expression remained carefully blank, but she saw his eyes flick to her satchel. "Yassum."

"Make sure you hand it to him—and no one else. I believe he'll be at his office in the city. Don't forget—the note is for his eyes only. You understand?"

"I only gives the note to Mr. Rand and not nobody else."

"That's right."

Ezra tucked the note into his pocket and nodded at Mercy. "I'll see to it," he said. "Now I gots wood to stack."

Mercy and Isaac both watched him walk away. Mercy crossed to Isaac. "Are you all right, Isaac?"

"Yassum, Miss Mercy," he said. "Thanks be to you he didn't get a chance to hit me this time."

For a moment, Mercy looked conflicted. "I hope I didn't make things worse for you by saying something."

"You was jes tryin' to help me," Isaac said. "Ain't no one done that before."

"Promise me you'll tell Mr. Rand if he hits you again, Isaac."

Isaac's eyes filled with tears. "I could tell you."

Mercy hesitated, then shook her head. "It needs to be Mr. Rand."

"Ezra say Mr. Rand will send me packin' if I tell. He say I be too much trouble to keep on here."

"Ezra's wrong, Isaac. Mr. Rand won't want you to be hurt. Do Kizzy and Letty know about this?"

Isaac looked down at the ground. "It just be the way things is."

Mercy put a hand on the boy's shoulder, wincing with the pain from her own wound. "It's not how things should be, Isaac. You're a good boy. A good worker. You don't deserve to be treated like that."

Isaac nodded but didn't look up. Mercy stepped back. "Would you saddle Lucky for me?"

"Yassum," he said. "Won't take me but a minute, Miss Mercy."

While Isaac made short work of saddling Lucky, Mercy took a last look around the cottage grounds. She should have known things were too good to be true.

Isaac brought Lucky to her. "I be ready to brush him down when you get back from yo' ride, Miss Mercy."

Mercy handed him the satchel and then tried to steel herself against the pain it would cause as she reached for the saddle horn and mounted the horse. Once astride, she held out a hand, and Isaac gave her the satchel.

"I thank you for the way you've cared for Lucky, Isaac. You have a way with horses," Mercy told him.

"Thank you, ma'am," Isaac said.

Mercy nodded, then gave Lucky a kick in the side, and they rode away.

Mercy's eyes were swollen and red when she knocked on the convent door. Deirdre answered and couldn't hide her look of surprise.

"Mercy?"

"I need to see Mother Helena, Deirdre. Please."

Deirdre nodded but looked past her. "Is Rand with you?"

Mercy shook her head and fought against tears. "No."

Deirdre drew her inside. "Wait in the common room. I'll find Mother."

Physically and mentally exhausted, Mercy dropped onto a wooden bench, wincing from the jarring pain in her shoulder. She wanted to be strong when she talked to Mother Helena. Wanted the nun to see she had grown and matured since her departure from the convent. All she needed was a place to stay for a few days until she could decide what to do with the rest of her life.

"Mercy?" Mother Helena stood a few feet away. Her musical voice was all it took for Mercy's carefully held reserve to crumble.

"Mother." Her voice cracked, and tears began to flow again. Mother Helena hurried toward her and kneeled at her feet. Mercy gripped the older woman's hands. Her voice was choked with emotion when she spoke.

"I didn't have anyone else to turn to," she said.

Mother Helena's brow creased as she looked up into Mercy's tear-streaked face. "What's all this about, child? What's happened?"

Mercy drew in a steadying breath, trying to stop the flow of tears. She wiped her nose with the back of her hand. "I'm not marrying Rand."

Mother Helena digested the news. "By the look of you, I'm guessing that he called it off?"

Mercy sniffed and shook her head. "It was me."

Mother Helena pushed herself to her feet and sat down next to Mercy. "Shall we talk about why?"

"I'm an awful person," Mercy said. "An evil, terrible, despicable person." She dropped her eyes to her lap. "I don't deserve him."

"I don't understand. Did you argue? Have some kind of disagreement that's left you feeling this way? Did Rand say those hateful things about you?"

Mercy shook her head. "He's never been anything but kind and loving toward me." She shifted on the bench so that she was facing the older woman. "That's the problem. He's been kind and loving to the woman he thinks he knows. But if he knew the *real* me … he wouldn't love me at all. He'd hate me. I had to leave him so I'd never see that hate in his eyes."

Mother Helena stilled. "You speak as though you've remembered something, child. Have you? Have you remembered your past?"

Mercy pulled in a deep breath. She wanted to admit it all: that Elijah Hale had threatened to expose her—that she'd set a fire and nearly killed a man because of her own selfish fears. But the bulk of the truth was stuck in her throat, and she couldn't force herself to push out the words. A version of the truth was all she could muster.

"I've remembered … something," Mercy admitted.

"But isn't that good news? I know you've prayed for your memory to come back to you."

Mercy's expression hardened. "Yes, I've been praying for that. Only God has seen fit to answer that prayer in part and parcel with information that makes it impossible for me to marry Rand."

Mother Helena's brows rose. "You've remembered a husband, then?"

Mercy shook her head, eyes filled again with tears. "No. I've not even remembered my own name."

"Then what?"

Mercy hesitated.

"What you tell me won't leave this room, child," Mother Helena assured her.

"I was a soldier in the war. A *Confederate* soldier." Somehow, saying the words out loud eased an ache in her chest. "I was Rand's enemy."

Mother Helena turned from Mercy and looked toward the window as her fingers found her rosary beads. Clearly thinking through what Mercy had just confided, she finally turned. "Your hair, the men's clothing—the binding around your chest. It all makes sense."

"Rand can never know the truth."

"The poor boy must have been devastated when you broke off your engagement," Mother Helena said. "It must have been a very difficult conversation."

"I couldn't face him, Mother. I had a servant deliver a note that said I couldn't go through with the wedding."

"So you lied."

Mercy sighed. "Right now it seems the least of my sins."

"Rand deserves to know the truth about this, Mercy. He may surprise you with his reaction. If he truly loves you, your past won't matter."

"I know how he feels about Confederates. I couldn't bear to have him look at me that way. And what if someone else were to find out? How would it look to have one of the biggest supporters of the Union cause married to a rebel soldier? It would be an embarrassment to his whole family. I won't do that."

"He won't be satisfied with a note, Mercy. He'll come here looking for you, and when he does, you need to face him."

"I don't think I'm strong enough to do that," Mercy whispered.

"Then pray for the strength," Mother said firmly. "I've told you this isn't a place to hide. But as long as you face Rand when he comes, you are welcome to stay with us until you know what you want to do."

Mercy's shoulders sagged with relief. "Thank you."

Mother Helena leaned over and hugged her. Mercy flinched from the pain in her shoulder. The nun pulled back and studied her.

"Are you hurt?"

"Just a little pain in my shoulder from a fall I took," Mercy said.

Mother Helena offered a sad smile. "'Tis a pain that will heal quicker than your broken heart, I'm sorry to say."

Mercy nodded. "I know."

Mother Helena stood. "All right then. See to your horse, and I'll let Oona and Deirdre know they'll have company in their room."

Mercy went outside and busied herself with Lucky's needs. She put him in the corral, forked some oats into a bucket, and stood with her hand on his neck as he dipped his head for the food and munched contentedly.

"There's no question that horse loves you," Deirdre said. Mercy turned to see the young postulant standing a few feet away.

"I suppose that's true."

Deirdre approached her. "Mother says you are back to stay for a while?"

"Yes," she answered, swallowing down the sorrow she felt in the admission. "But I will be the one to sleep on the floor, Deirdre."

"We can take turns again," Deirdre said. "Like old times."

Mercy tried to smile. "Old times."

"I won't pry," Deirdre said, "but when you're ready to talk about what happened, I'd be happy to listen."

When Mercy didn't respond, Deirdre took a step toward her. "Sometimes talking about something makes the burden a wee bit lighter."

Mercy knew if she told Deirdre, then the rest of the nuns would hear the news and she'd be spared offering the same explanation over and over.

"I've broken off my engagement to Rand, Deirdre. We're not going to be married."

Deirdre's eyes widened. "I'm so sorry, Mercy."

"No need to be sorry," Mercy said. "It's for the best."

"'Tis lucky for you to have realized you don't love him before you were married in front of God and everyone."

Mercy offered a sad smile. "Yes. Lucky for me."

CHAPTER TWENTY-SEVEN

It was Ezra's first time in the ornate building that housed the Prescotts' offices in midtown St. Louis. He was ushered by a stern-looking older man into an anteroom off the main lobby and told in no uncertain terms to wait there until he found Mr. Prescott.

It took only a few minutes before Rand opened the door. "Ezra? What are you doing here? Is everything all right at the cottage? There was some serious trouble at Congressman Henderson's house last night and—"

Ezra thrust the note out in front of him. "I promised Miss Mercy I would give this to you mahself, suh," he said, interrupting Rand.

"Miss Mercy sent you?"

Ezra nodded. "Yassuh."

"So there's no trouble?"

"Not at the cottage, suh."

"What is she up to?" Rand muttered. He tore through the wax seal and began to read the note. His demeanor quickly darkened, and he looked at Ezra through disbelieving eyes.

"She's gone?"

Slowly, Ezra nodded. "Seem like it."

"Where? Where did she go?"

Ezra shook his head. "Don't know, suh. She didn't say."

"Did she seem upset? Was she crying? Did someone come there and upset her? Did something happen?"

"Nothin' seemed wrong, Mr. Rand. Nothin' seemed off. She had Isaac saddle the horse this morning and left. That be all."

"And you're just now giving me the note?" Rand asked.

"Doing as the lady tol' me, Mr. Rand," Ezra said.

Rand frowned, ran a hand through his hair. "Do you know if she said something to Kizzy or Letty?"

"I know Letty say Miss Mercy had a painful head last night and took to bed early. But she be fine this morning. Miss Mercy even tol' Kizzy she be a fine cook."

Rand rubbed a knuckle over his jaw, glassy-eyed and stunned. "Thank you, Ezra. That will be all."

Ezra hesitated. "I be heading back to the cottage, then."

Rand nodded and started to close the door. "Let's keep this between us for now, Ezra. All right?"

Ezra nodded. "Yassuh."

Numb from shock, Rand shut the door and stared at the note that told him the love of his life was no longer able to marry him. What could have happened to make her change her mind? She loved him—of that he was sure. Why, then? Why call off the wedding—and where would she go? He felt a sudden chill when he realized she might have remembered something. Someone. He thought of the bald-faced lie he'd told his parents the night he declared his intention to marry Mercy.

And if she happens to wake up one morning and remember that she has a husband and a child or two tucked away somewhere? What then?

I don't believe that is going to happen, but if it does, I will bow out gracefully.

He wasn't going to bow out. He was going to fight. Fight for the woman he loved. He had to find her—assure her that no matter what had happened, they could work it out together. He knew there was only one place she would go.

The knock on the convent door came more quickly than even Mother Helena might have anticipated. Mercy knew before she opened it that Rand would be standing on the other side. She'd spent the last couple of hours trying to figure out what to say to him. The only thing she knew for sure was that she wasn't going to tell him the truth, no matter what Mother Helena said. There was nothing in her that would allow the words *I was a Confederate soldier* to pass through her lips.

When she opened the door, Rand stood in front of her with such an expression of pain on his face, she could barely stand to look at him.

"Have you remembered someone else?" he asked. "Is that what this is all about?"

She shook her head. "No."

He closed his eyes with relief. She hated herself—and she hated Elijah Hale.

Rand reached for her, but she shrank from his touch. "Please don't."

"I don't understand," he said. He held up her note. "This makes no sense. I'm not calling off our wedding based on some cryptic comments!" He opened the paper and began to read aloud. "'I cannot be the wife you deserve. I cannot be the woman you need by your side in the future you will have in your father's business.' What does that even mean?"

"It means I can't marry you," she said, her eyes filling with tears. "Please, just go away, Rand. Please."

"No. Not until you give me a good reason for all this. I don't understand why you suddenly changed your mind."

"It wasn't sudden. I've never hidden the fact I'm worried about my past. Or rather, my lack of a past. If someone, or something, should appear ..."

"It's not going to happen," he said, "and even if it did, there's nothing we can't face together. You're all I care about."

She felt herself soften, but she had to stay strong for his sake. "It's not just my past," she said. "It's ... so many things. The way I have to be coached before social events, the way your mother has to constantly watch me and prompt me to say or do the right things. I can't be part of your world, Rand. I constantly worry about saying the wrong thing, doing the wrong thing. Embarrassing your family. I can't live up to the Prescott name. I'm not the woman your parents envisioned for you to marry. And I never will be no matter how many lessons in etiquette I get or how much you spend on my clothes."

"None of that matters to me," he said. "You're denying our future based on something that's never happened—or on the off chance that there is some dark secret in your past?"

There is some dark secret, she almost screamed at him. *Darker than you can live with.* But instead, she looked down, afraid he would see how much she still loved him if he looked into her eyes.

"I don't accept this," he said.

"You have to. I'm sorry."

She started to close the door, but he slapped a palm against the wood.

"We'll run away together," he said.

"What?"

"I know you love me, Mercy. And I want to spend my life with you. If the Prescott name and all the trappings and pressure that goes with that is too much for you—then I'm done with that too."

"Don't be ridiculous, Rand. That's your family! Your name! I know what losing both of those things would mean to you. I miss my name and my family, and I can't even *remember* them!"

"I don't care about that. We'll start somewhere new where nobody knows us—pick new names."

"And have you resent me someday? No. I won't ask you to do that."

"You didn't ask."

"Your parents …"

"I'll tell them the wedding is off," he said.

Tears trailed down her cheeks. "Why are you making this so hard? Just go. Go and live your life with someone who deserves you."

He reached out and wiped a tear from her cheek. "I'm not leaving here until you agree."

"I'm completely selfish if I do," she said.

She saw the triumph in his eyes when he realized he'd won. "I'm the selfish one. I need you in my life." He grinned. "In just a few days we'll be Mr. and Mrs. ...."

She watched it dawn on him that they couldn't put their real names on a marriage certificate.

"Coming up with a name isn't as easy as you may think," she said. "I should know."

"We'll be Mr. and Mrs. Sherman," he said.

"After your horse?"

"Why not? It's a good, strong name. A general's name," he said.

She tamped down the ripple of unease that he was speaking of a *Union* general and smiled. "Mrs. Sherman. I like it."

"I'll need two days, maybe three to get some money together and tie up some loose ends without arousing the suspicion of my parents," he said. "Promise me you'll stay until I come back for you. I can't give up everything without your sworn word."

"I promise. I will be here." She leaned over and kissed him.

He cupped her cheek. "Not a word to anyone. As soon as my mother finds out the wedding is off, so will half of St. Louis."

Not only did she know it, she was counting on it. "I won't say a word—not even to the nuns."

Rand reached for her, drawing her close by grabbing her shoulders. She winced in pain and bit her lip.

"You're hurt?"

"It's nothing. I was being careless riding Lucky the other day and hit a branch with my shoulder," she said.

"Have you had a doctor look at it?"

"I'm fine," she said firmly. "Now go, so I can look properly sad again when I have to face the nuns."

"I'll be back soon," he said.

Mercy watched him ride away and took slow, even breaths. She couldn't believe it. She would still have Rand—and his love, respect, and admiration. It was almost too good to be true.

Rand paced back and forth in front of his mother and father, who sat in matching chairs in the drawing room. While Charles read the note, Ilene perched on the edge of her seat, her lips locked in a grim expression and her hand outstretched for the paper.

Charles finally looked at his son. "I suppose you have gone to find her?"

Rand nodded. "She's back at the convent with the nuns. She refuses to change her mind."

Ilene snapped her fingers for the paper, and Charles handed it over. She read it quickly while Rand downed the rest of his drink. When she looked up, her eyes were flashing.

"The whole world has gone mad!" Ilene said. "First the war, then the president shot while he's at the theater! The attempt on John Henderson's life by some crazed lunatic, and now this!"

"I hardly think the attempted murder of John and calling off a wedding carry the same weight," Charles said caustically.

"You aren't the one who has broken your back over wedding details and plans for the last five months!" Ilene rose out of her chair. "She is refusing the Prescott name, turning her back on all the extensive and expensive wedding preparations I've made for her. She's right, of course. She isn't suitable for you—she never was." Ilene pointed a finger at Rand. "I begged you not to get involved with her. I told you how foolish you were being, but in the end you had to have your way!"

"This is hardly the time to place blame, Ilene," Charles said evenly. "We were all enamored with the girl."

"I most certainly was not!" Ilene argued. "I have been onto her since the first time I laid eyes on her. She is nothing but a gold digger ..."

"If that were true, Mother, she would still be marrying me," Rand said firmly.

"There is one piece of good news here," Charles said.

"I can't imagine what," Ilene said.

"Better this all happened now than after she was legally a Prescott," Charles said.

"That's your attempt at good news?" Ilene snapped. "This will cause scandalous humiliation for me."

Rand said nothing. His father stood and put a hand on his shoulder. "I know it's a blow, Son, but you'll get over her."

"I'm not sure about that, Father," Rand said.

"I'm sure," Ilene said. "There are plenty of pedigreed women in St. Louis who have had their eye on you for years, Rand. Someone infinitely more suitable for you than Mercy was—someone bred to be a lady, who didn't have to be coached through the most mundane social event. Honestly, sometimes I thought that girl was born in the backwoods of Mississippi."

Rand boiled inside as he listened to his mother's disparaging remarks about the women he loved. "I didn't know you disliked her so, Mother," he said. "I thought you had warmed to the idea of our marriage."

Ilene waved a hand dismissively. "An act for your sake, my dear. We all do it for the ones we love, now don't we?"

Rand thought about Mercy's reservations regarding his family, his position—the problems he thought she'd imagined. But it was all true. He saw that now. He had been right to suggest they run away.

"Yes, Mother, we all do it for the ones we love," he said. "Now if you'll excuse me, I'd like to be alone."

"Chin up, Son," Charles said. "Tomorrow is a new day."

Rand nodded. He smiled as he left the room. Tomorrow was a new day indeed.

Chapter Twenty-Eight

It could have been so much worse. Although the entire wooden shed on the Hendersons' property was a total loss, the house had suffered little damage. Elijah could see black bite marks from the fire that had licked up the edge of the structure, but with the servants' help, he and John had managed to douse the flames before the whole house became a smoldering pile of ash.

The person responsible for this should be hunted down and locked up, Elijah thought. Just as he had told Mercy, the war might be over, but bad feelings remained. As the sun rose the morning after the fire, Elijah had been the first to see the paper fluttering from the hand of the lawn jockey. An old newspaper article about John Henderson and his efforts on behalf of the Union was pasted on a piece of parchment, along with words made up of newsprint that read: *Your debt must be paid, Henderson!*

Mary reacted as any wife would. She cried with relief that they were all still alive and hadn't been killed in the fire; she was angry that someone had actually attacked her home; she was frightened that the madman who had tried once might come back and try again to hurt her husband.

John did all he could to reassure his wife that everything would be fine. He telegraphed his good friend Allan Pinkerton in Chicago and asked him for advice on some added security for his home until the person or persons responsible for the attack were caught. Pinkerton, who owned the Pinkerton Detective Agency, responded swiftly. Less than a day later, Elijah stood and listened to one of the four agents at the Henderson place give John a briefing of their security plan.

"Vigilance at all times, Congressman," Tom McElroy said. "Two of us will be on the property twenty-four hours a day. We'll take turns operating in twelve-hour shifts. Mrs. Henderson gave me a list of your social engagements for the next two weeks. One of us will be at your side wherever you go."

"Your men are armed?" Elijah asked.

McElroy opened his jacket to reveal a revolver. "At all times."

A man on horseback came galloping down the Hendersons' road. McElroy looked at John. "Are you expecting someone?"

"No."

One of the Pinkertons stepped in front of the horseman and held up a hand. The man reined in the horse and stopped.

"I have a message for Congressman and Mrs. Henderson," he said, reaching into his vest pocket.

"Dismount," McElroy said.

"I just have a—"

McElroy drew his gun. "*Please* dismount."

Once the messenger was on the ground, one of the Pinkertons searched him. The man put his arms straight out away from his sides.

"I'm telling you, I'm just trying to deliver a message from Mr. and Mrs. Prescott," he said.

McElroy looked at John. "You know a Prescott?"

John nodded. "Yes. Let's have the message."

McElroy nodded to the messenger, who pulled the note from his pocket and handed it to John. John read it quickly and then looked at the messenger.

"No need for a reply," he said. "You may go."

As the messenger went on his way, McElroy raised a brow at John. "Anything I should be aware of, Congressman?"

John handed the note to Elijah but looked at McElroy. "As a matter of fact, you can cross one of those social engagements off your list. The Prescott wedding next week has been canceled."

Elijah read the note twice. It was impossible to know what had transpired between Rand and Mercy—had she told him the truth and he called it off? Or did she just walk away because the truth was too much to admit? Either way—the wedding was off, and Elijah was spared the distasteful job of having a very difficult conversation with Rand Prescott.

"Wonder what happened there?" John mused aloud.

Elijah shrugged. "Who knows?"

"If Rand was the one who got cold feet, his mother will make him pay somehow, but if this was Mercy's doing, then I shudder to think about how angry Ilene will be," John said with a half smile.

"If you'll excuse us, Congressman, Captain, we are going to make a trek around the perimeter," McElroy said. "Get a feel for the property."

"Fine," John said.

As they walked away, Elijah handed the note back to John. "I think you've got some good men looking out for you."

"Allan Pinkerton runs a fine organization. If he vouches for them, then I trust them with my life—and with Mary's."

"As long as things are under control here and I don't have a wedding to attend next week, I'm thinking I'll head to Kansas early," Elijah said. "I know my orders don't require me to be there for another two weeks, but I'd like to get settled in before I'm on duty and riding around the western half of the country."

"Fort Wallace isn't an easy post, Elijah," John said. "I wish you would have let me pull a few strings to get you assigned here."

"What would a cavalryman do in town, John?" Elijah smiled.

"I suppose that's true."

"Protecting the expansion of the railroad from the Indians is a mite better than fighting a war against my own countrymen," Elijah said.

"True again," John said. "If you ever head back this way, you know you're welcome."

Elijah looked pointedly at the armed men on the property and the black marks from the fire. He shook his head. "Now *that* would be too dangerous," Elijah said.

John laughed, and even Elijah chuckled at his own joke.

"What will be even *more* dangerous is telling my wife that the Prescott wedding has been canceled. Mary loves weddings," John said.

"She *has* been looking forward to it," Elijah said.

"Maybe you'd like to break it to her?" John asked hopefully.

But Elijah shook his head. "I'd rather take my chances with the Indians."

John laughed. "Me, too."

Deirdre couldn't figure it out. Mercy seemed ... different. Deirdre had seen her when she first arrived back at the convent—brokenhearted and hopeless about her future. Her eyes had that haunted, lost-love look, and her complexion had been sallow. Those things Deirdre could understand. She would have expected Mercy to look awful, considering the girl had just canceled her wedding to the most eligible man in St. Louis. But the things that were puzzling Deirdre now were the little things. Several times she had caught Mercy with a hint of a smile on her face and had heard her humming while she did the dishes. Not normal behavior for a woman with a broken heart. Deirdre tried to pin her down as they did the breakfast dishes that morning.

"How are you faring, Mercy?" Deirdre asked.

"I'm ... sad," Mercy said.

"Yes, of course, 'tis normal to be sad," Deirdre agreed. "I would be happy to listen if you'd care to talk. It might help a wee bit."

But Mercy shook her head. "I don't think anything will help."

"Can I ask you a personal question?"

Mercy hesitated. "I suppose so."

"What was it that made you realize Rand wasn't the right man for you? He seems pretty perfect to me."

"I really don't want to talk about it, Deirdre," Mercy said. "I'm trying to forget I ever knew Rand Prescott."

"Of course," Deirdre said, rubbing a speck from a plate with the dish towel. "I'm sorry. I didn't mean to upset you."

And you're lying to me, she thought.

"I'll be glad when our turn for kitchen chores is over next week," Deirdre said. "All those children make for a lot of dirty dishes."

"I like the children being here," Mercy said. "It makes the place a little livelier."

"Noisy, dirty, and chaotic is more like it," Deirdre complained. "Next week we have to turn out the beds and do all the linens. It will take all day."

"I may not be here next week," Mercy said. "I'm going to tell Mother Helena in the morning that I won't be staying."

"You just got back," Deirdre said, puzzled.

"I know. I just needed a safe place to think for a few days," Mercy said, "but the fact of the matter is that my situation hasn't changed since the last time Mother asked me to leave. I am not a nun. And I don't intend to become a nun. It's not right that I stay."

"Where will you go?" Deirdre asked.

"I don't know yet," Mercy said evasively. "Maybe west."

"I've heard there are a lot of hostile Indians in the West," Deirdre said. "Won't you be scared to travel alone?"

Mercy didn't seem to be aware that she smiled. "No. I won't be scared."

"But you'll be alone."

Mercy ignored the statement. Instead, she pointed at the table. "There's one more plate over there, Deirdre. Will you get it for me?"

Deirdre retrieved the plate, and when Mercy dropped it into the dishwater, she started to hum again.

If she's sad, she certainly has an odd way of showing it, Deirdre thought. *I'm the one who is grousing about the children; I'm the one who has no appetite and tosses and turns and can't seem to fall asleep at night. But not Mercy. She drops her nightdress over her head, brushes out her hair, and is sleeping in no time at all.* There was a time, she remembered, when Mercy would keep the flame lit long into the night so she could write in that journal of hers—but Deirdre hadn't seen her do that since her return. Strange, since the journal would be the perfect place for Mercy to pour out her thoughts about her poor broken heart. Maybe she had outgrown the need to write in the journal—or maybe she was too excited about her future to do any more thinking about her past.

Mercy was still humming as she hung up the dish towel and smiled distractedly at Deirdre before leaving the kitchen. And Deirdre was still wondering what on earth Mercy was up to and how she was going to find out.

Chapter Twenty-Nine

It was hard to pretend he was sad. But Rand dutifully and purposefully worked at a countenance that would show both his parents and strangers alike that he was just trying to get past the whole distasteful affair and soldier on with his life. His mother, racing to save face as best she could with the whole debacle, had been quick to place a small announcement in the city paper stating that the wedding was off. Telegrams were sent to those important enough to warrant them—and of course messengers were dispatched to close family friends. Rand and his parents had agreed on a pat response to the cancellation of the wedding: The bride and groom mutually decided it was in their best interest not to go forward. Differences were too broad to bridge.

Rand went back to work for appearance's sake and saw looks of pity from his father's employees. A few were bold enough to express their support of his decision not to go through with the wedding, but for the most part, people ignored the subject altogether, which was fine by him. He knew that when he disappeared with Mercy, tongues would wag again, but he didn't care. She was all he wanted.

He was checking things off his list—things he had to do in order to get out of town and never look back. The biggest sigh of relief had come after his visit to the bank. Mitch Bryant, president of St. Louis Trust, had balked when Rand asked him to pull almost all the money out of his account.

"That's a sizable amount for a honeymoon, Rand," Mitch joked.

"I may as well tell you, Mitch," Rand said with proper gravity in his voice. "The wedding has been called off—so obviously there won't be a honeymoon."

"I'm sorry, Rand. I didn't know," Mitch said.

"I'm sure you can understand if I don't want to get into specifics about what happened."

"Of course," Mitch said, then frowned. "But you still want to withdraw nearly all your funds?"

Rand nodded. "I need to do something to get back on track. I'm going to build my own house—with my own money."

"St. Louis Trust would be more than willing to loan you the money to build, Rand. You needn't liquidate your account to pay for that."

Rand shook his head. "I want to pay as I go. And quite honestly, I'm trying to do this on my own—without backing from the bank or my parents. The project will help me keep my mind off of ... current circumstances."

Mitch nodded. "Of course. It will take me a day or so to come up with that kind of cash. Can you come back tomorrow afternoon?"

Rand slid the valise with his cash under the bed in his room. He'd left things at his office neat and tidy with instructions for anyone taking over the accounts he handled. He'd decided he would take very little with him when he and Mercy left. There was a carriage that had seen better days in the back of the stables that would suffice to get them out of St. Louis. There was one last thing to do before he went to collect Mercy, and that was to retrieve her engagement ring from the cottage. It was the only thing of sentimental value he would take from his life as Rand Prescott. He smiled. In less than forty-eight hours, he and Mercy could be man and wife.

There was a knock on his bedroom door. Rand opened it and found Ellis standing in the hall.

"Someone is here to see you, Mr. Prescott," Ellis said.

Rand stepped outside to see Deirdre standing on the veranda.

"Deirdre?" he said, making his way toward her.

"Hello, Rand. I'm sorry to be showing up unannounced like this, but I need to speak to you."

"Is this about Mercy? Is she all right?" He couldn't seem to stop the unveiled concern in his voice.

Deirdre raised her brows. "Mercy is fine."

He relaxed. "Then might I ask what it is that brings you here?"

She hesitated. "The truth. The truth brings me here."

"What truth?" Rand asked.

"You are still in love with Mercy." He heard no question in the statement. Saw no hint that she was fishing for her answer. Rand could see that she firmly believed it.

"Not to be rude, but the way I feel should be of no concern to you," Rand said.

"I think of you as a friend, Rand. A personal friend and a friend to the Little Sisters of Hope. I am always concerned about a friend's well-being."

Rand's smile was strained. "I appreciate your concern, but you needn't worry about me. The feelings I had for Mercy have … faded. I am surviving the end of our relationship and will go on with my life just fine."

"Mercy seems as though she is surviving fine as well," Deirdre said in a speculative tone. "The poor girl was a wreck the day she arrived at the convent, but then strangely, she seems to have found a certain peace about the situation."

"That's good. Good that we can both look toward the future and not cry about the past."

Deirdre studied him. "The past. Yes. It's my guess that Mercy remembering her past is probably what ended your relationship."

His incredulous look was all Deirdre needed to confirm her suspicions.

"She hasn't told you, has she?"

"She's told me everything she remembers. Everything there is to tell—which is nothing at all," he insisted.

"Then you knew that she was a soldier in the war? A *Confederate* soldier?"

Rand's brows shot up, and he barked out a laugh. "You are a desperate, silly girl, aren't you?"

She shook her head. "I'm just trying to protect you, Rand. 'Tis all I've ever wanted to do."

He grew serious and lowered his voice. "No. You're just jealous and want to spoil everything. You want what Mercy has."

"You mean you?" She raised her brows. "That's insulting. I am all but married to the church."

Rand took a step closer to Deirdre, his expression an angry scowl. Deirdre backed up as he lessened the space between them.

"You want to wear pretty dresses and go to dances and be kissed in the moonlight," he said. "That is why you're making things up about Mercy."

He could see her flush at his assessment, but she remained firm in her resolve.

"It's up to you if you want to believe the truth or not," she said. "My wants and desires have nothing to do with the fact that your fiancée most likely killed Union men."

"I'm going to have to ask you to leave, Deirdre," Rand said, barely able to control his anger.

"You don't have to take my word for it," she said, holding out a leather-bound book toward him. "She has kept a journal since Dr.

Johnson treated her. It's all in here, Rand. In her own words—her own confessions."

Rand remained motionless as Deirdre continued to hold out the journal between them. "The truth can be a terribly painful thing to face—but God still wants us to face it," she said.

When Rand still didn't react, Deirdre dropped the hand holding the journal. "Fine. Don't read it. But you'll wonder for the rest of your life what's in that book."

Rand reached out and grabbed the journal from Deirdre. She inclined her head toward him. "I will say a prayer for your peace."

Without another word, she turned and left him standing there with the book she knew would change everything.

CHAPTER THIRTY

Rand sat in the study with the door locked. It was the only place he knew his mother wouldn't come looking for him. It would never cross her mind that Rand would consider entering his father's sanctum when Charles wasn't home. He wasn't sure how much time had passed since Deirdre's visit—an hour … maybe two? He held the journal in his lap and rifled through page after page of Mercy's neat handwriting, looking for the one inflammatory word that would prove Deirdre's claim. And then he saw it tucked in the middle of a page in a sentence that shattered everything for him.

I don't want to believe it—but I do. I fought for the Confederacy in the war.

He read the sentence over and over: *I fought for the Confederacy in the war. The Confederacy, the Confederacy, the Confederacy.*

He kept reading: *Why? What could have possibly driven me to dress as a man and take up arms? How did I get away with that? I have most likely killed men in the heat of battle. I look in the mirror and search my eyes for hints that I have seen death up close. But all I see is confusion and worry. What to do with this information?*

In a blind panic now, Rand practically tore through the pages, scanning, glancing, running his finger down the ink as he looked for more of the same truth that had already made him sick.

The clock is ticking, and unless I find a way out of this mess, he will reveal my secret.

Rand stopped and stared at the words. Someone knew about her past? Someone knew her secret? He read on: *I can't let that happen. Rand can't find out. It would kill me to see the look on his face that I can be counted among those he hates.*

I have no doubt that the Yankee will tell what he knows, so how do I stop the inevitable? How to keep the future I want without letting my past take it all away? I know this much—I can shoot. And I know I can hit my target.

I need only finish my mission to put this all behind me where it belongs. Apparently, I failed once before at my task—but I cannot fail again. Remembering tonight how the dogs flushed the birds from the bushes at the hunt with Rand. Hidden from view one minute, then out in the open—vulnerable to the hunter and his rifle. Her rifle. I can't use dogs—but there are other ways of flushing him out.

He turned page—*kerosene and some rags*—after page—*fire makes smoke. Smoke will drive him out*—after page—*done under cover of darkness.*

As Rand read the last words, *I hope God can forgive me,* he sat back against the wing-back leather chair and let the knowledge wash over him. He had fallen in love with the enemy—asked someone with a reb background to marry him. Someone who was attempting to kill even after the war had ended. With a look of resolve, he closed the journal, then wiped his sweaty hands against his trousers. Everything had changed.

Rand arrived at the cottage by midafternoon and handed Isaac the reins of his horse. "He needs water. I don't plan to be long."

The minute he stepped through the door, Rand could smell the perfume he'd given Mercy a few weeks before. It lingered in the air, hung like a mist in the room. He fought to get her image out of his mind as he went straight to the gun cabinet in the study. He knew the inventory of guns well, as he had always been the one responsible for their care. From the time he was old enough to know how to shoot, his grandfather had instilled in him the need for proper maintenance of firearms. Twice a year the rifles were broken down and cleaned, stocks oiled, barrels polished. It took only seconds for his trained eye to see that three of the rifles had been moved: a Springfield, a Colt, and a Henry repeating rifle. One by one he lifted them out of the case and examined them. The Springfield was the last rifle he picked up. He braced the stock against the floor and sniffed at the barrel. There was a definite odor of sulfur that made his gut wrench. He dipped a finger into the end of the rifle and scraped it around the steel, pulling it out to see the black powder residue that was a telltale sign someone had used the rifle but hadn't cleaned it. It didn't prove anything, he reminded himself. Ezra could have used the rifle—maybe even Isaac—though either case would be a violation of the law. He tipped the gun the other way and inspected the stock. There was a small dent on the butt plate—and something else. Rand leaned closer and squinted at the dark substance that was dotted across the grain of the wood. It looked like blood. He thought back to the moments alone with Mercy when they'd made their plan to run away. His hand on her shoulder and her involuntary wince at his touch. She had hurt herself. Bled enough to spatter the rifle. Could it be true?

Letty appeared in the doorway of the study. "Mr. Rand? Kin I have Kizzy fix you somethin' to eat?"

He ignored the question—held the rifle by the barrel and looked at her. "Have you ever seen Miss Mercy handling any of these rifles, Letty?"

"No, suh," she said, shaking her head.

"Do you know where she was the night before she left for good?" he demanded.

"She tol' me she had herself a powerful head pain and went to bed early," Letty said. "I even tucked her in with a hot brick for her feet."

"And she was in her bed all night?"

Letty fixed big brown eyes on Rand. "I can't rightly say that or not since I be sleeping in my quarters."

"But you didn't hear anything unusual?"

A shake of her head, then a small shrug. "Not till I heard her bawling around dawn."

"What are you talking about?" he asked impatiently.

"She be crying behind her door when I come in that morning," Letty said. "When I ask if she be okay, she say she be having a bad dream."

Rand propped the rifle against the wall of the study and brushed past Letty. "Get Ezra in here. Isaac, too."

Mercy's wedding dress was still hanging in front of the cheval glass in the corner of the bedroom, and it served as a punch in his gut when he saw it. The four-poster bed was neatly made; Mercy's things still sat on top of the bureau. His eyes swept over the memories scattered there: a playbill from the first time he took her to the theater, a yellow ribbon tied around a bouquet of dried pink roses, the long feather he had given her after the pheasant hunt. He picked up the feather and thought back to the day of the hunt and the astonishing natural ability she had with the rifle. Only it wasn't natural ability—it was training and a skill that was unnerving. Was the surprise on her face at her own aptitude an act? Or did she secretly laugh at the fools who had been so impressed with her shooting skills? Had she been laughing at him all along—especially when she had called off the wedding and he still professed his love and desire to run away with her? Was his judgment so clouded by her beauty that he failed to see how deadly she could be? He dropped the feather as if it were a hot poker and scanned the room. Newspapers were neatly stacked on a steamer trunk across the room. Letty hovered in the background, near the threshold of the room.

He crossed to the papers. "What are these doing here?"

"Miss Mercy liked to read 'em," Letty said. "Said it helped her fill in the blanks in her head."

He picked up the pile of newspaper so he could lift the lid of the trunk and was surprised to see bits and pieces of newsprint float to the floor like confetti.

"I clean that up right quick, Mr. Rand," Letty said nervously. "I gots to do a sweep of the whole room. Miss Mercy kept it neat and all, but I ain't had no time to get those grimy handprints off a the window."

Rand was distracted. "Did Miss Mercy have you wash out anything?"

Letty frowned. "What you mean, suh? I wash her things all the time."

"Lately! Did she give you some soiled clothes to wash right before she left?"

But Letty shook her head. "No, suh."

"Have you washed the bed linens?" he asked, heading toward the bed.

Letty hung her head. "No, suh, not yet. Miss Mercy had the bed made up real nice, and I haven't torn it apart and washed up the sheets. I be doing it directly, though."

Rand ripped the quilt from the bed—revealing nothing more than the bare mattress. "Where are the sheets?"

Letty's eyebrows shot up in surprise. "Don't know, suh."

Rand was pawing through the bureau drawers when Ezra and Isaac appeared. He pointed to the bed.

"See if there are any bed linens under there, Isaac."

Isaac scurried across the room and dropped to his knees to peer under the bed. He sat back on his heels. "No, suh, Mr. Rand. Nothing under there."

Rand looked wildly around the room. The dread he'd felt coming to the cottage was rapidly being replaced by rage. Then what Letty had said earlier dawned on him.

Rand crossed to the window. He leaned toward the glass and saw fingerprints on the lower pane near the sill. But Letty had been wrong about the grime. The fingerprints were made from blood. He turned the crank to open the window and saw it. A piece of ripped white cloth fluttering from the outside of the sill. There were footprints in the soft dirt leading away from the house. Small footprints.

He raked a hand through his hair and shook his head in amazement. "She went through here," he said under his breath.

"I'm sorry, suh," Ezra said. "You say something?"

Rand bolted from the room and nearly ran down Kizzy as she crossed the parlor. "Move!" he shouted as he made his way outside.

Ezra and Isaac followed him to the back of the cottage. Rand trailed the footprints that led to a thatch of cattails as tall as he was. Ezra was right on his heels.

"Can I help ya somehow, Mr. Rand? What you be looking for?"

But the blood was pounding in Rand's head. *Rebel soldier … traitor … arsonist and would-be assassin.* He insisted he wouldn't find what he was looking for, even as he dropped to his knees at a freshly dug place in the earth. He didn't wait for a shovel, just started digging at the ground. Ezra got down and helped him, and before long they unearthed the first bits of the end of his love for Mercy. The sheet was torn and streaked with blood; the men's trousers were intact, but the wool shirt had a sizable hole ripped across the shoulder and was caked in dried blood. Ezra pulled a large wooden spoon from the hole and held it up.

"Kizzy been looking for this," he said.

Rand slowly got to his feet, leaned down, and brushed the dirt from the knees of his pants. Everything he'd read in the journal was true. Mercy was a Confederate soldier at heart and was still at war—and she had tried to kill John Henderson.

Rand wondered at the speed at which love could turn to hate and started to gather the evidence to bring Mercy to justice.

CHAPTER THIRTY-ONE

It was shouting that roused Mercy from a sound sleep in the pre-dawn hours, and for a moment, she couldn't remember where she was.

The angry voices were incongruous with the soft-spoken sisters. She threw the quilt back on the cot and sat up at the same time Oona and Deirdre were also reacting to the noise.

"What in the world?" Oona asked, her sleepy eyes widening.

Deirdre pushed the covers back from her pallet on the floor. "It's some kind of a fight," she said. "Sounds like my brothers when they were about to come to blows."

Twelve-year-old Frankie and ten-year-old Thomas stood in the middle of the common room, fists clenched and eyes flashing with anger. Nearly all the nuns spilled into the room in their nightclothes—a sight Mercy had never seen and would have laughed at had it been any other circumstance.

"What is the meaning of this, boys?" Mother Helena stepped between the two boys circling each other.

"His father was a good-for-nothing Yankee," Frankie said.

"And his father was a dirty reb!" Thomas shouted. "Same kind of dirty reb that killed my pa at Antietam!"

"Maybe it *was* him!" Frankie yelled. "Stinkin' Yankees trying to steal away our way of life!"

"That is enough!" Mother Helena said. "I won't have that kind of talk in this house, boys. And I certainly won't allow physical blows on this property!"

The boys didn't take their eyes from each other, but they lowered their fists. Frankie's eyes filled with tears. "It ain't right I'm sleeping in the same room as someone from the Union side of things."

"I don't like it no better than you," Thomas said.

"We are not divided by North or South here," Mother Helena said. "And there is no place in God's house for the kind of venom you boys are spewing. The war is over, and it was ugly. What you need to remember is you have something in common now. You both know how it feels to lose a father you loved. If there is to be further discussion about your fathers, let it be about that."

The boys remained silent. Mother Helena put a hand on each of their shoulders. "I think we're done here, are we not?"

Frankie and Thomas nodded.

"Good," Mother Helena said. Then she looked at the audience of sisters standing around her as if seeing them for the first time.

"Well, Sisters, dawn is breaking. I suggest we get an early start on prayers once everyone is in proper attire."

Mercy followed Deirdre and Oona back to their room, uneasy at what had just transpired. She couldn't wait for Rand to come and get her and take her far, far away from it all.

The knock on the door came around midmorning when Mercy was in the middle of a board game with two of the children. She went to the window and looked out to see Rand's horse, Sherman, tied under a tree. Her heart leapt in excitement when she realized it was time. The day. The day when everything was going to change for her. She heard Deirdre go to the door and had the passing thought that she and Rand would have to make up a story for Deirdre. Maybe Rand would have to leave, and then she and Lucky would follow when no one was looking.

Deirdre came into the common room. "Mercy ... Rand would like to speak to you. I told him you wouldn't want to see him ..."

Mercy tried to still her nerves and put on a proper face for Deirdre. She sighed. "It's all right, Deirdre. I'll see him."

Deirdre nodded, then stepped aside as Mercy made her way to the door. Rand stood framed with sunlight behind him, and she thought he looked so handsome. She looked behind her to make sure she was alone, then let herself smile.

"I didn't expect you in the daytime," she said quietly, excitement underlying her words. "What will I tell everyone?"

"How about the truth?" Rand said. Mercy felt a twinge of unease at his stance, his expression. This wasn't the face of a man about to elope with his bride.

"What do you mean? Tell them that we're going to run away together?"

"That would be a lie," he said coldly. "But then, you're very familiar with the concept of lying to people who matter to you, aren't you?"

He stared. A glare so long and chilling that Mercy had trouble swallowing down the lump of fear that had formed in her throat.

"I don't know what—"

Rand reached out and grabbed her arm, and she grimaced.

"I'm sorry. Does that hurt?" he asked sarcastically. She shook her head, and tears trailed down her cheeks.

Rand's jaw trembled with anger. "I was ready to give up everything for you! My home, my family, my job—my birthright to the railroad empire my father has built! Everything for a rebel soldier!"

"Rand," she said in a hoarse whisper.

"I know you were the one who set fire to the Hendersons' house," he said.

She couldn't even think to deny it. "How?"

He lifted her journal into the air between them. "You told me."

Mercy's eyes grew huge at the sight of her journal. She hadn't even looked for it that day. Hadn't written in it for several days and assumed it was under her mattress.

"Where did you get that?"

He shook his head. "It doesn't matter. Nothing matters now."

"Let me explain, Rand, please!" she pleaded. "Let me tell you my side of things."

Again, he lifted the journal. "No need. I've read quite enough."

Mercy knew by the cold tenor of his voice, by his dark, pitiless eyes, that any feelings he'd had for her were gone. Her fear that the truth would kill his love for her had been realized. She swiped at the tears on her cheeks.

"I'm so sorry," she said.

Rand looked grim. He stepped back and waved at someone she couldn't see. "So am I," he said.

Mercy counted five law-enforcement officers coming toward her. Rand moved completely out of the way as they approached. Her knees *did* buckle then as they told her the charge against her: conspiracy to commit murder. She would be tried for treason for the attempted assassination of an elected official.

Mercy was vaguely aware of Mother Helena coming to her side—some of the sisters praying for her—Oona crying—and Deirdre … Deirdre was standing off to the side, not saying a single word. Mother Helena wrapped her arms around Mercy and whispered, "God be with you, child."

As the officer in charge led Mercy toward a police wagon, she saw Rand mount Sherman. He glanced her way, then gave the horse a kick. They galloped away, and he never looked back. If Mercy had ever wondered if a heart could break and still beat, she didn't have to anymore.

CHAPTER THIRTY-TWO

Mercy sat in her cell in Gratiot Street Prison, her heart pounding in a fear-induced cadence as her mind raced with what had happened. Rand's voice filled with hate, the nuns' faces as she was led away, the thought of spending the rest of her life in a prison cell. She had no one to turn to, no one to talk to—so she tried to pray. But the words she tried to form seemed to be drowned out by the voices of hundreds of men who had died within the prison walls, voices whispering despair in her ear. Did God hear their prayers? Would He even listen to hers when she had proven herself to be a liar and a manipulator?

Her tightly clenched hands lay in her lap, and she unfolded them against the gray of the prison dress they had given her upon her arrival. The minute it had dropped over her head, she'd thought of something Mother Helena had said right after they met. *Clothing is a way to communicate to people who we are and what we value.* The gray dress said she was considered a criminal, a blight so great on society that she had to be locked away behind bars.

It was hours later when a guard opened her cell door to admit a man. He was baby faced, with a leather satchel that looked as young as he did. As soon as the guard walked away, the man moved toward her.

"My name is Frank Collins, Mercy. I was appointed by the court to defend you, and to be quite honest, it isn't going to be easy. I've reviewed the evidence they have against you, and it's quite damning."

"You mean my journal?" she asked.

"Among other things."

"What else?" she asked, dreading the answer.

"They found torn and blood-spattered clothing and some blood-stained sheets buried outside of the cottage where you used to reside," he told her.

"Who found them?" she asked.

"Does it matter?"

"It does to me."

"It was Rand Prescott," he said, consulting his notes.

Tears slipped down her cheeks. Frank Collins cleared his throat and looked back down at the paper in his hand.

"Moving on … a Springfield muzzle-loading rifle at the same cottage was found to have been fired recently. There was blood on the stock."

"I forgot to clean it," she muttered. "How could I forget that?"

Collins looked at her with a trace of disbelief. "Don't say that in front of the jury," he said. "In fact, don't say that in front of anyone ever again."

Her chin quivered. "But it's the truth."

"Unless you are asked a direct question about cleaning the gun, that particular truth needs to be left unsaid."

Mercy nodded her understanding.

Collins continued. "There are several other things: missing kerosene, some bits and pieces of newsprint that can be traced to the note that was left outside of John Henderson's home. The injury on your shoulder, which was documented when you arrived here at Gratiot." His expression was grim. "The evidentiary case against you is very strong."

Again, her lip trembled. "The jury will find me guilty, Mr. Collins," she said nervously. "What will happen to me then?"

Collins shifted his eyes from her face and looked down at his notes. "They have charged you with treason."

"I know."

He looked back up at her. "Treason is a crime punishable by death."

She felt herself go numb. "But I didn't kill anyone."

"I know. But in the case of treason, it doesn't matter. If you're found guilty of plotting acts against the country, the army, or even elected officials such as John Henderson—then the death penalty is on the table. I wish I could tell you that I'm confident I can get an acquittal for you, but I don't know how to fight the evidence."

"What if I told you that it wasn't Henderson I was trying to kill?"

She could see the doubt on his face.

"They have a note that says otherwise."

She briefly entertained the idea of telling him about Elijah Hale, but who would believe someone who had proven to be so adept at lying? "I understand," she said in a monotone voice.

"I'm told you are suffering from amnesia," Collins said. "Is that right?"

"Yes."

"So if I ask you about your past—your upbringing—that means nothing to you?"

"The fact that I can't answer those questions means a great deal to me," she said.

"I'm going to do my best to dispute the treason charge so that the jury can't recommend death."

"Maybe we shouldn't fight it at all," she said, more to herself than to him. The thought of dying terrified her, but it was a way out of her nightmare. "At least it would bring it all to an end sooner."

"I won't just give it up without a fight, Mercy. My conscience won't allow it."

"Then do your job as best you can for your sake, Mr. Collins. I know what happens when a person doesn't listen to her conscience."

The courtroom was packed with spectators, and Mercy felt their eyes and their judgment with every step she took as Frank Collins led her to the defendant's table. She glanced over and got her first look at the prosecutor. She estimated Don Shepherd was in his midforties. He looked like a man who didn't have a tentative bone in his body. He studied her for a moment, then looked back down at the notes on the table in front of him. And just like that she knew he had no doubt he would win—and she would finally get a way out of the wretchedness that had become her life.

Frank pulled out her chair, but when she tried to lower herself into it, he put a steadying hand on her elbow. "Wait."

A bailiff entered the courtroom and crossed to stand in front of the judge's elevated platform. "All rise for the Honorable William Young."

Mercy heard the collective shuffle of feet, bodies rising, throats clearing all around her—and even above her. She glanced up to the side balcony at a sea of black faces peering down at the main floor of the court. Scanning the faces, she saw Ezra, Letty, Kizzy, Isaac—even Marjorie and Ellis from the Prescotts' estate. While the rest of the Negroes stayed stoic and stone-faced, Isaac forced a smile and wiggled his fingers at her. Ezra grabbed his hand and leaned into his ear with a scowl as he whispered something to him. Chastised, Isaac nodded and sat back.

Frank touched her elbow, and she realized the bailiff had called for everyone to be seated. As the bailiff read the charges against her, Frank leaned over and whispered into her ear. "Remember what I told you. Try not to react to things in a way the jury can hold against you. They *will* be watching you."

"Mr. Shepherd," Judge Young said from the bench, "you may begin your opening statement."

"Thank you, Judge," Don Shepherd replied. He slid his chair back and walked toward the jury box. He cast one disdainful look in Mercy's direction before he began to speak, painting a picture of a duplicitous, conniving woman who was true through and through to the Confederate cause—and, even at the end of the war, couldn't accept the South's defeat. He told the jury he believed she'd concocted the story about her memory and was in fact such a good actress that she'd gained the sympathy of a town doctor and a convent full of sisters and, ultimately, the love of a man who belonged to one of the most prominent and powerful families in St. Louis. A man whose family provided an introduction to the congressman she plotted to kill.

"In conclusion, gentlemen of the jury, I will prove, on behalf of the state and ultimately the federal government, that the woman who calls herself Mercy has not moved on from the war—has not accepted the defeat of the South and wanted to exact her revenge on John Henderson, a man who has given much to support the Union cause. A man who worked tirelessly to see the Southern way of life forever changed. A man who personifies the very words *hero* and *patriot*—and could easily represent all the Union men she hates so much."

Low rumbling murmurs filled the courtroom as Shepherd took his seat behind the prosecutor's table.

"Mr. Collins?" Judge Young said. "Opening statement?"

Mercy stared straight ahead at nothing and wondered how painful it was to die. Collins got to his feet and walked toward the jury.

"Gentlemen … this is a case of no ordinary measure and one with a possible outcome that could irrevocably change the course of a young woman's life. Our Constitution provides specific stipulations in regard to a conviction under law regarding treason." Collins held up two fingers and waved them in front of the men in the jury box. "There must be two witnesses to the act or an actual *verbal* confession from the accused." He took a moment to pause and let that sink in, then continued. "I assure you, gentlemen, today you will be provided with neither of those things."

Mercy heard all the witnesses who testified against her. Everything they said was true. She had shown up in St. Louis under mysterious circumstances, dressed as someone trying to pass as a man. She couldn't remember her own history but managed to remember everyday tasks and even proved herself quite capable at certain things. The issue of her incredible skill with a rifle had been recited by more than one witness who had been at the pheasant hunt. Frank Collins did his best to refute the growing evidence against her, but it was hard to put the truth in a box and hide it away. And then came the moment she'd been dreading the most. Rand walked past her and swore on a Bible that he would tell the truth.

Mercy held her breath, afraid Rand would look at her ... and equally afraid he would not. He looked pale and drawn, like a man who had suffered a great deal. The prosecutor went through the expected questions: He asked about Rand and Mercy's relationship, how they met, how well he knew her. How he felt when she unexpectedly broke off their engagement. Rand recounted his pain and confusion about the breakup. He talked about how good the family had been to her—providing her with a place to live, servants, money, clothes, and a very promising future. He finally turned and looked right at Mercy when he said he couldn't begin to describe the pain he felt when he saw the evidence that their whole relationship had been a ruse so she could get an introduction to their close family friend John Henderson—and plan his assassination.

"It turns out that Mercy was such a good actress, she should have been on the stage instead of sitting next to me in the theater," Rand said. "A female John Wilkes Booth, if you will."

Shepherd called his next witness. "The state calls Deirdre O'Hennessey."

Mercy watched Deirdre settle herself in the witness stand.

"Miss O'Hennessey, would you please tell the court how you know the defendant?"

"I met her when Dr. Johnson brought her to the Little Sisters of Hope Convent. I am a postulant of the order," Deirdre said.

"Would you say you and the defendant were on friendly terms?" Shepherd asked.

"I thought so," Deirdre said. She glanced over at Mercy. "We shared a room, meals, and some duties. I felt like I was someone she could confide in."

"And did she confide in you?"

Deirdre looked pained. "I used to think so," she said. "But it seems to me that things had changed between us when she came back to the convent after leaving Rand."

"How do you mean?"

Deirdre looked toward Mercy. "It felt like she had just … shut me out of her life. She didn't speak of her breakup with Rand. Didn't say what had happened."

"And how was her demeanor?" Shepherd asked.

"Sir?"

"How did she act? Was she sad? Happy? Angry?"

"She seemed sad when she first arrived, but after Rand paid a visit, I noticed that the sadness wasn't—genuine. I caught her humming, smiling—there was a hopeful gleam in her eyes." Deirdre stopped. "That might sound odd …"

"Not at all," Shepherd quickly assured her. "And her actions made you suspicious?"

Deirdre looked down. "A little—yes."

"Of what, exactly?"

"I got the idea Rand was still in her life. That maybe the two of them were going to run off together."

"But why? Why do that when she could have had the wedding of her dreams?" Shepherd asked.

Deirdre shook her head. "I didn't know. But I stumbled across the answer by accident one morning when I was cleaning our room. I was flipping the mattress on her cot when it just fell out onto the floor."

"It?"

Deirdre licked her lips nervously. "Her journal. I've seen her write in it dozens of times, and I never would have thought to read someone else's most private thoughts, but ..."

"But ... you felt as if something wasn't right with her? Is that it?" Shepherd asked.

Deirdre nodded. "Yes. At first I was just going to put it back under the mattress, but it had fallen open to a page that had some inflammatory information that I just couldn't ignore."

"So you read it."

"Yes, though I wish I hadn't. As soon as I read a few recent passages, I knew I needed to show Rand."

"You didn't confront Mercy?"

"No," Deirdre admitted. "I didn't want her to know what I'd found out. I didn't tell anyone but Rand."

"You didn't even tell Mother Helena, the woman in charge of your order?"

Deirdre looked down at her hands folded in her lap. "No."

"Why not?"

"I was worried she'd tell me that I was meddling in something that didn't concern me."

"But you felt it did concern you."

Deirdre nodded. "Indirectly, but yes. Rand and his family have been great friends and supporters of the Little Sisters of Hope. I just hated that he was being duped."

"Why didn't you go to the authorities with the journal?" Shepherd asked.

"I knew Rand to be a good and honorable man," Deirdre said. "I was sure once he knew the truth, he would do the right thing." She lifted her chin. "And he did."

As Deirdre left the witness stand, Don Shepherd looked at Mercy. "The state calls the defendant to the stand."

Shepherd asked Mercy to identify each piece of evidence he had introduced. She agreed that the clothes with the bloodstains were hers.

"And these are the same clothes that you buried behind the Prescott cottage the day you left?"

"Yes."

"Along with the bedsheets that were stained with your own blood?"

Mercy barely nodded. "That's right."

Shepherd walked to a table on the side of the courtroom and picked up a rifle. He carried it back to Mercy.

"Do you recognize this rifle?"

"Yes."

"Have you ever fired this rifle?"

Mercy looked at Rand, then back at Shepherd. "Yes."

"Yes. In fact, isn't it true that you fired this rifle on the morning that Congressman John Henderson's house caught fire?"

Reluctantly, Mercy dipped her chin to nod.

"Answer with a yes or no, please," Shepherd said.

"Yes, but I didn't mean to fire the gun. It went off accidentally."

Quiet, uneasy laughter rippled through the courtroom. Judge Young pounded the gavel on the bench. "Proper decorum from the spectators, please."

"You are telling me that you never intended to actually fire the rifle you carried from the Prescott cottage to the Henderson estate that morning?" Shepherd asked. "Remember you are under oath."

"I'm saying I didn't intend to shoot Mr. Henderson," Mercy said.

Shepherd turned to the men in the jury box and offered a small, disbelieving smile. "And I suppose you would have us believe that the fire you set was an accident also?"

Mercy cleared her throat. "No. Though I'm sorry about it now— it was deliberate."

"You mean sorry because you were caught?"

Mercy looked at him. "Well, sir, I'd be lying if I said no to that. Of course I'm sorry I was caught."

"Rand Prescott maintains that you fostered a false relationship with him in order to become acquainted with John Henderson," Shepherd said. "Is that true?"

Mercy saw John and Mary Henderson sitting beside Charles and Ilene on the prosecutor's side of the courtroom. She let her glance go from the Hendersons to Rand, who sat in front of his parents.

"No, that isn't true," she said. "My feelings for Rand were real."

"Yet you continually lied to the man you claimed to love," Shepherd said.

Again, Mercy looked down at her hands. "Yes."

"One last question," he said.

Mercy pressed her lips together and nodded.

"Were you a Confederate soldier during the war between the states?"

Mercy looked at the jury, then out at the faces of the people who seemed to lean forward in their seats to hear her answer. She knew with her next statement her life would probably be over, but she said it anyway.

"I'm so very sorry to say that yes—I believe I was."

If ever there was a time in her life she wished her memory would disappear, it was that time in that place, seeing Rand's contemptuous face as he watched her leave the stand and go back to sit beside Frank.

The summation in her defense was brief. Frank asked the jury to remember that Mercy had never verbally confessed to planning an assassination of Congressman John Henderson. Therefore, the charge of treason could not be constitutionally upheld. But Mercy knew, as did the rest of the spectators in the court, that Frank Collins was standing on the bow of a sinking ship.

It took the jury less than three hours to find her guilty of treason and attempted murder. Moments later the judge delivered the news of her fate: death by hanging.

Mercy heard the words and waited for the tidal wave of emotions she should be feeling—but instead, she felt herself die with the pronouncement. She was vaguely aware of Frank's words of apology, his sympathy, the ripple of vindication from the gallery of spectators.

As the guard led her away, she looked at Rand and saw a flicker of regret on his face before his mouth settled into a smirk of vindication.

Rand went to join his parents and the Hendersons as they stepped outside the courtroom.

"I'm sorry I brought that woman into your life, John," Rand said.

"Sounds like she would have found me with or without you, Rand," John said. "No hard feelings here."

"Still, I feel like a fool," Rand said.

"Nonsense," John said. "She is a beautiful, charming young woman. We were all taken in by her."

"I wasn't," Ilene said bitterly.

Charles sighed. "This isn't the time, Ilene."

"I'm just glad it is all over," Mary Henderson said. "I won't miss all the security men that have been camped on our doorstep these past weeks."

She looked at her husband. "You should let Elijah know. He was so worried when he left."

"I'll send a messenger to Fort Wallace right away," John agreed.

Under a hot sun the next afternoon, a lone rider galloped along a grassy river that led him into a valley dotted with canvas-walled tents, a long building made from pine lumber, and two storehouses. The rider dismounted in front of a large, singular tent twice the size of the others and spoke to the man in uniform who stood guard.

"This Fort Wallace?"

The soldier nodded. "Yup."

"Got a message here for one of your officers," the rider said. "Captain Elijah Hale."

The soldier held out his hand. "I'll see he gets it."

"I'm supposed to hand it to him myself," the rider said.

"Captain Hale is in the field."

The rider sighed. "Point me in the right direction."

The soldier offered a wry smile. "Okay, pal. Just know that between here and Captain Hale, there are countless Indians who ain't happy about the railroads chopping up their land."

The rider considered it, then handed him the message. "I'll consider it delivered."

The soldier folded the paper in half and stuffed it into his pocket. "It will be as soon as I see him."

CHAPTER THIRTY-THREE

It was late afternoon when Elijah rode back into camp at Fort Wallace. He had been gone for two weeks, traveling over the Smoky Hill Trail in western Kansas to protect the railroad surveyors from the increasing hostilities of the Plains Indians. The work was long, hard, and often dangerous on the trail, but Elijah found he preferred it to spending all his time at the fort. But now that he had a few days to relax, he was anxious to be out of the saddle. For the past few hours, it was the thought of a warm meal and sleeping on a cot that had kept him going. He brought his horse to the stables and then went to the mess tent for a coveted cup of coffee and some hot food.

He greeted a few familiar faces as he carried a tin plate to a table in the back of the tent. A young man looked up as Elijah sat down across from him. Sergeant Howard Peterson had a splash of freckles across the bridge of his nose and a bristly cap of hair that actually looked needle sharp.

"Hey, Captain, good to see you back in one piece," he said.

"Thanks, Pete," Elijah said. "Good to be back for a few days."

"Did Brownie find you?" he asked.

Elijah tucked into his food and shook his head. "Nope. Just got back about a half a second ago."

"He started lookin' for you a' couple a days ago," Peterson told him. "He figured it'd be sometime seen that we'd see ya."

"What does he want?"

"He had a message for you," Peterson said.

Elijah looked up from his food, alarm on his face. "From who?"

Peterson shrugged. "Don't know. When he couldn't find you, he said he was gonna take it to Captain Gordon."

Elijah hurried from the mess tent and made his way to the man in charge, Captain James Gordon. He executed a quick knock on the door that hung from the frame of the tent.

"What is it?" Captain Gordon called out.

Elijah went inside and found Gordon poring over drawings spread across a desk in the center of the tent. Gordon looked up.

"Elijah. Back to regroup?"

Elijah nodded. "For a few days."

"See any action?"

"A few skirmishes, threats—nothing that we couldn't handle."

"Good. Good. I've got to put in an acquisition request for more lumber and supplies. The rate we're going, it'll be winter and we're still going to be in these blasted tents."

"Do you have a message for me, James?" Elijah asked.

Gordon nodded and then started to lift up piles of papers on his desk. "Brownie brought it to me yesterday," he said. "It's here somewhere."

All kinds of desperate thoughts ran through Elijah's head—most of them having to do with his mother. What if something had happened and he never got a chance to tell her good-bye?

"Ah! Here it is," Gordon said, pulling the telegram out from under some drawings. He handed it to Elijah.

Elijah opened the telegram and read the words on the page twice: *Assassin caught. Rand's fiancée turned out to be a reb. Guilty of treason. Set to hang at dawn at Gratiot. May 3.*

"Hope it's not bad news," Gordon said.

Elijah couldn't believe it. If Mercy had been the one to set the fire, then he knew without a doubt that it wasn't John she had been after—it had been him.

"Elijah?"

He looked up from the telegram. "What's today's date?" Elijah asked.

"It's the first of May," Gordon said.

"I have to get to St. Louis," Elijah said.

"When?"

"Now. A woman is set to be hanged in front of Gratiot Prison at dawn day after tomorrow, and I need to stop it."

Gordon shook his head. "You'll never make it in time."

"I need a fresh horse," Elijah said. "Mine hasn't had time to rest."

"Neither have you."

"I have to go," Elijah repeated.

Gordon hesitated and nodded. "Fine. But I'm telling you, you're never going to get there in time."

"I have to try," Elijah said. He gave the captain a curt nod and hurried out of the tent.

The evening of May second, Mercy realized that she wouldn't be alive the next time the sun set. The thought made a small chink in the armor she had insulated herself with over the last couple of weeks, and she quickly pushed it away. They brought her a last meal—chicken and fried potatoes. Mercy wondered idly if anyone ever ate the last meal. She could no more swallow food than open the door of her cell and walk outside.

"Got some visitors," the guard said, moving into her line of sight between the bars. Behind him were Mother Helena and Oona. Mercy stood and felt her reserve start to crumble. Mother Helena offered a small smile, then turned and gestured to someone else. Mercy watched Deirdre step reluctantly into view. The guard opened the cell and made a motion for them to enter.

"You got ten minutes, Sisters," he said.

Mother Helena stepped into the eight-by-eight cell and opened her arms. Mercy rushed into them.

"I'm so sorry, child," Mother Helena said in her musical voice. "So very sorry."

"Thank you for coming, Mother," Mercy said gratefully.

Mother Helena stepped back and took Mercy's hands. "If this is to be your last night on this earth, then you need to make your peace with the Father. Ask for His forgiveness."

Mercy's eyes filled with tears. "Will He really forgive me for doing the things I did—for the things I planned to do?"

"Yes. It's called grace, and He says all we have to do is ask," Mother told her.

Mercy nodded. "I will."

"Mercy?"

Deirdre stood in the corner of the cell, her face a mask of misery. "I have no right to ask, but please forgive me for what I did."

Mercy hesitated, then heard Mother say, "In asking for grace, we also need to grant it."

Deirdre walked toward her. "I should have never looked at your private journal or given it to Rand."

"But you did."

Deirdre's eyes welled with tears. "Yes. I did. And I regret that more than I can ever say. I never thought … I never imagined that … this would happen."

"She's been tortured night and day since your conviction, Mercy," Oona said in a voice husky with emotion. "She never meant for Rand to do anything with the journal other than break off his plans with you."

Tears rolled down Deirdre's cheeks. "I was jealous of what you had with Rand, but please believe me when I say I never wished you harm. Things got … so out of control."

Mercy studied her. "I am sitting in this cell because of all the mistakes I've made. I'm the last person on earth to sit in judgment of someone else. If you need my forgiveness—you have it."

Deirdre's shoulders fell in relief. "Thank you. It means a great deal to me. I'm going home, but I didn't want to leave until … until I had a chance to see you."

"Home?" Mercy asked.

"I'm going back to Ireland," Deirdre said. "I'm leaving the order. I've been lying to myself and everyone else about hearing God's call."

Oona stepped closer. "You will always be my sister in Christ, Deirdre. And you, too, Mercy. Always."

"Three minutes, Sisters," the guard called out.

Mother Helena pulled a chain from the pocket of her habit. "I brought you something," she said, holding out the mercy medallion. "I found it with your things, and I thought you might want it, Mercy."

Mercy ducked her head so Mother Helena could slip the chain around her neck. "Thank you."

"We haven't much time left," Mother Helena said. "I'm a poor substitute for a priest, but if you're willing, I will perform the sacrament of the last rites for you."

Mercy nodded. Mother Helena held out her hand, and Oona placed a small vial of oil into her palm.

Oona and Deirdre bowed their heads. Mercy's eyes met Mother Helena's, and in them she saw nothing but compassion and love.

"Oh, Holy Host above, I call upon Thee as a servant of Jesus Christ, to sanctify our actions this day in preparation for the fulfillment of the will of God."

Mercy concentrated on the lyrical sound of the nun's voice, the words washing away the grime of her life, the moment tender despite the harsh surroundings.

Mother Helena continued, "Oh Lord, Jesus Christ, most merciful, Lord of the earth, we ask that You receive this child into Your arms ..."

Tears ran down Mercy's face.

"... that she might pass in safety from this crisis, as Thou hast told us with infinite compassion."

"I'm so sorry," Mercy whispered.

Mother Helena dipped her thumb into the vial of oil and made a cross on Mercy's forehead. "By this sign thou art anointed with the grace of the atonement of Jesus Christ, and thou art absolved of all past error and freed to take your place in the world He has prepared for us."

Elijah had been praying the same thing over and over since galloping away from Fort Wallace toward St. Louis. "Please, God, get me there in time."

He'd traded horses at an outpost when stars still covered the dark, cloudless sky. And while he rode, he went over and over in his mind what could have happened. He had so many questions about how Mercy had come to be tried and convicted and he hadn't even been subpoenaed. Surely she would have told someone about his part in all this—surely she must have told someone it wasn't John Henderson she'd been after, but Elijah. She was certainly culpable for some of her actions, but to be convicted without all the evidence was a tragic ending to the situation, one he didn't want on his conscience.

Dawn light filled the sky, and he pushed the horse even harder, hoping against hope that the animal would hold out until the end. Every muscle in his body ached, but the drive to get to St. Louis before the next sunrise was stronger than his fatigue. He pressed on.

Elijah didn't slow the hard gallop of the horse until he hit St. Louis proper just as dawn broke on the morning of May third. He all but stampeded past the buggies and horse riders on the street and made his way toward Gratiot Street.

People must have gathered in the predawn light because the noise from the crowd in front of the gallows could be heard a block away. The celebratory air of the spectacle was something Elijah had never understood, but he knew without question that as long as there were public hangings, people would show up to witness them. He caught sight of the gallows built at least ten feet in the air with steps that led to the platform. The executioner was slipping a noose over the head of a black-hooded prisoner standing with bound hands and feet.

The air of excitement among the spectators rose to a crescendo as the executioner moved to the side of the platform and put his hands on a large metal lever.

"No!" Elijah yelled out, pulling hard on the reins of his horse and stopping short behind the crowd.

The executioner looked toward a man on the other side of the platform who dipped his head once.

"Stop!" Elijah screamed.

The lever sliced through the air.

Elijah saw every detail of the prisoner's reaction: the shoulders tensed, the head thrown back as if the eyes under the hood wanted one more glimpse of the sky they would never see again.

"Oh, God, no," Elijah called out.

There was a horrendous screech of a pulley.

The crowd roared in anticipation.

The prisoner did a quick dance in the air, bound feet trying to find purchase as everything solid went out from under them.

Elijah felt the air go out of his lungs at the same time the prisoner's body jerked once beneath the space in the gallows.

CHAPTER THIRTY-FOUR

Sick to his stomach, Elijah stared in horrified disbelief. He had been too late to save her. Still on his horse, he watched as two men moved to cut her body loose from the ligature around her neck. A band started to play a hymn, and in his peripheral vision he was aware of a man moving through the crowd, selling paper cones filled with nuts.

She was dead, and Elijah wondered if there was something he could have done differently. Maybe he should have gone directly to Rand himself and not given Mercy a choice in the matter. It had proven to be too much for her, and for that he was sorry.

Elijah's eyes moved over the crowd, even as he wondered what they were all still doing there when the barbaric show was over.

From his vantage point on the horse, he saw a nun making her way toward the gallows, weaving in and out of people until she stopped at the edge of the wooden structure. Elijah remembered the diminutive stature of Mother Helena, and even without seeing her face, he knew it must be her.

A ripple of excitement went up from the crowd again. Elijah rose out of the saddle, standing in the stirrups—looking behind the gallows to see guards leading another prisoner to the platform.

His jaw dropped.

Mercy!

It *was* her. She was still alive. He tried to move the horse through the crowd, but they weren't budging. He bolted out of the saddle and started to elbow his way through the throng of people.

"Let me through!" he yelled. Some moved back out of deference to the uniform he wore. Some were so caught up in the excitement of the event they couldn't even hear him.

"Move! Move!" he yelled.

He could see them leading Mercy up the wooden steps to the platform and was close enough now that he could see John Henderson standing on the side of the platform near two other men.

Elijah pushed and shoved people aside. "Out of my way! Let me through!"

Elijah kept his eyes on the platform—saw a look of some relief on Mercy's face and followed her eye line to Mother Helena.

As he drew closer to the gallows, uniformed guards stepped into his path. "Sorry, Captain, no further," one man said, putting a hand on his chest.

Elijah shook off the man's hand. "Stop the execution!"

He tried to push forward, but another guard joined the first. He drew a weapon. "Stay back, Captain," he said firmly. "We don't want to fire on a soldier."

"Five minutes," Elijah said to the guard. Then yelled, "John! John Henderson!"

Elijah saw John turn and scan the crowd.

"John!" he shouted. This time John spotted him and said something to the man beside him before he hurried down the platform steps.

"Elijah? What's going on?"

"You can't let her hang!"

"She was found guilty of treason," John said.

Elijah's eyes flew to the executioner, who stepped up with a black hood to put over Mercy's head. The man on the other side of the platform looked grave, serious. He absently pulled on the end of his thick black beard. Elijah recognized him as the governor of the state of Missouri, Thomas Fletcher.

"She tried to kill me, Elijah," John said.

Elijah turned to him. "You're wrong! Tell Fletcher to stop. Trust me."

Tears streamed from Mercy's eyes as the hood came down over her face. The crowd, equally excited and horrified, murmured their approval at the final steps before her death.

Elijah saw the executioner look toward Governor Fletcher—while John sprinted toward them both. Even though he had reached the bottom of the steps, Elijah could see that the congressman was going to be too late. Before the guards by his side could react, Elijah drew his pistol from a holster on his hip and fired it into the air.

People around him screamed. One of the guards grabbed him while the other took his gun. Elijah looked up in time to see John pleading his case. The governor looked at Elijah, and it felt as though it took forever before he looked back to the executioner and firmly shook his head.

Elijah sagged with relief at the gesture, and as he was being handcuffed, he watched the executioner roughly yank Mercy off the trapdoor. The crowd, incensed at being robbed of a death, booed and yelled toward the gallows. The guards tried to get Elijah to move away, to turn his back on the gallows, but he stood firm until he watched the hood be pulled from Mercy's ashen face. He saw her confused eyes search the crowd for Mother Helena.

The guards yanked Elijah by the arm. "Let's go, Captain," one of them said.

"Elijah!"

John Henderson was striding toward him with the governor right on his heels. "This better be good," John said through clenched teeth. "My reputation is on the line here."

Governor Fletcher stopped just a foot from Elijah and nodded at the guards. "Turn 'im loose."

Elijah looked up at the gallows, where Mercy was being led from the platform.

"Your actions here today are outrageous, Captain," Governor Fletcher continued. "I was a colonel before I was governor, and I'm here to tell you, this could warrant a court-martial."

"I'm aware of your service record, sir," Elijah responded. "I've heard of your bravery at Chickasaw and Chattanooga. I know you to be a man who abhors injustice—and that's what it will be if you hang that woman today."

Governor Fletcher stared at him.

"Fifteen minutes, Governor. Give me fifteen minutes to tell you what I know," Elijah said.

Governor Fletcher looked at the guards still surrounding Elijah. "We'll use the warden's office."

It was an hour later when Judge Young, Prosecutor Don Shepherd, and Mercy's attorney, Frank Collins, all arrived after being summoned to join Elijah, Henderson, and Governor Fletcher in the warden's office. Elijah sat in a chair against the wall, his arms resting across his knees, his head sagging in exhaustion. A final tap on the door admitted Charles and Rand Prescott to the room.

They both looked surprised when they saw the group of men waiting for them. "We came as quick as we could," Charles said. "Governor, what's this about?"

"Captain Hale is convinced we were about to hang an innocent woman," Governor Fletcher said.

"Innocent?" Rand asked. "Perhaps you should have taken the time to catch up on your reading, Hale! Mercy's own journal is proof of her guilt."

Judge Young held up his hands. "We've agreed to hear him out, Rand."

"Am I the only one here who remembers that a jury of her peers found her guilty of treason?" Don Shepherd asked.

Elijah got to his feet, three days of beard growth on his chin, his eyes bloodshot and tired. He managed to square his shoulders as he faced Rand.

"They didn't have all the evidence," Elijah said.

"I'd say it's a little too late for that now, Captain," Shepherd said.

"She's not dead yet, Mr. Shepherd," the judge said. "I want to hear what he has to say."

"Go ahead, Captain," Governor Fletcher said. "Tell me why I stopped an execution today."

"The first time I met Mercy wasn't that night at your engagement party," Elijah said, looking at Rand. "I'd met her months prior—on a battlefield in Tennessee."

Elijah went on to tell the story of the day his brother died. The day his own life had been spared by Mercy. And he told them about the day he paid a visit to an excited bride-to-be and shattered her dreams of the future by insisting she tell the truth about a past she couldn't remember.

"You're lying," Rand said.

Elijah shook his head. "No. I wish to God I'd never seen Mercy again after that day in battle. But I did. When I recognized her, I wasn't sure if she was telling the truth about her amnesia, but I quickly came to believe she was."

"Her journal says she remembers being a soldier," Rand said.

"No," Frank Collins said. "All it says is that she *knows* she was a Confederate soldier—but now we know that's only because Captain Hale told her. There is never any mention of her memory returning."

"She plotted to commit murder—to kill a sitting member of our government," Charles said. "Surely no one here has forgotten that!"

"Her entries never refer to the congressman by name," Collins said. "They only say *he*."

"She admitted that she started the fire that could have burned down John and Mary's house," Charles said.

"She wasn't after John," Elijah said. "She planned to kill me. I knew her past and had threatened to expose her. With me out of the way, she could still marry Rand and keep the secret."

"Well, then, by all means, let's stop her punishment and throw her a party," Charles said.

"The point is that we can't execute a young woman for treason if she didn't intend to actually kill a government official," Judge Young said.

Rand pointed at Elijah. "Hale just said she planned to kill him. He's a member of the military—doesn't that make him a government official?"

"Admittedly, there is a gray area about that, but in my interpretation of the law, it has to be a duly elected member of the government that is killed or threatened before it constitutes treason. Captain Hale volunteered for his post."

"She still planned to kill a man."

"She changed her mind," Elijah said.

"We found the evidence that says otherwise," Shepherd said. "We have the round she fired."

"I won't argue with the fact that she fired," Elijah said. "But I am standing here to tell you, gentlemen, if Mercy had truly wanted me to die—I would be dead."

"She missed, is all!" Rand said. "She was too far away to hit her target. That is why you're here, Hale. Not out of some eleventh-hour cry of conscience on Mercy's part."

Hale shook his head. "No. She's too good. Too accurate. She changed her mind and spared my life—for the second time, I might add. Did she hate me? Yes. Why wouldn't she? I threatened to take away all her happiness by insisting she reveal a truth about herself that she didn't even remember. She was panicked, backed into a corner—and the clock was ticking toward your wedding. I had promised her I would seek you out and tell you myself, Rand, if she didn't."

"So what you're saying is that while she planned to kill you," John said, "she made it appear as though she meant to kill me. She wanted everyone to think she had it in for me because of my allegiance and support of the North."

Hale nodded. "She is guilty of plotting and planning revenge, Governor," he said, looking at Fletcher, "but you can't execute a woman for that. I would wager there's not a man among us who hasn't wished someone dead at one time or another."

"I would have to agree with Captain Hale," the judge said. "If what he says is true, and Mercy did not intend to kill the congressman, then hanging her is out of the question. Can you imagine the uproar among Southern sympathizers if it ever got out we hung an innocent woman?"

"It might be parallel to the uproar that's already happened because she wasn't hung this morning," Shepherd said. "The Radicals were out for blood, gentlemen, and they didn't get it. There have been some documented cases of women masquerading as male soldiers, and that in and of itself is disturbing, but this case escalates the degree of deception—and the thirst for revenge—even further. A Confederate soldier who was about to marry the son of one of the

Union's biggest supporters! I've already heard rumblings from the underground groups that go after Confederates who've stayed true to the Southern cause. It won't matter now to them if she's found to be innocent. They won't believe it."

"Who says she is innocent?" Charles demanded. "There's still no proof."

"That's right, Hale. Do you think we're just going to take your story as gospel, turn her loose, and let her go on her merry little way after all the misery she has put me—us—through?" Rand asked.

"He's right, Captain," Judge Young said. "I can't just let her go because *you* had a bout with your own conscience and want me to free her. We live in a civilized society with laws against taking matters into your own hands when you feel threatened."

"I would ask everyone in this room to remember that our civilized society just came through a bloody war because a way of life was threatened," Elijah said.

"The bottom line isn't that we have her plans on paper, or even that she set a fire that did minimal damage to some property. The fact that we have the minié ball she fired still screams intent to kill," Don Shepherd said. "You are here, Captain, because she missed."

"She does *not* miss," Elijah said. "And if you'll let me—I can prove it."

The men stared at him, but it was John Henderson who broke the silence. "What exactly are you proposing, Elijah?"

CHAPTER THIRTY-FIVE

The police wagon carrying Mercy came to an abrupt stop.

One of the armed guards opened the bars on the back of the wagon.

"Let's go," he ordered.

"Where are we?" she asked, not moving.

"Jake's Meadow," he answered. "Let's go. Now."

The handcuffs on her wrists made stepping out of the wagon awkward. The guard held her arm and kept her steady until her feet were planted firmly on the ground. She looked at the guard.

"What am I doing here?" she asked. He looked over her shoulder, and she turned to follow his eye line. There were men. A group of men standing and chatting together while they stared at her. She moaned out loud. Could they really be so cruel as to stop short of hanging her only to bring her to the middle of nowhere so they could take their time killing her? Or maybe death would be kinder than something else they might have planned. Her mind refused to participate in the rest of the horrible thoughts trying to push their way through. Instead, she focused on a man in the group with streaks of gray in his hair and a dark beard—the same man who'd stood on the platform of the gallows earlier that day.

He looks nice, she thought, as she turned her back on reality and closed her eyes. *He looks like a father should look.* She saw herself as a little girl, wearing a pinafore and shiny black shoes, ringlets cascading around her shoulders. A man lifted her off her feet and settled her on his knee, and though she couldn't see his face, she could smell pipe tobacco and soap. He hooked an arm around her waist and pulled her close and read from a book of fairy tales that made her smile when he made up voices. She felt so safe. So loved. She sucked in her breath and didn't dare move lest the memory disappear.

"Mercy?"

She felt herself jarred back to the present by a voice she never thought she'd hear again. Her eyes opened to see Captain Elijah Hale standing in front of her—or was this just another cruel joke of her mind?

"Mercy? Are you all right?"

Mirages didn't speak. She narrowed her eyes. "I haven't been all right since the day I met you, Captain." Her voice trembled, but whether from hate or fear she had no idea. At the moment, she had plenty of both.

"I didn't know about the trial until it was over," Elijah said, "or I would have come sooner."

"To see the spectacle—or gloat at the sentence?"

"To set the record straight," he said.

Her hand actually ached to slap him. To hit him and hurt him and make him pay for all the ways he'd ruined her life. But instead, she looked around. "What is this? Why am I here?"

Frank Collins and the man with the beard approached her. "Mercy, this is Governor Fletcher. He stayed your execution based on some new evidence that Captain Hale brought forth," Frank said.

"Hale says you're a crack shot, young lady. That you can hit any—and I do mean any—target you set out to hit."

She refused to look at Elijah. "What does that matter?"

"If you can hit anything you're aiming at, Mercy," Frank said, "then the court will have to concede that Captain Hale is alive not because you *missed* him when you fired that gun—but because you couldn't go through with your plan to kill him."

Mercy swallowed hard. "You mean Congressman Henderson."

Frank shook his head. "Captain Hale told us how he pressured you into telling Rand the truth. He has convinced us that he was the one you planned to kill."

Her eyes cut to Hale of their own accord, but there was no denial in them.

"Why didn't you tell them?" Elijah asked.

She stared at him. "One of the problems with a lie is that once you change your story, which lie will be believed?"

The governor cleared his throat. "There can be no lying your way out of today, young lady. Today is all about proof. There is a no-trespassing sign about a hundred yards that direction." He pointed toward the north end of the meadow. "See if you can hit it."

The governor nodded at one of the guards, who produced a key to unlock her handcuffs. "Bear in mind that if you so much as turn that rifle even a fraction of an inch toward any of the men standing here today, I've given standing orders to shoot you."

She nodded and looked over at the men who were still watching her. Rand's face remained impassive, but the other men almost looked as if they were watching some kind of sport. Don Shepherd was offering the judge a cigar, and Charles had clamped his pipe between his teeth.

With the cuffs off, she rubbed the soreness from her wrists. She still wore the mercy medallion, and her hand went to close around the medal. She saw Elijah's eyes go to the medal as he held out the rifle. "It's loaded."

He's actually handing me a loaded gun, she thought, turning loose of the medal and reaching out a shaking hand to take the rifle. "I'm not sure … I'm exhausted."

"We're both trained to work through our exhaustion," he said. His words rankled her. *How dare he assume anything else about me*, she thought.

"Besides, it's like walking, talking, and breathing to you. You don't miss."

She felt the weight of their stares—wanted to turn and plead with Rand that she was still the person he had fallen in love with, still the woman who wanted to make him happy and was so desperate to spend her life with him that she had taken foolish risks and told unforgivable lies. But she knew that in the end it wouldn't matter.

She trembled so hard she could barely lift the rifle. But when she did finally nestle the butt of the stock into a place on her shoulder that seemed made for it—she felt her nerves settle. She rested her cheek against the wood and slowly moved the barrel in tiny increments until she saw the target through the sight. A slight breeze had her lifting the barrel a fraction of an inch, and without giving it any more conscious thought, she squeezed the trigger and felt the satisfaction of the recoil when she fired.

She still hated him, but Captain Hale had been right about one thing. Shooting was as natural to her as breathing.

One of the guards was already trotting out to the sign to report back the findings. Mercy knew she'd hit the mark. What she didn't know was what was going to happen next.

The guard yelled, "Dead center."

There was a smattering of subdued conversation in the group of men. Mercy's heart hammered as she waited for some kind of pronouncement. But instead, Rand's caustic comment rang out and cut her to the quick.

"It's a hundred lousy yards! I could hit that sign from here. There was testimony at the trial that she shot from three hundred yards at John's that night. And they were moving targets, for crying out loud! This doesn't prove anything."

"Fine. Let's have a moving target at three hundred yards," Elijah said loudly. "I'll get on my horse and hold my hat in the air—she'll put a hole in it three times."

Mercy couldn't believe it. Had he completely lost his mind—or did he have a death wish?

John Henderson strode toward them. "Don't be foolish, Eli. We all appreciate what you're trying to do for the girl here, but you're not going to put your life on the line based on some crazy theory you have that she won't miss."

"Or just go ahead and shoot you," Rand called out. "It's the perfect opportunity to finish what she started."

Mercy flinched at Rand's words, but she shook her head at Elijah. "I won't do it."

"Yes, you will," he told her. "Three shots—three holes in the same hat."

"No."

He stepped closer to her. "Listen to me. I started this whole thing, and now we're going to finish it."

"I don't think …"

"Don't think. Just shoot," he said as he moved away to get his horse.

"Someone hand her a Smithfield," the judge said. "She needs something with some repeating action."

"Have we all lost our minds?" John Henderson raked a hand through his hair as he watched Elijah charge on his horse toward the far north end of the meadow.

"This is crazy," Charles said.

"He volunteered to do it," Rand said with a hint of satisfaction in his voice.

"If she hits him—they both lose," Shepherd said, chewing on the end of his cigar.

Mercy tried to still her stampeding thoughts. It was all a dog and pony show for these men. These men who held her life in their hands as if she were a bug they could squash and then promptly forget.

She watched Hale ride across the meadow, and she wanted to scream at him that she despised him for ruining her life. The only life she could remember with the only man she could remember loving. She could end it all right here and now. Shoot the man who'd taken everything from her, then set herself free from life in prison and assure her own death by committing cold-blooded murder in front of witnesses. Two deaths with a single shot. Now that was something worth standing in a field to see. But the part of her that demanded justice for her pain—demanded payment for her loss—didn't really care about the outcome at all. Her life was still in ruins. Her memory still gone. Her love still lost.

The weight of the Smithfield felt right in her hands. She closed her eyes and held it for a moment, drawing in deep breaths and waiting for her body to quit trembling. *It's like walking, talking, and breathing to you. You don't miss.*

Did he really believe in her so much that he was willing to risk his life?

She opened her eyes and saw him in the distance, riding the horse across the meadow, his arm in the air—his hat in his hand.

"Crazy son of a gun," Shepherd said.

"Does he have any family?" the judge asked. Then Henderson's answer. "A mother somewhere. He hasn't seen her since his brother died."

Pray me home, Eli … pray me home.

The thought skittered across her mind as she raised the rifle, put her eye to the scope, and tracked Captain Hale across the expanse of the meadow.

Shoot him. I hate him.

She sucked in a breath and made a minute adjustment with the scope.

Shoot him. He ruined me.

She fired, and his arm remained high—the hat still in the air.

Shoot him! He deserves it. Surely goodness and mercy ...

Again she found him in her sight, let her reflexes find their sweet spot, and fired. *Goodness and mercy shall follow me all the days of my life.*

Ten seconds more and she fired again—and it was all over.

Mercy. Not mine. His.

She lowered the rifle to the grass and backed away from it. Every muscle in her body trembled.

Elijah galloped toward the group. He stopped and was met with stunned silence when he held up his hat with three round holes dead center in the brim.

Mercy felt hot tears pour down her face at Elijah's tangible act of forgiveness. She didn't deserve it, hadn't even sought it, but he'd given it to her.

Her shoulders shook from the sobs that tore through her. No one said a word. The men in their circle of judgment remained silent. Elijah dismounted and came toward her with his hat still in his hand. And still she continued to cry, head bowed, hands clasped.

Finally, he reached out and put a hand on one of her quaking shoulders. She shuddered from sheer weariness and relief as she brought her eyes to his. He pulled a handkerchief from his pocket, handed it to her, then turned to the men.

"Gentlemen," he said. "We need a plan."

CHAPTER THIRTY-SIX

"Mercy?"

Something jarred her, but she resisted.

"Mercy?"

Then a shake drew her out of a muddled dream. She blinked away images that still hovered in the darkness around a weak splice of light floating in midair. In another moment, she recognized the man behind the light.

Disoriented, Mercy sat up on the cot in her cell. "Mr. Collins?"

"I need to talk to you."

He sat down on the cot next to her, putting his briefcase on the floor.

"I slept." She frowned. "That hasn't happened in …" She looked at him. "What time is it?"

"A little after midnight," he told her.

"I'm never sure in here," she said. "The guards light lamps and extinguish them at their will. Night and day have no meaning for me anymore."

"It will now," Frank said, "because you are going to be released into the night. *This* night."

She stared at him, then slowly shook her head. "No. I'm still asleep, and you are part of my dream."

He smiled. "This isn't a dream. They *are* setting you free tonight."

"I don't understand."

"With the new evidence that has come to light and the way you shot with such remarkable precision yesterday, you are free."

Her eyes filled with tears. "As simple as that?"

Frank shook his head. "Hardly simple. But it's done. At least it will be when you walk out the prison doors."

"I don't believe this," she said.

"Trust me. I'm as surprised as you are," he answered.

"You're sure this isn't some kind of ... trick? I'll step foot outside, and they'll say I tried to escape or something?"

"No trick."

"But I admitted to setting the fire at the congressman's house. I planned to kill ..."

"Henderson dropped the arson charges," Frank said. She studied him. Even in the meager light, she could see the tense set of his jaw, the rigid way he held his shoulders.

"What aren't you telling me?" she asked.

"Nothing," he said quickly, before amending his answer. "Well, actually, a couple of things. We had a lengthy meeting in the field yesterday after you left. The prosecutor wanted certain conditions met in order to secure your release, and the judge agreed."

"Just tell me what I have to do to get out of this place," she said, starting to accept that what he was saying might be true.

"Everyone agreed that for your own safety, you need to leave Gratiot under the cover of darkness. As soon as we're done talking, I'll escort you out of the prison."

Her thoughts raced. Not only would she live, but she was going to be allowed to live as a free woman. There had been the smallest shred of hope after she'd been in the field with those powerful men. Hope that maybe they would spare her life ... but it had not even occurred to her that she could be set free. Yet freedom was at hand, and she needed to figure out what to do with it. Her mind went immediately to the safest place she could think of.

"I can go back to the convent," she said, more to herself than to him.

"No, Mercy, you can't. That's the second condition. You have to leave St. Louis—in fact, you have to leave the state, and if you ever come back, they can arrest you just for walking on Missouri soil."

She let that sink in. "All right."

"Even though the judge has overturned your conviction based on the new evidence, there will be a lot of angry people once the news of your release is made public. The war may be over, but people have long memories about the damage that was done. They have strong opinions."

Rand's face filled her mind. "I know."

Frank opened his briefcase and withdrew her journal. "I thought you might want this back."

She fingered the leather of the book. "I suppose I was foolish to write down all my thoughts."

"Not foolish. Your own words helped convince the judge to give you a chance at shooting in that field. Without that plan, well, we obviously wouldn't be having this conversation."

"I don't know how to thank you," she said.

He shook his head. "The credit goes to Captain Hale. He must have moved heaven and earth to get here from his post in Kansas in time to stop your execution. It was his idea to have you prove your skill with the rifle." He shook his head. "Bravest thing I've ever seen a man do."

She agreed, but all she could think to say was, "How soon can I leave?"

Frank smiled. "Now. But there is one more condition to your release."

"Anything."

"Captain Hale is going to escort you to the state line. It's for your own safety. You are obligated to stay with him."

"The man has already done so much for me. Did they really need to order him to accompany me?"

"It wasn't an order. He volunteered," Frank said. "Are you ready to get out of here?"

"I don't think I could *be* more ready."

Mercy followed Frank through the labyrinth of Gratiot Street Prison. It was the same route through the same dark halls with the same permeating smell of death and despair, but this time she wasn't going toward death. This time she was walking toward life.

They reached the front of the prison, and Frank stopped at the small alcove. "There is a matron in there who will give you back the dress you were arrested in," he said. "I'll wait while you change. Then the warden will meet us by the door, and that will be the end of your stay here at Gratiot—and the beginning of a new life."

She entered a small room where a dour-looking female guard shoved her clothes into her arms and jerked her head toward a privacy screen in the corner. "You can change over there."

Mercy made quick work of the buttons on the gray prison dress, revealing the mercy medallion that the guards had failed to take away when they brought her back to her cell. She dropped the dress on the floor and stepped out of the pooled fabric, and in the next instant she pulled her own dress over her head. It mattered little to her what dress she was wearing, because in truth, she had chosen neither. Was the yellow dress that settled itself with a whispered hush around her feet something she would have worn *before*? Were the shoes in which she slid her feet something she would have picked out and admired? Did she even care about clothes before? Did she have closets filled with beautiful things, or had she lived a more modest existence so that the dress she now wore would have been considered fancy and expensive? Did she love to read, to sing, to dance? Had she been a sister or an aunt or a cousin to someone? Had she been a shy little girl or rambunctious? Did she have a best friend somewhere she had whispered secrets to and laughed with? What about a mother who had held her tight and a father who had kissed her head? She needed those memories—or at the very least, needed to find someone else who knew some of her history.

Mercy realized there was only one way for her to have a new life. She had to go back. Back to wherever her old life had been. A new life without the foundation of her past was like trying to build a house on shifting sand. She stepped out of the room with a new resolve: to search until she found her home—so that she could finally find herself.

Frank and the warden were waiting for her. She signed her name to a paper that said she understood the conditions of her release—especially that she was never to come back to Missouri. With nothing left to say, Frank and the warden flanked her as they walked to the door.

The air smelled fresh and held the light scent of a recent rain shower when Mercy stepped outside. The crescent moon gave off just enough light for her to see Captain Hale standing immediately to her right between two horses. It took her only a moment to realize that one of them was Lucky. She crossed the few steps to the captain.

"I, ah …"

"We need to get going," he said without preamble, handing her Lucky's reins.

She slipped her journal into a saddlebag, then took a moment to brush her hand lovingly over Lucky's neck before she mounted the horse.

Captain Hale mounted his own horse, and in seconds, she was following him across the expanse of the prison yard. As they reached the road, Mercy glanced over her shoulder at Gratiot. Her eyes swept the building silhouetted against the dark skyline, but then her gaze caught on something else. Not something—but someone partially obscured from view. Her heart stuttered in her chest. Rand? It had to be. She recognized the way he sat on his horse, the tilt of his hat—even the outline of his shoulders in the semidarkness.

"Let's move," she heard Captain Hale say. She turned back in the saddle and in moments had Lucky galloping, putting the shadow of Rand and the horror of Gratiot behind her.

She heard nothing but the sound of the horses as they moved over the ground. Lucky had always run for the joy of it, and she could actually feel him straining to restrain himself. She knew he could go much faster if only she'd give him his head. But she had no idea where they were going. She'd waited for Captain Hale to say something—anything—but he remained silent. They pushed on through the humid night through acres of forested trails. Finally, she pulled up short, and Lucky stopped. She waited a moment, then felt a tug of relief mixed with trepidation as Captain Hale brought his horse back around.

"Why did you stop?" he asked brusquely.

"I want to know where we're going."

"I thought Collins explained the stipulations of your release to you," he said.

"He did. I know I have to leave the state. I'm just wondering which way you're taking me."

"We're headed north."

"I want to go south," she said. "It's the only place I'll find the answers I need."

"It doesn't matter what you want right now. North is the safest route to the state line, and that's the direction we're headed."

"Why not head east to the river? Lucky and I can board a river boat and be in Illinois before anyone knows I'm missing," she said. "You could be on your way, and I would be forever out of your life."

He studied her for a moment. "We're going north. It's not up for discussion."

He urged his horse into a trot again, but instead of following him, Mercy wheeled Lucky around, and with a nearly imperceptible command, she urged the horse off in the opposite direction.

She didn't look back, just leaned down low over Lucky's neck and felt the night air stream over her face. She gave Lucky a free rein, holding fast to the pommel to hold her seat. They flew in and out of the cover of trees, but the farther they went, the more the trail opened up—leaving the rider and the horse more exposed than before.

A mile later, Mercy felt Lucky's sides heaving beneath her, and she dared to glance over her shoulder just before the moon slid behind a cloud. She didn't see Elijah following her and couldn't believe her luck. Maybe he'd given up and said good riddance to a problem. The cloud swallowed the moon, and the landscape darkened. She felt a rush of relief and slowed the horse to an easy gallop, amazed at her own moxie. *I told him I wanted to go south*, she thought, just before something came out of the dark and caught her. She felt herself being lifted up and out of the saddle, then heard her assailant grunt when she landed on top of him. Before she could say a word, she felt a hand slip over her mouth, and someone lifted her up and started to carry her away. She struggled against him, still unable to see his face because of how tightly he held her. Her heart hammered as hot breath hit her neck.

"Don't say a word," Elijah's voice hissed into her ear as he deposited her behind some bushes.

Mercy wrenched away from Elijah and whipped her head around to stare at him, but he put a finger to his lips and adamantly shook his head. He pointed into the darkness, and that's when Mercy heard it—the sound of a horse's hooves galloping toward them.

CHAPTER THIRTY-SEVEN

Mercy felt Elijah's hand tighten around her arm, and she wanted to reassure him she had no intention of running into the path of whoever was coming at them in the dark; but there was no time for that. One moment he was holding on to her, then he was leaping from the meager cover of the bushes toward a horse and rider that seemed to materialize right in front of them. Elijah connected soundly with the rider, and she heard a surprised grunt as he was swept from the back of the horse. She could see the dark form of Elijah as he drew his pistol and leaned down over the man on the ground.

"You've been following us for miles," Elijah growled.

"Yassuh." The voice was thin with fear. "I has been."

Mercy frowned at the familiar voice and searched the memory that usually did her no good.

"Don't … shoot me, suh, please."

Mercy rushed toward them. "Isaac?"

"Yassum," the boy said. "Yassum, Miss Mercy, it be Isaac."

"Let him up," Mercy said. "I know him. He's one of the Prescotts' servants."

Elijah looked down at the black man still prone on the ground. And then he realized it—he was no man. He wasn't much more than a boy with wide, frightened eyes.

"Get up," Elijah said.

Isaac scrambled to his feet.

"Why are you following us?" Elijah demanded.

"When Mr. Rand came to the cottage, I hear him tell Ezra that Miss Mercy not gonna be hanged."

Isaac turned to Mercy then and smiled. "God saw fit to save you, Miss Mercy. I am mighty glad 'bout that."

"Thank you, Isaac. Me, too," she said.

"That doesn't tell me why you're here, Isaac," Elijah said.

"Mr. Rand say she be needing Lucky to get to the state line," Isaac said. "I tell myself that if Miss Mercy gonna leave St. Louis, then I am gonna go with her."

"Did you lose your job with the Prescotts?" Elijah asked.

"Nasuh. I be a hard worker and ain't give nobody call to cut me loose, Cap'n," Isaac said. "I jes wanna leave that place, is all. The only thing that been keepin' Ezra from beatin' on me was that he be scared you gonna catch him, Miss Mercy. Once they toted you off to prison, he gone back to his old ways, and I can't stand it no more."

Mercy's eyes welled up, and she looked at him. "I'm sorry, Isaac."

"We wish you luck, Isaac," Elijah said. "I'm sure Mercy appreciates your concern for her, but we need to be pressing on now."

"I know, Cap'n. I be pressing on with you."

"No," Elijah said quickly. "You can't come with us."

"Please," Isaac said, looking directly at Mercy. "Please take me with you. I got no one—no place."

"I'm going south, Isaac," Mercy said. "You don't want to go there."

"We're turning around and heading north," Elijah said.

"But, I—" Mercy said.

Elijah interrupted her. "I'm not having this argument with you."

"Yes, you are. Why should I go in the opposite direction of where I'm so obviously from? I need to head south. That's where I'll find answers about my past. That's where I can begin to look for my family—my home."

She could see Elijah shaking his head. "No. We're going the route I have planned, and that's the end of it. Do I need to remind you about the conditions you agreed to upon your release?"

"No, Captain Hale, you don't need to remind me, but for the life of me I don't understand why it matters which way we get out of the state as long as I get out of the state!"

Elijah blew out an irritated breath. "There is a bounty on your head, Mercy."

"Bounty? I don't understand …"

"A price. A prize. A good deal of money has been offered to anyone who kills you."

"But they've exonerated me. Doesn't that mean anything?"

"There are a lot of angry, hateful people who can't let go of the war. Groups that commit vigilante acts in the name of their cause. They believe anyone who fought for the South should pay—either with prison time or death. They were already riled up about the delay of your execution. When the judge made the stay permanent, the underground groups made it clear they intended to serve up their own brand of justice should the opportunity ever arise. The way some prison guards can be bought, I have no doubt the word of your release is spreading and people will be looking for you."

"So we are taking the northern route because it's the least likely?"

"Yes," he said. "But here we stand under the moonlight, out in the open, chatting like we're at a tea party."

"Pardon me, Cap'n," Isaac said, "but seems to me if I kin find you, so kin the bad men who be looking for her."

"Don't think I haven't already thought of it, Isaac," Elijah said.

"I could help you look out for the bad men, seein' as how I blend right in with the dark," Isaac said. "I can fetch things, bring wood, rub down the horses."

"Speaking of horses, Isaac," Elijah said, "do I want to know where you got yours?"

A look of guilt crossed Isaac's face. "He be an old horse at the cottage that nobody never paid mind to," he said. "I left all the money I have in the world and a piece of paper that says I'll pay more some day."

Elijah blew out a breath. "An amnesia victim and a horse thief. An unlikely pair."

Mercy rolled her eyes at him, then looked at the boy. "Captain Hale is only taking me as far as the state line, Isaac," she said. "We won't be traveling long enough to need your help."

"Then once you get to the state line, I be going on with you," Isaac said firmly.

"We can stand here and argue all night, or we can get going right now," Elijah said. He mounted his horse, and the other two did the same. Elijah looked over at Mercy. "No more arguments about which direction we're headed?"

"No."

"Good. Now, we all need to stay close," he said. "I've had enough surprises for one night."

She let Elijah set the pace and rode alongside him while Isaac brought up the rear.

Mercy glanced over her shoulder at the boy, then looked at Elijah. "Do you really believe it was a good idea to let him come with us?"

"No, but at least this way we can keep an eye on him."

"Who knows about the bounty?" she asked.

"Everyone who was privy to your release tonight," he said.

"And that includes Rand?"

He looked over at her. "Yes. It's one of the reasons he insisted you ride Lucky. He said you could outrun anyone on that horse."

"Except you," she said. She could just make out the ghost of a smile on his face.

As the sun rose, Elijah reined in his horse in a secluded spot near the river, and the others followed suit.

"We'll stop here for a few hours," Elijah said. There was palpable weariness in his voice.

Mercy and Isaac dismounted, and Isaac, in an obvious effort to seem useful, hurried to take care of the horses and brought them to water.

"We'll take turns keeping watch," Elijah said. "An hour at a time. Agreed?"

"Yes. I'll take the first watch," Mercy said. "I slept a few hours after—after you let me shoot at you in the field."

"I didn't let you shoot at me," he said. "I let you shoot at my hat."

"In any event, I don't think I could sleep if someone tried to force me right now," she said. "I'm fine to keep watch."

He withdrew a pistol from the waistband of his pants and handed it to her. "Here. I hope you won't need it, but just in case ..."

She nodded. "Just in case."

He pulled a bedroll from behind his saddle and dropped it on the ground. "Wake me in an hour."

"All right."

He closed his eyes and was asleep before Isaac even returned with the horses.

Mercy sat with her back against a tree trunk and smiled at the huge yawn Isaac tried to hide.

"Why don't you sleep for a while, Isaac?" Mercy asked quietly, so as not to disturb Elijah.

"No, ma'am. I'll watch with you," he said, even as he yawned again.

"If that's what you want."

He nodded, eyes huge as if he was fighting to keep them open. "That be what I want."

"You know, Isaac, I'm still not convinced that you should go with us."

"I need to, Miss Mercy. I need to leave this place."

"I meant what I said to you at the cottage. You're young and healthy—good with horses. You could pick any place to go and you'd be fine. You are free."

"I always been free. Never been no slave, even though Ezra treat me like one," he said. "I pick to go with you."

She looked over at Elijah, still sleeping soundly as the sky continued to brighten. "I'm not sure where I'm going, Isaac," she said quietly. "After Captain Hale takes me to the state line, I don't know what's next for me."

"I don't mind not knowin'," he said stubbornly. "I knows where I come from, and I knows I don't want to go back."

"Now, see, that's where we're different," she said. "I don't know where I come from—so I don't know how to find my way back. I just know I have to."

"I s'pose that's what be next for you then," he said wisely. "Trying to find out where you used to be."

"*Who* I used to be," she said thoughtfully.

"Seem like you has had a bunch of trouble you didn't deserve, Miss Mercy," Isaac said.

"Trouble doesn't discriminate, Isaac. We all do our turn," she said.

Isaac stretched out on the ground next to her. "Yassum, I s'pose that be true," he said. His heavy eyes started to close. "I be happy to help ..."

He fell asleep in the middle of his thought. Mercy leaned her head back against the trunk of the tree and thought about the future she hadn't expected to have.

Elijah woke, and his eyes went to the sun directly over his head. He sat up quickly and looked around. Isaac was stretched out under a tree, sleeping, his arms thrown wide, his mouth relaxed and slightly open. Elijah looked for Mercy but didn't see her. Getting to his feet, he felt a ripple of unease at her absence. She was nowhere in his line of sight. *Maybe off taking care of some personal business,* he thought. *Maybe washing her face in the river?* He looked toward the water, trying to shake off the dregs of his much-needed sleep, but he didn't see her. He turned and looked toward the horses that were tied to a tree. His horse was there. Isaac's mare was there. But Mercy's horse was gone.

"Isaac!" he said, shaking the boy awake. "Where's Mercy?"

Isaac sat up and frowned. "She be right at this tree and talking to me, but I must'a gone directly to sleep, Cap'n. I don't know where she be off to."

Elijah looked at the horses with a grim expression. "She's taken her horse and gone south. Stubborn woman. This is bad," he said, more to himself than the boy. "We're still a few hours from the state line ..."

He went to put up his bedroll and saw it. The mercy medallion had been wound around a rock, and the rock held down a piece of paper. Elijah pulled the chain from the rock and stared at the medallion until Isaac came up beside him.

"What's it say?"

Elijah began to read aloud. *"Elijah and Isaac—I'm sorry, but I'm going on alone. I have done enough damage, disrupted enough lives—and I won't have the two of you in harm's way because of me. You have a post to get back to, Elijah—and, Isaac, it's time you thought about your own life for a change. Go north and find those opportunities you spoke of. You have a big heart and a great capacity for compassion. I know you will find the happiness you deserve.*

"I left you the medallion, Elijah. It seems only fitting that you have it—especially considering it is your family heirloom, not mine. I need to find my family. My name. My past. I know that I can't go forward with my life until I go back.

"After all, what are we if not the sum of our memories?

"Thank you for saving me ... Mercy."

Elijah stuffed the note into his pocket and started to bundle up his bedroll. "If you just head due north from here, you'll be fine, Isaac."

"But you said Miss Mercy gone south," Isaac said.

"That's right." Elijah lashed the bedroll to his saddle. "Which means she could be headed to any number of places."

"She be smart," Isaac said. "She won't go the way you s'pect her to go."

"You're right about that," Elijah said. "It would be like looking for a needle in a haystack with the number of hours she might already have on us."

"You makin' it sound like it be impossible to find her," Isaac said.

"Could be," Elijah agreed. "That's why I think you should head north. Go get yourself a new life."

"I ain't going north, and I ain't going back, Cap'n," Isaac said firmly. "Only way you can make me is if you pull out that gun of yours and shoot me."

Elijah looked at the resolve on Isaac's face and shook his head in frustration. He slipped the mercy medallion around his neck and then mounted his horse. Isaac stood and looked at him, hands fisted at his side.

"Well?" Isaac demanded.

"Well, what?"

"Well, what do you say?"

"I say get on your horse," Elijah told him. "We're going to find Mercy."

... a little more ...

When a delightful concert comes to an end,

the orchestra might offer an encore.

When a fine meal comes to an end,

it's always nice to savor a bit of dessert.

When a great story comes to an end,

we think you may want to linger.

And so, we offer ...

AfterWords—just a little something more after you

have finished a David C Cook novel.

We invite you to stay awhile in the story.

Thanks for reading!

Turn the page for ...

• **From the Authors**

From the Authors

After sixteen years of working together, there are two questions that routinely surface about our writing partnership: *How did you meet? What is your process for working together?* To answer the questions from our respective points of view, we thought we'd defer to the **He Said – She Said** format since we never work in the same office, let alone the same state.

He said: I grew up in the film business with a father who was not only a successful actor, but a writer, producer, and director as well. Though I wasn't interested in acting, I was passionate about becoming a filmmaker. I learned my craft both on the job and through formal education, and like most filmmakers serious about earning a living, I was working on multiple projects. In 1997, a screenwriter, Rick Ramage, who had attended AFI (American Film Institute) with me, called to say he had a screenplay he thought I might be interested in directing. It was written by his sister—who had absolutely no experience in the business. I asked him to define "no experience," and he told me she was a Lamaze instructor who had tabled her dream of writing to raise three kids. This was her first screenplay.

Alarm bells started to go off, but in the next breath he said something that got my attention. The script was inspired by Margery Williams' children's classic *The Velveteen Rabbit*. There is only one way you can add another iron to the fire—you have to have a certain belief in the viability and success of the project to take it on. For me, at the time, the belief was in the title of the book and the idea that no one had made it into a long-form, live-action story. I told him to send the script.

She said: Growing up, my dream was to become a professional writer. But as is so often the case, life happened, and the dream stayed just that—a dream. I had no formal education in creative writing, but I filled journals and wrote poems and family Christmas letters. After some urging from my brother, I finally wrote my first screenplay. When Rick called and told me he was going to send that script, an adaptation of *The Velveteen Rabbit*, to Michael Landon Jr., I couldn't believe it. "You mean Little Joe's son?" I asked. He said yes. "Charles Ingalls' kid? *That* Michael Landon Jr?!"

Yes, he assured me. "He's a nice, *normal* guy who happens to be a really good director with an amazing background in the business."

I was thrilled, of course, but after our conversation, I knew I was in way over my head.

He said: I read Cindy's script and told Rick it needed a ton of work and warned him that I would want to scrap most of it. He told me to go easy on her. "Don't forget—she's my sister." I called Cindy and told her I'd always loved the story of *The Velveteen Rabbit* and its theme that love makes us real. I didn't want to damage either her confidence or her spirit as I prepared to discuss my notes with her. I told her that while her adaptation had some interesting elements and charm, she needed to understand that wholesale changes would be made if we moved forward. At the end of the conversation, we decided to start working together from page one. I remember hanging up the phone and saying to my wife, "What have I gotten myself into?"

She said: When Michael called to discuss the script, I had butterflies the size of bats in my stomach. He was very nice and told me how much he loved the idea of turning the classic children's book into a film, but he had some ideas of his own about the tone of the story. In other words, he had some notes. I learned very quickly that "some notes" meant we were rewriting the whole thing. By the end of our initial conversation, I had such terrible writer's cramp I needed to ice my hand. But I was undaunted, and even though I had taken copious notes, I was still floating on a cloud, thinking that I might actually become a professional writer. I hung up the phone, turned to my husband, and said with a big grin, "He loved it!"

He said: We worked together almost every day for six months on the rewrite of the script. What Cindy lacked in experience, she made up for with hard work. She'd rewrite a scene five, six, *ten* times until we were both satisfied we had it right. In the end, we were both very happy with the screenplay.

She said: At the end of six months of rewriting, I'm pretty sure all that was left from my original draft were the kid's name and the attic where all the imagining takes place. Michael is all about the work.

It didn't take long for me to forget that I was talking to the son of a television legend because he never played that card. He's just a guy who has a talent and a passion for good storytelling.

He said: With *The Velveteen Rabbit* under our belts (the film was released several years later once animation was complete), the collaboration between us became more solidified when we wrote *Love Comes Softly*. A typical day when we're doing a project begins early. I start my day at 4:00 a.m. to review the pages Cindy has sent the previous night. I'm rewriting, making notes, and laying out future story beats, so by 8:00 I'm on the phone with Cindy to go over the day's work.

She said: It's not unusual for my phone to be ringing by 6:00 a.m. when we are working on a screenplay or novel. Our conversation usually begins with, "Got your pen handy?" And so we begin to discuss the scenes we've done and the scenes we still have to do. If we've been stuck on a scene or a certain story point, sometimes the phone call starts with him saying, "I've figured it out. Here's what needs to happen." He describes it—and then I write it. He sees things in pictures—I paint the picture using words. Sometimes when we're stuck on something, I'll say, "How about we do this?" Usually his reply is, "No. What else have you got?" I'll pipe up with another idea—and hear another succinct no. On the other hand, he can get quite tangled up with the actual words. "I took a pass at rewriting that last scene you did. I think it's working, but could you just do your thing and clean it up a bit for me?" It just works out so well that he loves story and I love the words.

He said: So after sixteen years, a dozen screenplays, and now two novels, our process hasn't changed much at all. One thing that has changed, however, is how much Cindy has grown as a writer. I feel blessed that we've been able to work together the way we have.

She said: It still amazes me how it all came together. Inexperienced mom of three has a dream to write; experienced filmmaker believes in the project enough to make it happen. Who knew that *The Velveteen Rabbit* would be just the beginning? There's been so much more—more than I even dreamed. I am truly blessed.

We said: In one of our first conversations, we both agreed that we wanted to tell stories that would be appropriate for entire families to enjoy together. Stories that would reflect our worldview and our faith—and we would never compromise for the sake of commerciality. While the work has evolved over the years, we are proud of the fact that we've stayed true to our conviction. Our hearts are in the same place they were all those years ago. We want to tell stories that are inspiring and to speak to the truth of the brokenness of humanity and the wholeness that is only found in God.